I0840793

Under a Pelican's Wing

A Surfing Adventure, a Dangerous Love, and the Heroic Journey to Save a Woman from Captivity

Giovanni B. Sciurba

First edition

This book is a work of fiction. Any names, characters, companies, organizations, places, events, locales, and incidents are either used in a fictitious manner or are fictional. Any resemblance to actual persons, living or dead, actual companies or organizations, or actual events is purely coincidental.

Copyright © 2024 by Giovanni B. Sciurba

All rights reserved. No part of this publication may be reproduced or transmitted in any form or by any means, electronic or mechanical, including photocopying, recording or any information storage or retrieval system, without prior permission in writing from the publisher or author. For rights and permissions, please email: gsciurba@hotmail.com

ISBN PB: 979-8-9912388-0-9

ISBN HB: 979-8-9912388-1-6

ISBN Ebook: 979-8-9912388-2-3

Library of Congress Control Number: 2024915745

To
My Beloved Father

***

"Father, if you are willing, take this cup from me; yet not my
will, but Thy will be done."

— Luke 22:42

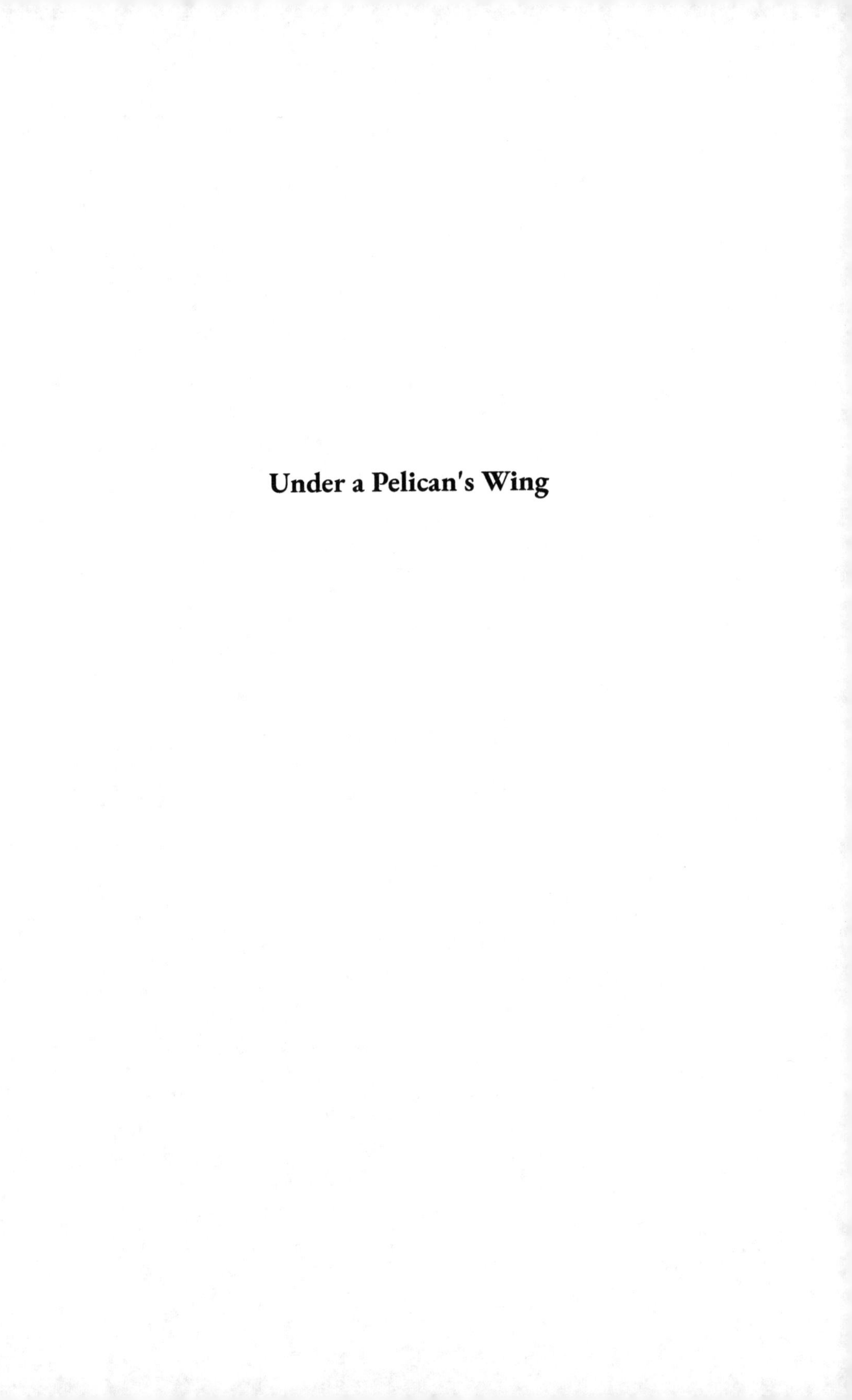

Under a Pelican's Wing

Chapter 1

"Luca!"

"Yeah, Dad," I said.

"Get the phone!"

I handed the change of a ten-dollar bill to my last customer, a lawyer who lived down the street. A strange genius who drove his old Cadillacs in to fill up every Friday. He owned three of them old boats—all from the 1960s. He was always bugging my father to start a chapter S corporation on the cheap. It was a decent idea, but it was a hard sell for my father; he hated change.

Lenny scurried out of the sales office toward the old lady in the Chevy Nova. She gave him the keys to her gas cap and asked him in her sweetest voice to fill up with regular unleaded.

I jogged past Lenny, past the sign in the window that read cash or credit same price to the pay phone at the far corner of the sales office. My father walked in behind me and stood behind the counter, where he sorted money collected from the last shift. Along the back wall, quarts of motor oil and transmission fluid lined in rows on long shelves. The door to the service area was wide open—it always was. Al's impact wrench hammered and ceased before I put the phone up to my ear.

"Hello," I said.

Scott's voice blared, "Head-high waves, dude! Can you get to Park Avenue?"

"I don't know. Steve isn't here yet, and I have to cover for his sorry ass."

"Bro, the waves are pumpin', and I'm goin'—you comin' or not?"

"I can't. We're a man down." My dad heard me, but he feigned interest. He organized the money, sorted each bill by denomination, and stacked them face up in neat piles.

"Dude, you're missing out big-time," Scott said.

"Like I said, I can't. I'll be there later. Hey, Scott—" But he hung up on me before I could ask him about the party.

My father's furrowed eyebrows and creased forehead always made him look pissed off about something. "You can go," he said. "I'll work with Lenny."

"No, I won't," I said.

"Why?" he snapped. "You think I'm too old?"

"Because it's my job, Dad. I'm not leaving and that's it."

A line of cars formed outside as if all at once. I hurried out to the gas pumps to help Lenny.

"Go help Lenny," my father shouted after me.

Steve showed up an hour later, looking pitiful. Of course, he was late on a day when the waves were amazing.

I stood at the gas pumps looking into the sales office—it was more like a waiting room. The front of the building had large windows facing the pumps so anyone could look in. My father remained calm as he explained the obvious to the prick; Steve looked down and nodded. I pumped a few cars and finished one, then Steve walked out of the sales office and up to Lenny to apologize. Lenny never took his hand off the pump handle as Steve spoke. His plea looked convincing as Steve raised his hands to his chest and shook his head. Lenny smiled and nodded, letting his teeth shine through his mustache. With that finished, Steve stepped up to me in an indignant manner, his hand out for the shift money.

"Sorry I'm late. I had trouble getting here," he said with a hint of regret.

What a doofus. Why did my old man put up with this crap? Whatever, I was finally leaving. I handed him the shift money and walked into the sales office. My father was still counting.

"I gave Steve the shift money."

"You can go."

"You sure?"

"Yeah, go," he said, keeping his eyes on the money.

"I'm working the afternoon shift tomorrow."

"I know," he said as he wrote down the cash totals on a piece of paper.

With much haste, I drove home. Without saying anything to my mother, I changed, grabbed my surfboard, and left as quickly as I came.

The patchy clouds moved eastward. The aftermath of a storm off the coast was a gift. The weather report was one a surfer from New Jersey would hear once or twice a year.

I parked behind Scott's Samurai and Jamie's pickup truck, near public access to the beach between old mansions along Ocean Avenue. The sandy path ran straight, shadowed by a row of six-foot-tall boxwoods. On the open sand, my feet began to cook. I knelt near the water and rubbed surf wax on my surfboard while I watched where the waves crested and crashed. It was true. The water was glassy, and the waves crested head high.

Beyond the breakers, my friends floated on their surfboards facing the horizon. I paddled out to meet them.

"There's my man," Jamie said. "These waves are monsters, bro. I'm glad you made it."

"How big? Overhead, right?" I said.

"Dude, some are bigger than that," Scott said.

"That's awesome," I said.

Jamie caught a wave and surfed to shore. He disappeared beyond view, behind a mountain of water. I cheered.

Jamie and I grew up in the same neighborhood. We were acquaintances at first, but became true friends after we fought over something he said about my dog, Nicky-boy. When I told him to apologize, he refused. The fistfight ended with us on the ground gripping each other's throat. Jamie submitted before he passed out. Later, he apologized. He's like a brother to me now; the tensions between us purged that day.

I met Scott a few years back in 1989 on the high school soccer team. He was the goalie, and I was the center back. After his parents divorced, he stayed with his mother in New Jersey. Through a dare, he talked me into surfing with him one quiet Sunday morning. He gave me a spare surfboard to use. I fell and tumbled into the waves so many times I had seawater dripping out of my nose for a week. That night, I had trouble sleeping. I dreamt of being under water, flailing my arms below the waves, reaching for the light. Rather than moving on, my desire to surf again haunted me. I called the surf report daily and drove to the beach often enough to annoy the hell out of Kelly, my ex-girlfriend. I never stopped surfing after that. The desire was the same for Jamie. Surfing was it, and we had Scott to thank for it.

As a wave crested, I went for it. I stood up on my surfboard and turned on the wave. I leaned back to slow down and took short steps to steady myself and keep balance.

"Nice ride," Scott said.

"Yeahhh," Jamie shouted with his fist raised.

As the afternoon passed, the wind blew from the west. This flattened the swells and drained the ocean of energy. The fleeting day sank with the sun, leaving me thinking the good days always were that—fleeting.

Back at the cars, I was last to strap in my surfboard and load my stuff. Jamie rolled down his window and leaned his head out, "I'm starving. Let's get some wings."

"Let's go, Luke," Scott replied from his Suzuki.

I nodded and jumped in my old Mustang. We sped off down Ocean Avenue and onto Highway 35 toward Eatontown. Feeling charged up and obnoxious, I played "My Name Is Mud" on the cassette player. The strong flow of hot August air battered my ears, and I adjusted my wet surf trunks for comfort. Scott drove up in the adjacent lane. He smiled and bobbed his head to the music. I laughed. He let go of the steering wheel and swung his arms in sync with the bass tempo. That bitch almost sideswiped me. Jamie was close behind; he hit his horn a few times to add to the delinquency. Looping around the traffic circle, we parked at the chicken house and ordered food. We sat down at a picnic table near a chain-link fence.

"Two more days, fellas," Scott said.

"Damn right. I'm already packed," I said. "My dad's taking us to the airport. It's definite."

"Dude, I'm ready," Jamie said. "My mom tells me the doctors are terrible there, and that I'll die of some strange jungle disease and whatnot."

"What?" I said. "Dude, if you get sick, just take something over the counter. Tell your mom we're not going into the jungle anyway . . . What about your dad—what's he saying about our trip?"

"I don't care what he says. The guy's a dickhead. You think we'll ding our surfboards on the flight?" Jamie said.

"If we do, we can rent boards at the surf shop there. I wouldn't worry about it," Scott said.

"Yeah, Scott's right. I wouldn't worry about it."

Scott looked at me. "You're hitting the clubs with us, right?"

"Yeah, you better come with us," Jamie said, joining in.

"I can't handle a cage, man," I said in my worst Patrick Swayze impression from the movie *Point Break*. We laughed.

"Great movie," Jamie said. "But seriously, you are clubbin' with us. Kelly's gone, right? You're not going back to her, are you?"

"Of course not. We broke up," I said.

"Good. Just making sure," Jamie said.

"Kelly's coming to the party, bro. Don't even think about hooking up with her," Scott said.

"Dude, I just said it was over. Do we really have to talk about it?"

"Hey, I have an idea. Hear me out. Why don't you keep Kelly on the side and when the next hottie comes around, dump her," Scott said.

"C'mon, you know I'm not that smooth," I said.

"Well, it's not as hard as you think, bro," Scott said.

We laughed again.

Scott declared he would bring the alcohol to the party and that we'd pay him later. We debated on what to bring. We settled on Eisbock and a bottle of cheap whiskey.

"All right, fellas . . . I'll be at Hunter's around ten thirty. See you there," Jamie said.

"I'm Audi 5000," Scott said.

At home, I hosed down my surfboard and placed it in the garage. I went around back and opened the sliding door to the kitchen where I smelled garlic and clams. My father's favorite dish, linguini with red clam sauce. I loved it, too, but I was full of chicken wings. My mom said dinner was ready as she filled a water bowl for the dog. Dad sat at the chair near the television, watching the *Nightly News* with Tom Brokaw. He still had his work clothes on.

"Michele, non dimenticate di prendere l'insulina . . . check your sugar," she said in a commanding voice.

"All right," he said.

He got up for the bathroom; his eyes fixed on the television. For years, he had trouble managing his blood sugar. Recently, he focused more attention on his diabetes, moving it up his priority list, behind work, money, and pasta. When he fell off the sugar-free wagon, my mom tried her best to straighten him out.

Nicky-boy was busy eating table scraps mixed in with his dog food.

"I didn't know you were making pasta tonight," I said to her, trying to divert attention away from the elephant grass growing on the yard.

"Vuoi che io scaldare, there is some pasta left. I warm it up for you," she said.

"I'm full, Ma, thanks. I ate with Jamie and Scott."

"E qui se lo vuoi, Luca. When are you cutting the grass?" she said with frustration.

"Tomorrow, Ma, I promise."

"You're lucky your father doesn't say anything—vergogna."

Resigned, she turned to clean the dishes, making me feel inept and shameful. I deserved it though. Given the choice of either surfing or mowing the lawn, I say let the yard go to hell. Let the grass grow like the Serengeti—I don't care. Oh, but the guilt. The guilt my parents made me feel was biblical; they were pros at it.

When Nicky-boy finished his scraps, he bothered me for a walk by standing at the sliding glass door. I let him out where he immediately pissed on the nearest tree. The street was quiet. The neighbors nestled in their homes. I clipped the leash on his collar. My restless sled dog pulled me down the sidewalk, found a place to plant his nose, and sniffed. He pulled me again, leaving a squirt of piss here and there. I stood near the neighbor's fence to let him sniff for a while.

What would I do if I saw Kelly at the party? For a moment I pondered not going at all but that was stupid. Things were great at first with us: the boardwalk, the park, watching movies at her house. Then one day I broke it off. I felt awful about it, but I realized one day she was too much for me and I lost interest. I hoped she wouldn't make a scene tonight.

We got back. Nicky-boy drank from the bowl, moved to his favorite place near the air vent, and slumped down. He groaned a little as he placed his snout on his forepaws.

"Good boy," I said.

I walked upstairs to my bedroom. The window was open, and the curtain swayed gently with the summer breeze. Across the street, a bat flew around a bright streetlight. I thumbed through my collection of CDs. I placed Jane's Addiction's *Nothing's Shocking* into the stereo and hit play. The alarm clock was set to go off in an hour. I lay on my bed and closed my eyes. My mind raced as I imagined things: *What do I wear?* An image of me surfing down a monster wave as girls watched from the beach. The thought of a girl I knew in English class senior year. *What's she doing now?* She was beautiful. One morning, between periods, she asked me out; she wanted to go to the movies and then to her house. I made her wait for an answer, like a dork. I said no to her. Why? Why did I do that? I was stupid and a coward. A stupid-coward. I was a dumbass. After that, she killed the small talk and left me alone in the hallway. She never spoke to me again, probably because I was a moron—no, definitely because I was a moron. She ended up dating some other guy. It's been years now. We would have had fun. Next month, I'll start my junior year at Columbia where I would finally begin my core courses in engineering. The vision of a beach in Costa Miel flashed before I faded into sleep.

The alarm woke me. I switched off the stereo and took a shower. I put on my gray cargo shorts and black long-sleeve shirt. I laced up my boots and rushed out to start my long walk to Hunter's place. The night air was calm and pleasant. I looked up at the bat as it flew around and around the streetlight before it disappeared into the summer night.

Chapter 2

Parked cars stretched along the street and around the cul-de-sac. The sound of heavy metal music played as I stepped up to the front door. Hunter stood outside greeting each guest, holding a beer in one hand and a cigarette in the other. He hugged the girls and shook hands with the guys. As a gracious host, he explained where the beer keg was and which bathroom to use before entering the house.

"Luke, what's up guy? Good to see ya." He smiled. We connected in history class a few years back, but I avoided getting too close due to his druggy clique. He was gregarious and eager to invite anyone over to hang out and party. It was a good way to sell the weed he grew and other stuff.

"How the hell are ya? What're you up to?"

"You know, working, surfing."

"Dude, we're going to see Biohazard on the twenty-third. You wanna go?"

"I'm leaving for Costa Miel with Scott and Jamie on Sunday. We're going for a week."

"That's right. I wasn't sure about the date. That's awesome, dude. Enjoy." He paused to take a drag from his cigarette. He exhaled. "Go inside and enjoy yourself. The keg is in the garage and only use the bathroom downstairs. If you want anything, don't be afraid to ask." He stepped aside to let me pass.

"Cool," I said.

The music was loud. There was this smell of pot in the air. People huddled in their circles here and there, drinking from plastic cups. A few heads turned, glanced at me, then turned back to chat and drink. In the dining room, four guys were playing poker. A few onlookers were talking as they leaned against the credenza. In the living room, two guys—I thought I recognized one of them—sat on folding chairs watching *Beavis and Butt-Head*. Scott sat on the sofa with some girl I didn't know. He saw me and waved me over.

"Jennifer, I want you to meet Luke. Luke, Jennifer."

"Hi," Jennifer said.

"Hi," I said.

"Jennifer is going to NYU in the fall and we have a lot to talk about," Scott said, winking at me.

"Don't let me bother you two. I'm looking for Jamie," I said.

"I think he's out back," Scott said. "Hey, there's a six-pack of Eisbock in the fridge. Don't drink from the keg, dude. They pumped it full of air. Our stuff is much better."

"Got it. Thanks for the heads-up," I said and waved goodbye to Jennifer.

Curious sounds drew me to a door. I opened it to see the garage doors opened with about a dozen or so drinkers and smokers separated by gender. The guys listened to some dude ramble on as they smoked. The girls guffawed between idle gossip. They touched one another after a compliment and leaned on friends for comfort. Discarded plastic cups, wine coolers, and cans were strewn across a folding table. The sweaty beer keg was on the ground near the open garage doors.

I looked out on the driveway—my stomach ached at the sight of Kelly talking to my sister, Sofia. I felt exasperation as Kelly caught my gaze. I closed the door and winced. *Crap*, I thought, as I paced to the kitchen for a drink. The Eisbock was still warm, but whatever; I took one more bottle. I guzzled the first one right away and immediately put a dent in the second.

I cut through the living room to the back of the house. My stomach was full. I thought about going back and getting a third bottle, but no. Jamie was playing a game of beer pong outside. Onlookers, mostly females, watched. Jamie played against a large jock-type. He was brawny with his hair cut in a Mohawk style. There were guys like him, too, sporting the same look. They cheered him on with visceral grunts. The score was even with two cups left on each side of the table. Jamie's eyes were glassy. It was the jock's turn to toss. He concentrated as he aimed. Jamie stood still, moving a Ping-Pong ball between his fingers. The burly oaf lobbed the ball, but it hit the rim of a cup and bounced off. The crowd groaned and then mumbled to itself. The jock immediately threw his arms up in disgust as a caveman would when he misses with a spear. Jamie slapped his hands together and got ready. I stood off to the side, so he wouldn't know I was watching. The crowd let out a groan when his ball splashed in the cup. He raised his arms in victory. The jock removed the wet ball and drank the contents of the cup. He seemed disoriented and upset. Jamie fed on it. I stared at the guy's Mohawk, the way his pale, white scalp met his spiky black hair. I couldn't take my eyes off of it—it was an absolute blunder. I finished my second Eisbock and started to giggle but resisted cackling to avoid getting punched in the face. The jock repositioned the last cup and his friends shouted a few encouraging words. He leaned forward and reached his arm out to judge the distance of the throw. He cocked his arm back and tossed but overshot completely and missed the table. Jamie prepared, and with an easy toss that even surprised me, his ball landed into the last cup of beer to win the game. The crowd let out a communal heavy sigh and dispersed in disgust. I stepped up to him.

"That's awesome. How'd you end up playing that monster?" I said.

"Thanks, man. Yeah, when I got here, I walked around looking for you. That's when that punk-ass bitch asked me to play him. I said, 'Okay, then, get ready to lose, bro,' and there you go."

"Nice." I giggled.

"Yeah. I play better drunk sometimes—it makes me brave. Anyway, did you find Scott?"

"Yeah, he's inside talking to some girl."

"Nice, real nice. I should be doing that."

Kelly approached. She came around the side of the house. Her arms crossed. Jamie smirked and without a word walked away, leaving me to die. He stepped into the house and slid the patio door shut. I waved for Kelly to follow me away from the house in case we argued. We stood under a pine tree. It was dark, but the outdoor light gave me a good look at her. She was beautiful. She wore jeans that fit well. Her long blonde hair hung full over her shoulders. Her skin was tan under her black tank top, and she smelled like peaches.

"Hi," she said.

"Hi."

"You never returned my calls," she said.

"Kel, I've already explained myself."

"I just want a better reason after all we've been through," she said.

"We're not compatible. We're on two different wavelengths—simple as that."

"Wait, we've been together for like two years and that's the reason? Really?"

"Yeah, no. I mean you're just too controlling. I'm sorry."

"And that's it . . . Just like that, it's over?"

"You're not gonna change, Kel. I tried, but—"

"But what?" she interrupted. "God, you're such a baby. You're such a coward, you know that? You don't even want to try to make this work."

"C'mon, Kel, let it go."

She leaned in and pointed her finger at me as a mother would to a disobedient child. "That's a sorry excuse for breaking up with someone you love. I love you, Luke. We have a long history together and now you're giving it up?"

"Whatever . . . I don't want this anymore," I said.

"I don't believe you. You're gonna throw away two years?"

"It wasn't two years," I said.

Kelly did her best to stay calm. She leaned in with a concentrated stare. "You're going to regret this. You know, I'm too good for you."

"Whatever," was the last thing I could say.

She turned and walked away. Her arms still crossed. She didn't look back. I tilted the empty bottle up to my mouth without realizing it was empty. I felt beaten. One and a half years of misery. That's not true. It was only miserable for the last few months. "Whatever," I mumbled to myself.

I sauntered back to the house and made my way to the kitchen. I drank from an open bottle of whiskey on the counter, not caring about getting sick. I wanted to be alone. The surrounding eyes disregarded me as I passed. I walked outside and found a chair to sit on. The whiskey did it for me. The night air was cool, and my skin was warm. Sofia approached from the garage. She dragged over a chair and sat beside me.

"I know why you're here," I said.

"Kelly's gone, Luke. She drove off without saying anything. Look, I never bother you, and I always mind my own business, but what did you say to her? She left me without saying anything."

"I told her how I felt, that's all. It's not my fault she couldn't handle it."

"She's still my friend, though, and she has feelings."

"That's fine. I got it, but I let her know it's over, that's all."

"She loves you."

"That's not my problem, Sis. I don't love her."

"Then why did you let it go on for so long?"

"Well, she was fine at first, but after a while she got too possessive. I'm not right for her anyway. We're not the same."

"Well, let me teach you something. Men and women don't think the same. You should know that. I'm starting to wonder if you loved any of them."

"What do you mean?"

"Have you ever loved any of your past girlfriends?"

"Kelly was my only serious girlfriend. But I guess not."

Sofia let out a sigh. "Okay, I'm glad you said that. That means you haven't found the right one yet."

"I'll agree to that," I said, feeling drunk and bloated. I looked away.

"Luke, all I'm saying is be nice next time and break it off as soon as you know it's not going to work—don't let it drag on. That's all I'm telling you. Oh, and don't be like Scott. He's a pig."

"Okay, thanks."

"So . . . Where're you going again?"

"Costa Miel, in the town of Playa Sueños."

"You must be so excited."

"Yeah, I can't wait; it'll be my first time out of the country. The surfing will be awesome."

"You're lucky. I can't hang out with my friends for a week," she said.

"Really? I thought you were close with them."

Sofia let out a heavy sigh. "They're all right, but they can get bitchy after a few days."

"Well, we'll be surfing most of the time so we'll be busy doing that," I said.

"Don't forget to give Mom your itinerary. She'll worry, ya know."

"I know. Hey, how are you getting home?" I asked.

"Susan will take me. Don't worry, she's fine. She's been good. Why do you ask?"

"Nothing, only checking," I said.

"Want a ride?"

"No, I'll walk. It's not far. Thanks anyway." I smiled.

Sofia got up to leave. She turned and said, "You know Dad and Mom are very proud of you."

"They're proud of you too," I said. "You'll be a great nurse." She smiled and headed to the garage. I thought of following her, but I wanted to go home. I'd talk to Jamie and Scott tomorrow. I felt tipsy. Scott was with that girl anyway. I'll be fine—whatever.

The walk home felt short. The kitchen light was on through the window. I walked around the back to see Nicky-boy sleeping on the deck. He got up and wagged his tail. I kneeled low and gave him a kiss between the ears; he went back to sleep. I left the kitchen light on for Sofia and went upstairs. I heard the TV in my parents' room. I stripped down to my underwear, turned off the light in my room, and went to bed. The walls moved and my stomach was sick. I rolled over and looked out the window. The breeze felt soft on my face. I focused my sight on the distant streetlight—three bats circled the light in a chaotic rhythm. When the spinning in my head slowed, I fell asleep.

The sound of the constant barking woke me. I got out of bed and went to the window to see why. It was a bright, hot, and humid morning. My father cleaned the pool with the long leaf skimmer. Nicky-boy barked at a raccoon perched still on our fence. My father had enough of the annoyance and used the leaf skimmer to push the raccoon over. The creature resisted. With a final push, it fell into the bushes and disappeared. The dog stopped barking and peered through the fence to see where it had fallen. The raccoon was gone. Nicky-boy went back to the deck as if nothing had happened.

I had a slight headache, so I took aspirin and drank lots of water. The smell of toast and coffee made me hungry. I had to mow the lawn and work the second shift later. I could have used another hour in bed, but I didn't want to hear it from my mother for the tenth time.

After getting dressed, I went down to the kitchen. I took a cup and went directly to the hot, brewed espresso. I put a few slices of warm toast on a plate. Mom wiped the kitchen counter.

"Hey, Ma, is Sofia sleeping?"

"Yes."

"How's Dad been?"

"He has swollen feet again. His sugar is fine, but I'm worried."

"Did he say how he's feeling? You know, about his blood sugar?"

"No. You know how he is," she said.

"Yeah, I know. You have to be a mind reader with him," I said.

"So, you're packed?"

"Yup, I'm ready." I spread butter on my toast and poured a little milk into my espresso.

"Hey, Ma, I want a tattoo." She ignored what I said as she cleaned the dishes.

She scrubbed the dishes harder. "I thought you were smart," she answered. "You go to Columbia University. Why do you need a tattoo?"

"Everyone's getting one. It's beautiful."

She dropped a plate. It made a loud clunk in the sink. "Why do you want to be like everybody else?" she said with consternation.

"It's not a big deal, Ma. It's art. Why are you so against it, anyway?"

"Because criminals have tattoos. It makes you low, like a cockroach," she said, picking up the plate and wiping it.

My father slid open the patio door and walked in with the dog following him. The last thing I needed was to get double-teamed about getting a tattoo. I said good morning to my father and headed to the garage to start the lawn mower. Later, while I emptied the grass bag, my father drove off in the CJ-7 with Nicky-boy in the passenger seat. Every Sunday, he took the dog to the park for a walk. I thought about the tattoo I wanted. The inspiration came from an illustration in a surfing magazine. A phoenix rising from the ashes in a tribal style. Jamie drew it for me already. I would do it after I got back from Costa Miel.

After finishing the yard, I went to work. When I got home, I called Scott.

"Hey, what's ya doin'?" I asked.

"Gettin' my buzz on," he answered.

"Can I come by? We can talk about tomorrow."

"Dude, come over. Jamie's already here and we're playing pool. I was gonna to call you, but I thought you were at work."

"I'll be there in a few," I said.

When I got there, the front door was open behind the storm door. I peered in to see Scott and Jamie drinking beer in the kitchen. I knocked; Scott waved me in. We took the stairs to the basement. The wood paneled walls and the painted floors did a bad job of covering the mold smell. The dehumidifier was noisy, so we turned up the stereo volume. We played a round of eight-ball and chatted about the trip. There were folding chairs and an old sofa that smelled worse than the mold. We stood near the pool table. Jamie took the triangle and racked up the pool balls.

"Didn't you drink enough last night, or is this round two?" I said.

"Na, we're celebrating," Jamie said as he raised his bottle.

"And you didn't wait for me? Wow, great friends I have," I said.

"Relax dude, we'll drink more," Scott said. He grabbed a beer from the six-pack lying on the floor and handed it to me. The bottle was cold.

"Guys, don't get too drunk. We're leaving in the morning," I said.

"C'mon, it's a vacation," Scott said.

"You know what I mean," I said before taking a swig.

"I told Scott you spoke to Kelly last night. How did it end? Are you two back together again?"

Jamie and Scott laughed.

"Very funny . . . I told her it was over. She wanted me back, but I can't deal with being under her thumb all the time. You know."

"To be honest, I'm glad she's gone. We barely saw you. She hates me, dude," Scott said.

"Nah, we hung out. Anyway, yeah, she was extreme, but those days are over. How'd you make out at the party last night?" I asked Jamie.

"I felt cocky after beating that jock, so I went to the garage and found some people to play quarters with. I lost, of course." We laughed. "I ended up so trashed that I slept there. I drove home this morning and slept most of the day."

We laughed again. We looked at Scott, giving him the audience.

"Jennifer was a talker, dude. I don't think I got a word in." We laughed. "She gave me her number, so I'll call her when I get back from Costa Miel."

Jamie and I looked at each other and smiled.

"So how did it end?" Jamie asked Scott. "Come on, tell us."

"Dude, we didn't do anything. She kept talking and then she said she had to work in the morning. Then she left. I'll call her when I get back. If things go right, I'll go see her. I'm not gonna sweat it."

"Definitely call her. Going to parties in the city would be awesome," I said.

"Going to NYU to party—nice, real nice," Jamie said.

We laughed.

"Let's play a round of eight-ball," I said.

"Let's do it," Scott said.

Chapter 3

The morning sky was clear. We arrived at the airport on schedule, checked in our surfboards, and made our way to the gate. My father was quiet. I expected him to say "be careful" or "stay together"—instead, he shook my hand with the notion of a final farewell. He had the "learn from your mistakes" and the "discover things on your own" mentality. My mother reminded me to be aware of the scammers out there and the desperate people eager to take advantage of me. She was quite cynical about the world. She called it being realistic. I found out later they were both right.

We sat together on the plane. I sat in the middle seat, Scott near the window, and Jamie closest to the aisle. We said the word *awesome* like forty times before takeoff. Our exhilaration met with a hint of disbelief. The plane landed in Miami to pick up more passengers. After that, we landed again outside the United States, but not in Costa Miel. We were parked on the tarmac. Scott nudged me and pointed to the window. Military tanks and fighter planes were parked along the runway. Scott and I looked around with intense curiosity. Jamie tapped me on the shoulder and asked what was wrong.

"Don't worry, bro. There are some tanks and fighter jets out there. I guess the military uses the airport for storage or something," I said.

Jamie shook his head and laughed. "Oh man, I can hear my parents now. 'I told you it was going to be dangerous, blah, blah, blah. You should always listen to us, blah, blah, blah.' When we get back, don't say anything about this to them. I'd rather be in a Colombian prison than hear my parents say I told you so for the rest of my life."

Scott and I giggled.

A few men who looked like farmers exited the plane. A young lady holding a baby boarded and sat up front. She wore a white dress with rainbow colors across the bottom of her skirt. After a long wait in the hot plane, we took off. As we rose in altitude, I leaned over to look out the window. We cruised above the patchy clouds casting shadows on the mountains below. Dense jungle covered the mountaintops and spread out like a plush blanket over the valleys. Looking out farther, the heat formed a haze between the mountains. I imagined this was how the earth looked thousands of years ago. It struck me as a godforsaken wilderness, primeval, and not yet touched. What unknown secrets of nature lay under the jungle canopies?

Across the aisle, one row up, a young man wearing sunglasses leaned over to Jamie and asked if we were surfers.

"Yeah, we're goin' to Playa Sueños for a week," Jamie said.

"We're going there too," the dude said as he nudged the guy next to him. "I'm Bobby and this guy here is Kevin." Kevin's lazy hand lifted to greet us. They were older and appeared well seasoned. Bobby wore dreadlocks and Kevin had a shaved head and a thick beard. They were heavily tattooed, grungy, and smelled like incense.

"Have you been there before?" Scott asked.

"Sure, many times—you're going to the right place. Sueños has decent breaks. You should also hit the waves at Playa Curvo."

"Where's that?" I said.

"It's south of Sueños—about a twenty-minute drive." He paused and dropped his expression of serenity to one of earnest. "But remember, give the blind man at the gate some money or he won't let you through."

"Blind man? What—" Scott said.

"Wait," I interrupted. "A blind man has to let you on the beach?"

"Yup," Bobby said.

"Dude . . . We're definitely going to Playa Curvo," Scott said.

Bobby smiled and said with a smooth tone, "Riiiight. Just give the blind guy a few coins and he'll be more than happy to let you through. No problemo."

"How difficult is it to get to Playa Sueños from the airport?" I said.

"It's not. When you leave the airport, follow signs for the west coast. Then take the route south to Playa Sueños," he said, pausing for a moment to think. He turned back to Kevin, and after a moment, he faced us again.

"If you want, you can follow us. We're goin' there anyway, so that's fine with us."

"Yeah, thanks. We appreciate that," I said.

"Yeah, no problem," Bobby said.

I looked at Scott in case he had something to say, but he sat there with a silly grin, smitten with bro-love.

"When you get your stuff, meet us at the car rental," Bobby said. Kevin never said a word to us; he was half asleep.

Scott put up his hand to high-five me, then I high-fived Jamie. A short time later, after the plane took a few dips, we landed in Costa Miel. The terminal had large windows where the mountains stretched wide across the horizon. The vista showed the foreground riddled with palm trees. Farther back, more trees formed a hedge around the airport. It was a hot afternoon below the patchy clouds. Jamie was so excited he took copious amounts of photographs. It intensified after we picked up our surfboards at the baggage claim. Jamie got bold and asked a standing transit officer if he could take photographs of us. When simple English wouldn't do, Jamie persisted by using hand gestures. Under the officer's thick mustache, his straight face switched to a wide smile as he reached out for Jamie's camera. We posed like dumb gringos, looking around with idiotic awe. Next, we playfully stood side by side with arms crossed. We drew in a few women and children curious to watch our clownish display. The policeman took one last photograph and handed the camera back to Jamie. Jamie thanked the officer, and in pure Jamie-style, took things to the next level and asked him to pose arresting us. To our surprise, the officer agreed. He got a kick out of the whole thing. I wanted to hit the road, but screw it, it was funny, so why not. Bobby and Kevin were halfway to the coast anyway. We placed our hands against the nearest wall and spread 'em. Scott looked guilty about something. He always looked guilty of something, but that's another story.

Jamie told the officer to stand with authority behind Scott and me. Somehow they were able to communicate and Jamie clicked away. Some children nearby gazed with eager curiosity; others were enthralled. With my head down and my hands against the wall, I looked over at an old woman whispering into a boy's ear. The child moved his hand over his mouth and smiled through his fingers. That's when I lost it and started to laugh as Jamie handed the camera to Scott and switched roles. The picture taking continued. The child's rapture was contagious. Jamie took one last photograph of us posing side by side with the officer. We shook hands and wished him well.

When we arrived at the rental car center, the lady told us no pickup trucks were available, only subcompacts. We got screwed. By some miracle, we were able to strap our surfboards to the top of that glorified go-kart. We drove around the parking lot looking for Bobby and Kevin, but no sign of them. They wouldn't wait around for a bunch of baby-girls giddy about being on a vacation for the first time, so we headed for the exit. Would you believe our new surfer buddies waited for us on the side of the road? We didn't. Bobby pointed west, and we followed. Scott let out a heavy sigh when he saw they rented the last pickup truck. I was like, whatever, and Jamie took more photographs out of the tiny window from the back seat. Off we rolled down the highway in our little surf-mobile.

The vegetation was lush all around. Hotels, buildings, and homes scattered across the thick green landscape. The airport was in the center valley, so for a time, as we drove west, it was flat. Bobby and Kevin sped so I did my best to catch up. Jamie ran out of film. Scott soaked in everything as he tapped his hands on his knees. We were smiling the whole time. With no air-conditioning, it was hot, but the wind was cool and the air smelled fresh and different. Leaving the valley, the road narrowed as we drove up a mountain. The highway stretched and bent around thick growth, and the landscape displayed striking colors. Here and there rocks protruded along the mountainside. I looked down to see a small waterfall cascade from a deep crevice between the rocks. My ears popped from the high altitude. Looking down, along the base of the mountain, I saw a small house surrounded by grazing cattle. All the fun ended after we descended from the peak. The brakes began to smoke, and I struck enough potholes to give me a panic attack. I mean they were everywhere. I hit one pothole that felt like the floor dropped out from under my feet. I looked out the rearview and was relieved to see no fallen car parts. I knew we should have reserved a pickup truck; I should have done that a month ago. Now we were going to break down in the middle of this strange country and starve to death. At the bottom of the hill, the road leveled off. The harsh smell of burnt brake pads made us cough, and the last pothole felt like the oil pan fell off. I wanted to pull over and check the vehicle's condition, but to be frank, I was afraid to look. We were still moving so that was good enough for me. Bobby and Kevin were way ahead of us at this point. I imagined them laughing uncontrollably at us and our little clown car.

"Damn, the potholes are killing me. I hope we get there in one piece," I said.

"Do you see any warning lights on the dashboard?" Jamie said.

"No," I said.

"Then don't worry about it. We don't want to lose those guys. Keep up with them," Scott said as he strapped on his seat belt.

"Dude, everything's fine. We're only bottoming out every five minutes instead of every two minutes. Things are improving," Jamie said, giggling.

"Keep going. You're doing fine. Stay close to them. If we break down, we'll deal with it then," Scott said with confidence.

"Look, if we break down, hit the horn so they hear us," Jamie said.

"You think they're gonna stop for us? Please, give me a break," Scott said.

"God, I hope so," I said.

On top of all the potholes, the smoking brakes, and the narrow roads, we had the one-lane bridges to deal with. You had to see them. If you didn't stop in time, it was over. I mean kiss-your-ass-goodbye over. If you didn't stop to negotiate who crossed the bridge first, it was a game of chicken with oncoming traffic. This happened several times along the way. I guess for the locals it was no big deal, but to my amateur ass, it was life or death.

Back on a flat road, my anxiety waned. We passed a small town. On the roadside, street vendors sold pottery, fruit, and clothing. People in town played soccer or gathered in groups, or both. We took the next jug handle and followed signs for Playa Sueños, which put us back on the highway. Over time, I got better at maneuvering around potholes.

Scott pointed ahead. Bobby and Kevin were pulled over by the police. One of the officers waved us over. I stopped behind their pickup truck. The officer was tall, thin, and wore a tie with his uniform. Without a word he leaned in close and took a whiff, stepped back, and said a few words in Spanish. After a little back-and-forth, he said Jamie and I were in violation for not wearing seat belts. As a result, we had to pay a fine and take a mandatory trip to the police station. It took a moment to process the officer's demand. A trip to the police station was a major diversion, not to mention scary. I wasn't getting help from my friends, so in my best Italian, I apologized, and said I was new in Costa Miel and I didn't know. Rather than scowl me, he asked if I was Italian. When I told him I was American, his tone changed. He said if I gave him twenty dollars, a trip to the police station wasn't necessary. When I repeated what he said in English, Jamie tapped my shoulder and handed me a twenty-dollar bill. I didn't think twice about it. I grabbed the money and handed it to the officer followed by one big gracias. We were all smiles after that—even the policeman. The transgression was resolved. Bobby and Kevin must have done the same thing because they were already waiting for us to haul ass. Adios, highway patrol. By the time we reached Playa Sueños, it was dark. We thanked Bobby and Kevin, who gave us the shaka sign and drove off.

Our hotel was near the center of town. We checked in, leaned our surfboards against the wall, and dropped our bags on the floor. The balcony outside the room faced the courtyard. A thick hedge buffered us from the swimming pool. We punched each other with excitement and left. We walked past the tiki bar, the swimming pool, and down a sandy trail to the beach. It was dark but the moon's reflection hit the crests of the waves and the sea sparked under the moonlight. The beach stretched out, ending in both directions by cliffs descending into the sea.

"Wow, you feel that? The ground shook when the wave crashed," Jamie said.

Scott chimed in, "We're in for a double head high day tomorrow, guys—get ready!"

"That's the Pacific Ocean, baby," Jamie said.

"We'll be the first ones here tomorrow," I said.

We wandered away from the sea toward town. Our feet stepped onto the main strip called Calle Principale. Like moths in the night, we followed the bright lights to the open shops and restaurants. The sound of reggae music told us we'd arrived. We passed a small plaza, a souvenir shop, and a few more restaurant-bars until we found the Onyx Club. It resembled the Trade Winds back home, which caught our attention. Scott gave us this look and we headed straight for the door. Tables and chairs surrounded the dance floor. The DJ played dance music from a small stage in the corner and the lights were dim. We sat at the bar. The bartender looked American with dirty blond hair and a deep tan. He wore an Onyx Club T-shirt with a parrot logo.

"Do you speak English?" I asked, almost shouting above the music.

"Sure, what can I get ya?" he said.

"Tres Cervezas, por favor," I said.

"Where are you guys from?" the bartender asked.

"New Jersey . . . near Asbury Park," I said.

"No way!" He smiled. "I'm from New Jersey. Have you been to Cherry Hill?"

"No, what exit is it?" I asked.

"Na, it's not off the parkway; it's nearer to Philly."

"We know Philly, but not Cherry Hill," I said.

"No worries."

Scott tapped my shoulder and motioned for me to listen. "Dude, this guy lives here. Now, that's what I'm sayin'. He's living the dream."

"Definitely," I said. I looked at Jamie. "How are you doing?"

"Pretty girls here. You checkin' this out?" Jamie nodded toward the crowd.

"Definitely," I answered. I doubt he heard me, but I nodded in agreement and looked out to the dance floor. The girls outnumbered the guys. There were some American girls—at least I thought they were American. They grouped together with drinks in hand, whooping and laughing with one another. Looking on, my eyes fixed on one girl in particular. She danced with another beauty. They were like sisters. She stood out among the swaying background in a yellow dress. Whenever she looked in my direction, I peered away. I found myself gazing back at her. The bartender placed our drinks on the counter. I paid. Scott mentioned he would buy the next round.

"I'm Ryan," the bartender said. "If you guys need anything else, let me know."

"Thanks," I said. The music changed. She swayed to the music back to the bar with her girlfriend. They sat down and ordered drinks. As she waited, she caught me looking—our eyes met long enough for her to smile. That did it for me. She stored her gem in my heart. I had to have her.

"Scott, she smiled at me," I said, losing self-control.

"So go over there and talk to her," Scott demanded. "Don't be a pussy."

What if she didn't speak English? I thought. My Spanish skills were nil. I could use some Italian words to bridge the gap. I don't know. She glanced at me again, whispering into her friend's ear. I held down my fear of rejection long enough for me to move in, so with little hesitation, I went for it. I handed Jamie my beer and I walked over. Scott and Jamie watched me like fans watching the Chicago Bulls win the NBA Finals. As I neared, her girlfriend inspected me as if I were a racing horse. She stepped back to give me room. At this point I was going on pure determination. I smiled at both of them, and I leaned in so not to yell over the music.

"Hi, my name is Luca. You dance very well," I said, hoping like hell she spoke English. Thinking back, I should have said Luke, rather than Luca. I always referred to myself as Luke growing up; only my parents or relatives called me Luca. It is my real name, though, and at that moment, it felt Latin-like to say it. I thought something was wrong when they started chatting in Spanish. "What's your name?" I said over the chatter.

"My name is Eva and this is my friend Rosa," she said politely, placing her hand on Rosa's shoulder. Her accent was heavy but clear.

"Nice to meet you," I said. "How long have you two been dancing?" I asked Eva.

She gave Rosa a strange look. Eva turned to me and asked, "You mean tonight?"

"No, I mean when did you first learn how to dance? How long ago?"

"Since we were young. Dancing is part of being Latina. We love to dance," Eva said.

"Oh, so all Latin women are great dancers, right?" I asked with eager curiosity.

The girls stared at each other again and giggled. I got a little nervous when Eva covered her mouth. I felt myself blush. All I did was smile back. I clammed up, waiting for her to say something. That's when I opened my mouth again and said, "Rosa, do you speak English?"

"She can understand more than she can speak," Eva interrupted. Rosa said something to Eva in Spanish. Eva nodded and waved her hand away. I stood there looking like I knew what they were saying. I took some Spanish back in high school, but they spoke so fast I couldn't follow. Eva insisted Rosa say something in English, but Rosa refused.

I asked if I could buy them both a drink. They agreed. In my peripheral vision, I saw my friends give each other a high five.

"Coca-Cola light," Eva said.

I got excited. I got brave and said, "Me gusta Costa Miel." The few words I remembered from Spanish class.

"Oh, you speak Spanish?" Eva said.

"I took it in high school so I'm not very good—hablo poco."

"That's okay," Eva said and smiled.

Her smile gave me hope. I ordered drinks. I thought it was a good time to call over my friends. They could handle Rosa for me.

"Estoy aquí con amigos. Would you like to meet them?" I said. They agreed, so I waved them over.

"Eva, please correct my Spanish if I don't say it right: Estos mis amigos, Scott y Jamie. Did I say that right?"

"Si, muy bueno, but you don't have to speak Spanish. We can understand English," Eva said.

Scott interrupted, "Yeah, Luke, forget the Spanish, man. Can't you see these girls are fine without you?"

"Yeah, okay, chill out, bro. Jamie, this is Eva and Rosa," I said.

Without delay, Scott walked up to Rosa and made himself known to her. Jamie helplessly stood by.

"I'm so glad you speak English," I said to Eva. "I was getting worried."

"I will try."

"Muy bueno. I think Rosa doesn't like me," I said.

"No, she's okay. We protect each other, but sometimes she makes me crazy."

"Why?"

"Yes, she is my friend; she thinks she knows what is best for me."

"Well, that's good, isn't it?" I asked.

"Yes, but sometimes I don't think so—sometimes we argue," Eva said.

"Yeah, my sister is like that with me sometimes. If I don't agree with her, I walk away before she gets angry. You know."

"Yes," she said. "But Rosa will say it again, and again, and again." She smiled.

Dance music with a familiar tempo played. "Would you like to dance with me?" Eva gave me a look of hesitation. "Just one dance," I said. "We'll go slow."

After a slight pause, she agreed. I followed her to the dance floor. We zigzagged around the other dancers like dragonflies. She faced me and held my hands. She looked down to show me her legs. She kept it simple. Her steps were short and slow. I felt her lead as she pushed and pulled on my hands. I tried not to look down, but I was afraid to step on her feet, so I looked down anyway. Someone bumped into me, but Eva adjusted, slowing down until we were in sync again. She was patient. We danced through a few songs before she waved to me and spoke in my ear. "I have to go back." I agreed. My friends were getting along with Rosa; Jamie was starting to lighten up and Scott was all smiles. Rosa looked nervous but engaged. I asked Eva about Playa Sueños: When were the festivals and how strict were the police? I told her what happened to us on the highway and she said the police do that sometimes. Rosa approached and said it was time to go. Rosa looked over her shoulder at a man standing near the bar. I waited for Eva to look at me. I asked if I could see her again. The request sent a pause between the girls and then a slight back-and-forth. Finally, Rosa shook her head at Eva. I felt she wanted to rush Eva away, but she didn't move. Instead, Eva smiled back at me and said, "Yes."

"Can I meet you here tomorrow?" I said.

"Tomorrow is okay," she answered. "Twelve o'clock. We can eat lunch together."

"Yes," I said. I smiled and waved goodbye as they walked away.

"So, what happened?" Scott said.

"I asked her out and she said yes. I'm gonna see her tomorrow."

"That's awesome, dude. You're the man," Scott said.

"What about Rosa—what's her story?" I said.

"She was real friendly, but there was something up with her. She kept looking at this guy at the bar. When you came back with Eva, she got weird—something about them leaving early," Scott said.

We looked for this man at the bar, but he was gone.

"Hey, you guys want to head back to the hotel? I'm tired, and I wanna hit the waves tomorrow," I said.

"Dude, you're on a roll. Hang out with us longer," Scott said.

"It's been a long day. Besides, I want to get up early and surf."

Jamie tapped Scott's arm and said, "Let him go, Scott." Jamie looked at me and said, "Go, dude. We're gonna be here for a while."

"All right, but remember, we're surfing first thing in the morning."

"Don't worry," Scott said as he waved me away. "Bye."

"You gonna be all right walkin' back alone?" Jamie said.

"Dude, he's not a pussy. He proved that tonight. He's more than fine," Scott said.

"I got lucky with Eva . . . I'll be fine getting back. You guys have fun."

"Watch out for the federales," Jamie said as he slapped my shoulder.

"I'll be a good little gringo," I said. Part of me wanted to stay, but with so many first times in one day, all I wanted was sleep. I kept thinking of Eva. I also felt like a bitch for leaving my friends behind.

Chapter 4

"C'mon," I said, nudging Scott's shoulder. He rubbed his face as he woke.

"What time is it?"

"It's time to surf, bro. Jamie's waiting outside," I said.

"Ah, man. Okay, I'll catch up," Scott said as he realized the time.

"Okay." I grabbed my board and left.

The color of the sea matched the blue sky. Behind me the sun rose over the mountains and warmed my back. Jamie and I stood on the sand for a few minutes to inspect the surfing conditions. Swells formed waves and crashed with the weight of a billion gallons of water. The largest waves I had ever seen. As we paddled out, you felt the abiding energy of the earth and the raging currents of the sea. A fear creeped over me. With prudence, I caught a small wave, which for me was large, and it carried me to shore. I realized they were too big for me, but I couldn't quit now. Fearful, I paddled out, cautious to avoid having a wall of water fall on my head. I got past the breakers and sat on my board and watched. I took deep breaths to calm down. I looked for the smaller waves to ride. Jamie paddled to me. He proclaimed with utter enthusiasm that he would surf until nightfall. He added that if a shark swam up to him and bit a piece out of his ass, it wouldn't change his mind. Scott paddled up.

"Oh my God," Scott said as he sat on his board. "Dude, this is definitely not Jersey. Am I right, bros?"

"Not even close. These waves are monsters, so be careful," I said.

"Dude, chill, we'll be fine," Scott added and paddled away.

"What happened last night?" I asked Jamie.

"Nothin'. Scott drank his ass off, so I had to put his sorry ass to bed. He was loud and obnoxious the whole way back. I should've gone back with you."

"Na, you guys did the right thing. You gotta use every waking second here, ya know."

"Ah, man, he bitched the whole night. He got rejected once and he was like, 'This bitch is this and that bitch is that'—feeling sorry for himself, ya know."

"Well, once he gets laid, he'll calm down," I said.

"Yeah, he should do it and do it soon. To be honest, I need it too. I saw a few hookers walking around last night. It shouldn't be a problem as long as they're not crazy-expensive."

"Yo, heads-up," I said, pointing to the horizon.

Jamie shifted on his board to catch the wave. He paddled past me as the crest formed over him. The swell lifted me and I dropped for what felt like twenty feet and Jamie was gone. The wave crashed, churning sand upward. The color of the blue ocean around me changed to an eddy of clay-colored water. I looked for Jamie—nothing. A sense of dismay crept over me every second I lost sight of him. Every passing moment meant he was under. I looked back for any approaching waves before I paddled to shore. My heart raced. How would I explain this to his parents? Time slowed as I began to panic. I didn't see him. Finally, I looked down the shoreline to a figure; it was him, stumbling out of the water. I ran over. Jamie was out of breath and exhausted.

"You all right, Jamie?!"

He answered me between breaths. "I was under for a long time." A breath. "I'm all right though." A breath. "I'm good." A breath. "I got drilled." A breath.

"Dude, forget this," I said. "Let's go back to the room and chill. The waves are too big today. We'll hang out in town and check conditions tomorrow."

"Na, I'm good," he answered as he gained control of his breathing. "Just give me a few minutes."

"Are you sure?" I said.

"Yeah, yeah, I'm fine. Wow, that kicked my ass."

"I'm gonna ask you one more time, Jamie. You don't have to go. We can come back tomorrow."

"No way. I'm fine. I'm going back out," he said.

Jamie's determination inspired me. I paddled out with him, keeping my prudence paramount. I noticed more surfers riding as the morning progressed, which made me feel ashamed of my fear. I wasn't worried about Scott. He surfed well. I pondered whether I should use a longboard in the future. I paddled to where the waves were smaller, and rode the ones I could handle. After a while, I motioned to Jamie that I was heading back. He gave me a thumbs-up.

Back in the room, I changed and headed to the Onyx Club to meet Eva. I arrived a little before twelve o'clock. It was slow and Ryan, the bartender, was working again. Latin music played over the speakers—no DJ. Ryan recognized me with a smile and nodded. "The Jersey boy is back," he said. "Where're your friends?"

"They're not coming," I said as I sat at the bar.

"What happened? You guys got into a fight over those girls last night?"

"Na, I'm here to see one of them."

"Oh, very nice."

I smiled. "Yeah, I'm the lucky one."

"You are. You are the lucky one. Can I get you something to drink while you wait?"

"Sure, I'll have an Imperial."

"All right."

"Ryan—your name is Ryan, right?"

"Yup."

"I wanted to ask you how you ended up here."

Ryan chuckled. "I get that question a lot. I came here on vacation about three years ago and loved it. You know, the beach, the mountains, the easy life—the people are friendly too. Anyway, when I found out I can handle things financially here, I was sold."

"What about your family? Were they cool about it?"

"Yeah, my parents supported it. It got me out of their house." We laughed.

Eva stepped up to the bar. She wore a blue sleeveless dress with a pleated bottom that flowed with her legs. She smiled at Ryan.

"Hola, Ryan," she said.

"Cómo es usted, Eva?" Ryan asked.

"Bien gracias."

"Hello," I said. "You look great—beautiful dress."

"Thank you," Eva said, smiling.

"Would you like something to drink?" I said.

"Coca-Cola light, please."

"Sorry I'm dressed this way. I didn't bring much with me on this trip," I said. I had on my only short-sleeved polo shirt among the T-shirts, surf trunks, and cargo shorts in my travel bag. I took a mental note to buy something decent to wear.

"You look good," she said sincerely.

"I was so impressed with your dancing last night. Can you show me a few more dance moves? We can eat afterwards."

"Okay, you were very good last night. I can show you some steps, but I am not a good dancer," Eva said.

"Don't worry. Go slowly and I'll copy you."

She paused for a moment and giggled. "Okay, I will go slow," she said.

Ryan put down our drinks. I left money on the bar, and he nodded. "If you need anything else, let me know," he said.

I took Eva's hand and led her to the dance floor. We stood apart as I watched her switch her weight from her left foot to her right and back. Her hips shifted with her steps. She called it the Merengue. She counted 1-2-3-4-5-6-7-8 as she stepped and shifted from the left to the right. She repeated her steps, and I followed. It was simple. Next, she took my hand and told me to start with my left foot. She put my other hand on her hip and encouraged me to lead. I pulled her close to me. She told me not to sway my shoulders so much, but to move my hips only. The music played a heavy drum and horn mix. I stopped looking down as I moved with the music. She let go of my hands as we danced freely. I remained calm and focused with what she taught me, trying to keep tempo. She was amazing. I'm not sure how I looked, but she didn't seem to care. Her eyes closed, and she withdrew, looking self-absorbed, dancing and swaying with a sexy grace. It got hot, and after a while she stopped and led me back to the bar.

"See, you are very good. Excuse me, my English is bad. Did I teach you good?" she said.

"Yes, thank you. Your English is fine. I'm sorry for not speaking Spanish. My parents are from Italy and I have a hard time even remembering Italian words. I'm horrible at learning languages."

"You're Italian? Tell me more." Eva sipped her drink.

"Well, I was born in the United States, but my parents are from Sicily. They came to the U.S. in the late 1960s."

"Where do you live in America?" she asked.

"New Jersey, about an hour from New York City."

Eva's face lit up. "Oh, I love New York City."

"Have you been there?" I said.

"No, but one day I will go."

"Do you have family in America?" I said.

"No, my family is here—me and my mama."

"Well, if you ever come to New York, I'll show you around. I'll take you anywhere you want to go; we'll see everything."

She smiled before taking a sip.

"Let's have lunch. Would you like to eat here?" I said.

"No, is that okay?" she answered with slight apprehension.

"Sure. No problem. Where do you want to go?"

"The Colonial is very good."

Eva waved to Ryan, and I thanked him. Walking along the sidewalk, we passed shops, cafés, and places to eat. It was hot and my skin was getting red. I'd surfed without wearing sunscreen and I was starting to pay for it. Over the din of the midday noise, Eva pointed to The Colonial. The dining tables were outside on a patio under a tin roof held up by wooden posts. Short palm trees in large pots decorated the corners. A warm ocean breeze cooled my sunbaked skin. Eva chose a table off in a cozy corner, away from the street. I pulled out a chair for her.

"Thank you," she said.

"You're welcome. Wow, it's busy here."

"Yes, the food is good here."

The waiter arrived to hand us menus.

"Something to drink?" the waiter said.

"So many choices," I said. She agreed. Eva ordered a virgin piña colada.

"I bet it's because you saw Ryan making one before," I said, smiling.

"That's true," she replied with a smirk.

"I'll have an Imperial, please." The waiter walked away.

"What do you recommend?" I said.

"Oh, there is beef, chicken, or fish," Eva said as she pointed to the menu.

"Looks like everything comes with rice and beans."

"Do you like rice and beans?" she asked.

"I do. I'll have rice and beans and chicken. What rice and bean combination are you getting?"

"No, I will get the vegetable tapas," she said.

I smiled. "I guess you're tired of rice and beans."

The waiter arrived with the drinks. He took our order and we added an appetizer of cheese quesadillas.

"It's a beautiful day. Thank you for being with me. The dress you're wearing looks beautiful."

Eva looked down with a coy smile. "Thank you. It's a nice design."

"It's a pretty design. Last night you had on another pretty dress. You have an eye for it."

"Oh, I love clothing design. When I am off from work, I like to draw new designs and think of the colors."

"You have a talent."

"No, I don't. It's something I love to do for fun, but I work too much. Thank you for saying that."

"What do you do for a living?" I said.

"I work as a waitress at a nightclub."

The waiter arrived with the cheese quesadillas.

"What is your job back home?"

"I'm in college. I'm going into my junior year. When I'm on break, I help my father with his business."

"What is the business?"

"It's a gas station with auto repair."

"You can fix cars?" Eva asked.

"Yeah, I can do most repairs. I love engineering, especially robotics."

"Oh, the car makes a noise when I start it. I don't know why."

"If you're worried about it, show me the problem. I can see what's wrong."

"Okay, yes. Thank you."

"Do you hear the noise all the time or only sometimes?"

"Only when I start it. After I drive, it goes away."

"Maybe it's the belt," I said.

The food arrived. She gave me a tapas to try. It was delicious. The food was fresh and the meat tender. Eva smiled. I tried not to stare. I would spend the whole vacation fixing her car if she asked me. "How did you learn to speak English so well?"

"Well, we have so many Americans who come here. I have to learn English. I also learn from the movies and reading the American newspaper."

Our conversation shifted from how I met my friends to styles of Latin music and how to dance to each one. I asked about the local wildlife. She said to watch for falling fruit while parrots feed overhead. She said it's strange to see a lone monkey because they tend to live in small groups.

I finished my second beer. The breeze picked up and the crowd thinned. I thought of asking her to walk with me on the beach, but it felt like it was too much too soon. She finished her virgin piña colada.

"Eva, I have to ask you something." She nodded to my words. "I want to visit the Adora National Park tomorrow. If you're free, would you like to go with me?"

She looked a little surprised. "Oh, I have work tomorrow . . . Will I be back before four o'clock?" she asked.

"Yes, the tour bus leaves at nine in the morning and the tour lasts five hours."

"Oh, yes. I will go," she said.

"Great. Have you been there before?"

"A long time ago with my mother; it is a beautiful place."

I told her where I stayed. The waiter placed the bill on the table, and I paid. "Is your car close by?" I said.

"Yes, it's down the street."

"Can I walk you to your car?" She agreed.

We walked in silence again, this time side by side. I thanked her for her time and the dance lesson. She started the car. The engine let out a loud pitch and a squeaking sound. I leaned down to the driver's-side window and said, "It sounds like a loose belt. After our trip tomorrow, I'll look at it. You should be fine getting home."

She thanked me with a nod.

"See you tomorrow morning," I said.

She smiled, and drove away. I stood there like a dork. I walked back to the hotel feeling light-footed. I felt both a sense of relief and accomplishment. I thought of what to say to impress her.

The midafternoon heat was almost unbearable. Scott and Jamie were sleeping when I entered. Wet beach towels were strewn across the floor. The room smelled like board wax and seawater. Each took a queen-size bed for themselves. Jamie took up less space, so I lay next to him. I woke him.

"How'd it go?" Jamie whispered.

"Great. She's coming over tomorrow, around nine."

"Nice."

"We're going to the park," I said.

"Is she bringing her friend?"

"No, but I'll put in a good word for you."

"That's cool," Jamie said. He turned over and went back to sleep; I told him to move over, and I fell asleep beside him.

Later, Scott woke me and told me they were going out for dinner. It was almost 8:00 p.m., much later than I thought.

"I slept for four hours. What the hell," I said.

"Jet lag, bro, and surfing all day," Scott said. Jamie stepped out of the bathroom. I got up and got ready.

The concierge told us the restaurant was upstairs. Food service was buffet style. I got shredded beef, beans, and fried plantains. I sat down at a table next to the railing overlooking the courtyard. Jamie arrived with a burger and fries on his plate. He had a Pilsen like me. I remembered someone drinking it the night before, so I gave it a try—good flavor.

"Luke, I swear to God, if that wave held me down any longer, I would've drowned," Jamie said.

"I panicked when I didn't see you. You scared the crap out of me."

Jamie laughed, but it wasn't funny to me; I remained solemn as I ate my dinner. Scott showed up with his tray full of fried chicken wings and bacon.

"Those waves were monsters. I thought about turning tail and running away like a baby Ewok," Jamie said.

"From what I remember, Ewoks were brave and kicked ass," I said.

"C'mon, dude. Ewoks were made up by the movie producers to keep the kids happy. The Ewok concept ruined it for me."

I laughed. "Jamie, I'm with you—the empire is badass. All I'm sayin' is the Ewoks were brave—that's all."

"Ewoks ruined my life . . . They made *Return of the Jedi* into a Laurel and Hardy skit. Isn't that a shame? I swear I'm gonna write a letter to George Lucas and tell him," Jamie said.

"Yeah, you do that. Hey, some of those surfers out there were real pros today," I said.

"One guy was way the hell out there, and I was thinkin', why? Then I saw that baby tsunami form and he caught it. I duck-dived under him to get the hell out of his way. The dude knew his stuff," Jamie said.

"What do you think so far, Scott?" I said.

"This place is awesome—I wanna move here," Scott said.

"The waves didn't look so big from the shore, but when you're out there—oh my God," I said.

"Some guy told me there was a storm offshore that's caused the large swells, but I'll tell you, they're not that big. Go to Hawaii—now that's big wave surfing, fellas," Scott said and turned to me. "Luke, I saw you miss a wave about double-head high. That bitch would have knocked you into next week if you fell under it. You know which one I'm takin' about?"

"No," I said.

"Dude, you know. You know. You're lucky you didn't catch that one. That would have been your ass," Scott said.

"I admit it was crazy out there. I had fun with the small waves," I said.

"By the end of this week, we'll be surfin' like pros," Jamie said, as he winked at Scott. "Scott, you're gonna be the big kahuna out there."

"Yeah, right," Scott said. "How was your date, Luke?"

"It was good. We danced a little, then we had lunch."

"Danced? In the middle of the day?" Scott said.

"Dude, around here, people dance anytime," I said.

"All I gotta say is you better tap that ass while you have the chance. In a week we're outta here and she's gonna be history," Scott said.

"He's playing it cool," Jamie said to Scott. "You are, dude. Don't deny it."

I chuckled. "Look, I'm having fun. It's a vacation, right? Whatever happens, happens."

"Yeah, well, while you're having fun, we'll be hangin' out at the bar trying to get some." Scott pointed to Jamie. "Whoever gets lucky gets the room for the night. The rest of us sleep on the beach."

"What if we all get lucky?" I said.

"I don't know about that. You know, sex on the beach is nice, too, but I'm still gettin' the room," Scott said.

"What's the matter? You don't want sand up your ass? I'll do it anywhere. I don't care," Jamie said. We laughed.

"Nice," I said. "Watch out, Jamie. A crab will crawl up your ass and pinch your balls."

"Yeah, really, but I don't care where I have sex as long as I'm gettin' some," Scott said.

"Yeah, none of us care where we do it as long as we do it," I said. We chuckled.

After dinner, we walked out onto the town and visited the local surf shop. Jamie bought a pair of board shorts and Scott got a new board leash. I got myself a few linen-cotton shirts and a pair of Bermuda shorts. We decided to turn in early and hit the waves in the morning. I went to bed excited to see Eva again.

Chapter 5

The morning light through the open patio door woke me. A warm breeze brought in the smell of the courtyard, and I could hear waves crashing.

Scott got out of bed. He entered the bathroom and closed the door.

Jamie sat up quickly and turned to me. "Luke, you up?"

"Yeah," I said as I stirred.

"You wanna go surfing before you see her?"

"What time is it?" I yawned.

"It's eight."

"Dude, I have to get ready and buy the tickets. Maybe I'll surf when I get back."

Jamie got up and sat on the other bed, facing me.

"How much are you gonna hang out with this girl?" he said.

"I don't know. If she wants to hang out, I will. I ain't missin' this one. Sorry, dude."

"Yeah, I know. But we've been talking about this trip for like over a year and now you're completely out of the picture—I'm just saying."

Scott left the bathroom and grabbed his surfboard. "You guys comin' or you gonna make out?" he said.

"Go ahead. I'll catch up to you," Jamie said.

"I'm not goin' . . . I'm taking Eva to the park," I said.

"Yo, remember, you can always find a girl back home, but you can only surf like this here. I'm out, fellas," Scott said and left the room.

Jamie waited for the door to close. "Hey, I admit. If I was hanging out with Eva, I'd forget about us too. But all I'm saying is before you disappear, try to spend a little time with your friends."

I nodded in agreement. I was sure Eva would be their top priority if they dated her. I knew they were upset, but oh well, that's how it goes.

After Jamie left, I took a shower and put on my new clothes. I looked down and thought I should buy sandals—mine were old. Kelly never liked it when I wore walking sandals; she preferred the slider type. I walked into the lobby and bought tickets. I headed to the tour bus. A short line of people stood waiting. Eva drove in and parked. She carried a small beach bag and a bottle of water. She wore neat jean shorts and a red short-sleeve shirt. Her hair tied back in a ponytail. She wore a New York Yankees baseball cap.

We hugged. "Hola," she said. "Did you wait a long time?"

"Na, I just got here. I got the tickets and I'm ready. Are you ready for the jungle?"

"Oh yes."

There are so many beautiful women in the world, too many to count, but her beauty struck me as natural, and tireless. I wanted to know her age. I knew she was older, but my curiosity was piqued. I made a mental note to find out somehow.

The bus door opened, and the driver stepped out to collect the tickets. Eva and I sat near the back. We were among the youngest on the bus. There were mostly older couples. The bus headed north out of town. The land was rich and fertile—life blossomed. A small number of red parrots, floral in décor, flew across an open field and veered off. Their bright yellows, reds, and browns dashed and disappeared into the dense forest, like a dream. Eva pointed at them in awe. She looked at me and said how much she loved animals. They're so innocent, she said. I gazed farther into the countryside at the splendor of the mountains. Soon my eyes wandered upon her as she stared out the window. I studied her face and followed her lines down her cheek, passing the curve of her neck.

"Can you teach me a little Spanish?" I said.

She gave me a look of inspection and with an intelligent half smile said, "Okay, like what?"

"How do you say: 'I am very happy today'?"

Eva leaned her head to one side, looked at my lips, and said in a whisper, "Hoy estoy feliz."

I leaned in closer and asked her to repeat it. Her lips curved and fluttered upon her gentle breath, sweet and soft. Her eyes smiled. I repeated the phrase. She asked me to correct my pronunciation a few times. She admired my effort. I thought for a moment and asked, "How do you say: 'I enjoy your company'?" She leaned her head back slightly and said, "Me gusta su compañía." I repeated the phrase with more enthusiasm, more vigor. She held back a laugh by covering her mouth. Between my questions, she pointed to things along the road and asked me what they were called in English. She requested English names for fruits she described with hand gestures. She spoke English very well.

We arrived at the park, the driver told us to remain seated and wait for our guide. Soon, a young man stepped onto the bus. He smiled and introduced himself both in English and in Spanish. "Good morning, ladies and gentlemen. My name is Philippe, and I am your guide today. You will follow me through Adora park, and we will experience this very special place. Adora park is special because it's a transition zone, which is a place between the dry region to the north and the wet region to the south. This zone attracts many animals from both regions and you will see a wide variety of plants as we walk together. Please do not touch any plants or animals during your visit. Follow me and stay close. I will stop and explain things to you as I see them. Now come." Over his shoulder, Philippe carried a spotting telescope on a tripod. He led us down a mud-dried trail. Above us, the thick treetops shaded the sunlight completely. Vines hung down and over buttress roots and branches. The trail was strewn with large leaves and small puddles. The movement of something above us caught the group's attention. To our utter amazement, a pair of monkeys swung and jumped along the branches high on the canopy. One stopped for a moment to look down, and with its curiosity satisfied, it moved on. We hiked through the forest with the occasional pause from our guide to explain the surrounding plants and animals. He spoke of the black and yellow spiky caterpillar, the banana spider, and the kapok tree.

"This place is amazing," I said. "I'm glad you're here with me."

"It is. I'm happy you like it."

"How about you—do you like it?" I asked.

"No, I hate it." We chuckled.

"Yeah, this place sucks," I said.

Eva reached down, plucked a small, bluish flower, and carried it for a while. With eager concern, her eyes squinted as she focused on my ear. She told me there was something in it, and she wanted to remove it. I got worried. I thought a poisonous ant had crawled into my ear and that I would suffer chronic hearing loss or even death. Although I didn't feel anything, she looked concerned for my well-being.

"What's the matter?" I asked anxiously. "What is it?"

"I don't know. Let me see." She placed her hand over my ear, and with a slight tug, placed the flower she held behind it. I waited for something else, but she stepped back, pointed, and giggled with her hand over her mouth.

"Very funny." I reached up to remove the flower, but she lunged at me and clutched my arm.

"No," she said. "Mi gusta. You look so handsome."

"You're funny, you know that? You want me to wear a flower on my ear like a hula dancer?" I said.

"Keep it on for me," she begged with a soft voice. "Please." She rubbed against me like a cat, caressed my arm, and moved down to hold my hand. I was so smitten by her, I wore the stupid thing.

I was surrounded by magnificent trees that reached amazing heights. The buttress roots on certain kapok trees were taller than me and were hundreds of years old. An older man approached me with his camera and asked me to snap a photograph, so I obliged. He placed his arm over his woman's shoulder as they stood between the roots. They did their best to ignore the flower I wore over my ear. The curious woman with him murmured as they wandered away and said what young men do for love. Eva reached up to my ear to reposition the flower to her liking. Philippe called out to the group for attention. We huddled around him. He pointed up to the canopy and explained rainforests like this one contain over half of all animal and plant species in the world. The tops of the trees can be as high as eighty meters. The organic matter that falls is eventually recycled back into the earth and nourishes the ecosystem. He went on for a while about that. Finally, he pointed to a few trees near the trail and spoke of the rare hardwoods native to the region. He was easy to listen to. We then continued down the trail.

"Eva, you said last night you were here once with your mother. How was it?" I asked. "Was it fun?"

She was nice enough to take the flower off my ear before answering me. I guess the prank wore off.

"Oh, I was a little girl, maybe seven or eight years old."

"What do you remember most about that day?"

"I remember a monkey took a banana from her hand. She was mad at the monkey, but I laughed and then she laughed with me."

"I didn't think monkeys were that brave. I thought they were scared of people," I said.

"When I got older, I learned monkeys can be dangerous, especially when the mama monkey has her baby. You should never go near them."

"I guess there was no guide with you at the time."

"No guide. It was a long time ago."

"What's your mother like?" I asked.

"She is a good mama. She worked hard to raise me, but now she is not feeling well."

"I'm sorry to hear that. I hope she's okay."

"She has depression. Sometimes she's fine and other days she's not."

"What do the doctors say about her condition? Is she getting treatment?"

"No doctors. My mother doesn't like drugs."

"Why? A doctor can help her."

"She saw a doctor and she took the drugs he gave her but she was not the same. She told me she felt old and her stomach hurt."

In a sudden gesture, Philippe raised his hand. He requested we remain quiet as he placed his tripod and scope down and directed the lens to the treetops. After a moment of adjusting and moving the scope, he said in a low voice, "Okay, okay, I found it, everybody. We're lucky." The group in unison looked up hoping to spot what he saw. Philippe stepped back and said, "Please make a line and look into the telescope. Not too long. I want everyone to see it."

The first person looked like a college professor on sabbatical. The group waited in anticipation, and the man finally uttered his revelation. "It's a toucan," he said.

"Yes," Philippe said with his finger pointing upward. "A toco toucan. Please don't stare for too long. I want everyone to see it. The largest of all toucans in the world." I tried to spot it by eye, but I couldn't. When it was our turn, I let Eva go first. With her eye to the lens, she whispered something to herself in Spanish. Her voice was soft and low, as if she whispered to a child. I was the last to peer into the eyepiece and gaze upon the giant toucan. The animal was all beak. I mean the beak was as long as its body, not including the tail—it was yellow with a white chest and appeared stately. It sat there and bathed in the sunlight, which may explain why it remained still for so long. It faced the sun in a small opening in the canopy. I moved aside to let the others see it again until it flew away. We continued down the trail. Eva offered me water.

"No, I'm fine."

"You're not thirsty? If you want some, ask me." She put the bottle back in her bag.

"Eva."

"Yes?"

"Thank you."

"For what?"

"For coming with me today. To be honest, I didn't think you were going to say yes."

"You're right. I had to think about it," she said with a smirk.

I giggled. "I don't remember waiting so long for your answer." We smiled at each other.

"So, do you have fun like this with your girlfriend back home?" she said.

"No," I said.

"Ah, so you have a girlfriend?"

"No, I didn't say that. I had a girlfriend, but not anymore."

"Was she nice?"

"Yeah, she was nice when she wanted to be."

"What happened?"

"I left her."

"Why?"

"It wasn't serious. We were young."

"Young? How old were you?"

"We met in high school—senior year—like seventeen. I'm twenty-one now. It was like puppy love."

"Oh . . . Was it like throwing away old shoes?"

"No . . . It was like I couldn't breathe with her."

She discerned my answer for a moment and said, "That's good."

"Are you still in school? How old are you?" I asked.

"Oh no, no school. I'm twenty-six."

"You look young. I thought you were nineteen."

"Oh, thank you. You're so nice," Eva said.

"When we get back to the hotel, I'll look at your car. I want to see what's up with that noise. I'm curious."

"Okay, if you want to."

"I do," I said.

"Okay, but only because you want to."

"I do," I said.

She smiled.

Chapter 6

My hands sweltered as I lifted the car hood. I leaned down. My arm snaked between the radiator hose and the belt pulley. Sweat rolled off my nose and fell somewhere. The engine belt had cracks and too much slack against the pulley. Eva stood by, watching. I told her to wait under a palm tree to stay cool, but she didn't listen. A lonely breeze gave only a slight relief from the heat of the day. The hotel parking lot was quiet, and the tour bus was long gone.

"I'm sorry, Eva, but the belt is bad. It's old and cracked. It needs to be replaced."

"Is it hard to change?"

"No, it's not a problem. If you tell me where I can find an auto parts store, I can buy a belt now and replace it for you. It's not a big deal."

"No," she said. "I only wanted you to check it. I will get it fixed."

I straightened up and leaned against the fender. "It's not a problem for me. It's easy." Her skin glistened with sweat—a light coating on her forehead. Her eyes looked troubled. "If I had two wrenches, I could fix it in ten minutes. It's that simple."

"Only ten minutes?" she said with uncertainty.

I chuckled. "Okay, how about this. I get the belt and the next time I see you, which I hope is soon, I'll replace it. Very simple." She fell silent and looked down. Her cap brim covered her eyes. She looked up with a gentle smile.

"You're very nice," she said. "I want to see you again."

"How about tomorrow?" I said.

"Yes," she said. "You know I work nights."

I paused for a moment. "We can have lunch again—is that okay?"

"Yes. Okay."

"I'll pick you up at your house?"

"No, no. I will drive here. It's not easy to find my house. I will come."

"Okay, not a problem. Where'd you like to have lunch?"

"I like Colonial."

"Perfect."

She reached out her arms and we hugged.

"Todo bueno," I said, smiling.

"Si," she said. "Todo bueno."

"Will you teach me more Spanish?" I asked as we relaxed and faced each other.

"If you teach me more English."

"Girl, you already know English."

"I want to know more," she said.

We laughed and hugged again. I closed the hood. Eva got in the car and lowered the window. I leaned down, hoping for a kiss, but I got a provocative stare and a heartfelt good-bye. I watched her drive away.

Back at the hotel room, I crashed on the bed and thought about the last two days. It wasn't a problem to have a long-distance relationship. A lot of couples did it. We needed to be more disciplined, that's all. We'd contact each other often and set future goals. One goal would be to bring her to the U.S. in about a year. No, I should take her back now. No, I still lived at home. No, I needed to make money. What about her mother? It was probably bad timing right now. I had to have her. I was only twenty-one years old.

I got up from bed and looked down at our unzipped travel bags stuffed with crap. I rifled through my bag and found a shirt to iron. I remembered seeing an iron in the closet. I ironed my shirt, and with the iron hot, I ironed the rest of my shirts and hung them in the closet. Jamie and Scott walked in, still wet from the ocean, laughing and chatting. They hushed when they saw me. Jamie leaned his surfboard against the wall and asked amiably, "How was the park?"

"It was fun," I said. I turned to Scott. "Hey, Scott, I want to say I'm sorry. I thought about what you said before and you're right." Scott let out a quick sigh as he leaned his surfboard against the wall.

"Dude, all I want is for us to have fun together and not to be separated by some bitches."

"C'mon dude, you know I can't help it. She's hot. See it from my side for a sec."

"What's happened since you guys have been hangin' out?" Jamie said as he sat on the bed. Scott sat down next to him.

"We danced, we had lunch, and we walked in the park. Now I'm gonna fix her car."

"Oh, so you're banging her now. That's awesome," Scott said triumphantly. "I'm taking back all the things I said about you. You're the man, Luke! Give it here, bro!" Scott held out his hand.

"What'd you say about me?" I said.

"Na, forget it. I was pissed off before. Now it's all justified. We're celebrating tonight," Scott said.

I shook my head. "No, I don't wanna bust your bubble, bro, but we didn't have sex. We're having a great time, and I like her. I like her a lot."

Scott and Jamie looked at each other with uncertainty. After a short silence, they gave me a cold stare.

"Wait, you mean you love her?" Scott said.

As if for the first time, my mind was lucid, and without doubt, I nodded in agreement. Scott began to laugh. Jamie stood up and placed his hands upon my shoulders, guided me down as I sat on the other bed. Scott fell back on the bed and continued his wicked, derisive laughter.

"Dude, we're going home in a couple days. I hope you realize that. We don't want to bring home a basket case. Think about it, bro—it's a little crazy, man. Think about it," Jamie said. Scott's laughter continued.

Scott sat up and coughed a few times to clear his throat. "Man, you're gonna be thinkin' about her all the time now. That sucks, big-time," he said as he tapped Jamie's shoulder to assist.

Jamie looked at Scott and then back at me. "Luke, my bro, Scott's got a point. You're setting yourself up for disaster. Do us all a favor and end it now."

"I don't want to," I said.

Scott interrupted, "Yeah, man, you do want to. It's real easy. Just go into the bathroom and jerk one out. Then we head back out and surf till nightfall. Tomorrow, we'll start over again until we go home. Put her in the rearview."

Jamie interjected, "Yeah, think about it. Once you're back in the States you'll never see her again. Okay, you might write to each other, and talk on the phone, but after a while you'll drift apart. The long-distance relationship thing doesn't work."

"I'll make it work. I don't care. I'm seeing her again. And if it fails, it's because she wants it to fail."

Jamie let out a sigh. "When're you gonna see her again?" he said.

"Tomorrow around noon."

"I'll see you on the plane ride home, bitch," Scott said, disgusted.

"Chill, dude. She's working tonight. We can hang out now. Let's have dinner and then go to the club," I said.

"This makes me think of something. You know back at the club that night—you remember those women off to the side? The ones dressed a certain way?" Jamie said.

"You mean the whores?" Scott said. "I told you to hook up with one of them, bro. There is nothing wrong with that."

"Maybe I will," Jamie said.

"Why do you wanna get with a whore?" I said.

"Dude, he needs it," Scott said to me.

"Let Jamie answer the question. Tell me, bro. Why do you need to be with one of them?"

"I know what you're thinking. And I thought about it a lot. You guys know how nervous I get around women. It'll help me build confidence in myself," Jamie said.

"I told you, bro. He needs this," Scott said.

"Hold up. Hold up," I said, raising my hands. "Jamie, I know you and you don't want your first time to be with—"

"I decided I'm doing it," Jamie interrupted.

"I don't want you to feel any regrets in the future. Think about it," I said. Jamie looked down at the floor. "I know you're not listening to me, but why not go for a hand job? You know, baby steps."

Jamie thought for a moment and nodded. "Okay, that's fair."

"Dude, let's eat," Scott said.

"All right," I said.

"There's a rib house not far from here. We can walk," Jamie said.

We paraded under the colorful signs, the souvenir shops, and the eateries. The streets were quieter under the hot afternoon sun, but the shops were busy. A few stray dogs ran along the street. They stopped, circled one another, and swarmed like bees down a narrow dirt pathway away from the road. A street vendor played the pan flute and sold CDs. Along the walls of a shop read the hand-painted words: ceviche y carnes. The only clouds in the sky rested above the mountains. The rib house was set back from the street surrounded by palm trees and an iron fence. There were concrete picnic tables covered over by a cloth canopy held up by wooden posts. Back farther was a square choza covered in Spanish tiles. The smell of cooked meat and burnt wood lingered. We ordered ribs and beer. We got comfortable and Scott started with his dream of visiting Playa Curvo before we left. We made plans to go the day after tomorrow. The waves in Playa Sueños were diminishing in size. We hoped the waves would be bigger there. People with children sat by us. The kids were horsing around enough to make us leave.

It was too early for the club; instead, we gravitated to the beach. Jamie and Scott spoke of the ocean waves in a philosophical way. My eyes followed the shoreline to the end where a cliff descended into the sea. During my time in Playa Sueños, I would look at it often as I surfed. The granite peak was enveloped in a cloud and I was drawn to it for no particular reason but to simply be there and climb it. I felt the need to make that excursion on my own, so I didn't say anything.

After a long walk along the beach, we wandered back into town, past the narrow streets and the colorful casas. Men played soccer on a grassy field and children played tag. The jungle thinned after crossing a narrow bridge, and we found ourselves in the center of town. We entered a café and sat down next to a large window. A woman sold flowers on the street, and we drank coffee. Across the street, construction workers put away their tools as the sky turned a dark opal. No one spoke for once, absorbed in the scene of a typical day in Sueños. We witnessed the end of the day in a tropical, coastal town. We left and found the Onyx Club. The sky was dark. A man unloaded boxes from his truck onto a cart outside a restaurant. An old man smoking a cigarette watched from his metal folding chair. He tossed the finished cigarette and told the delivery man where to stack the boxes. The sidewalks filled with eager travelers and wanderers.

A drunk tourist yelled out among his friends like they do back at the Jersey shore. The street was well-lit and the signs colorful. I realized it was true when they say the best way to know a city is by walking its streets.

We entered the Onyx Club. The women were gathered around, some standing and others sitting. We sat near them. I was nervous, but Jamie more so. Scott wanted to buy us drinks. He lifted his hand with three fingers up; Jamie and I nodded, and he left. Jamie told me which girl he liked, and I told him to follow me. A woman who we thought was the madam said hello. She had short blonde hair and was businesslike. She made us feel comfortable—not pretentious or aloof. I began to ask the madam if she knew English. She said no. I spoke to her in my best Spanish. I conveyed that my friend needed service from *that* young lady in the tube top with long auburn hair. Anyone watching could see my anxiety as I fumbled my way through the deal. She wanted $100 for her girl to give a hand job. I pointed two fingers up to signal $20. After some back-and-forth, I got her down to $70. It was going to be the best hand job of his life, she demanded. I thought for $70 Jamie could get a lot more than a hand job. I insisted on lowering the price. After more talking and interesting hand gestures, we agreed on $50. Without hesitation, I felt Jamie hand me the money under the table. With discretion, I handed the money to the madam. She put the money in her handbag and introduced the girl to us; her name was Sabrina. The madam spoke to her for a moment and Sabrina smiled at Jamie. We followed Sabrina outside under the bright streetlights. Sabrina took Jamie by the hand and led him into the darkness somewhere behind the club. Scott handed me a beer and we chuckled. After a while, the couple emerged from the darkness splitting up with a quick wave goodbye. Rather than talk about it, Jamie rushed past us, and we followed him down the street, away from the club. Scott and I caught up to him. Jamie focused ahead, moving with swift determination.

"Well?" Scott said. "How was she?"

"She was all right," Jamie said. "It was good."

"So, you're good?" I asked.

"Yeah, I'm good. Let's head back to the hotel," Jamie said.

Scott pointed at a surf shop we visited earlier and spoke of the women from the club he thought were hot. I listened and agreed, nodding. We debated on what makes a woman hot—is it her hair, her legs, her ass? Scott even spoke of sexy hands or feet as being a good reason for what makes a woman hot. After going over the subject for a while, we determined it could be anything. It can be one single feature that guys find irresistible. That's how simple we are. Jamie kept quiet but listened without interest. His mind was somewhere else.

Chapter 7

The sun rose with a fury and brightened the mountains behind us. We stepped onto the beach where I followed my friends' footprints into the sea. As I paddle out, I smelled the pineapple scent from my surf wax mixed with the salty seawater. The ocean was choppy with white caps here and there. Waves formed, crested, and fell till all that remained were white frothy lines, one after another. We duck-dived past the breakers. I felt less anxious. The big waves were gone. After surfing for a while, we floated together and let the current drift us slowly with the southern wind.

"What are you doing with Eva today?" Jamie said.

"After lunch, I gonna find an auto parts store in town. After I replace the belt, who knows what's next?" I said, smiling

"My man is getting some," Scott said. He took his finger and thrust it into the air. I smirked. Scott shifted his attention to the horizon. He turned his board and caught a wave, leaving Jamie and me alone. I watched a series of swells roll in. The first one formed a peak and began to crest. I caught it, but stood up too fast and lost balance. When I moved back to compensate, I fell. I relaxed my muscles as the ocean tossed me like a leaf in the wind, tumbling underwater. Before panicking, I surfaced. I took a few heavy gasps. When I felt revived, I mounted my surfboard and paddled to Jamie, who looked concerned for me.

"Are you all right?" Jamie said.

"Yeah, I'm okay. The wave held me down too long, that's all."

"You wanna take the next one?" he said.

"Na, go ahead."

Jamie caught the next wave and rode it to shore.

I thought of Eva. I wanted to see her again.

"Dude, what's wrong?" Scott said as he paddled to me.

"What do you mean?"

"You missed a nice wave, bro. If you don't watch out, someone'll take it."

"I got drilled on the last one. I guess I'm getting anxious," I said.

"Dude, we all wipe out. The last one wasn't that bad." Scott pointed at an approaching wave. A wave formed with a high peak. "Take it!" Scott commanded.

I paddled to catch the approaching wave. Its peak was already too high, but I remained committed; the face of it was high and massive. I lost balance and fell off the board. My surfboard hurled over me. I hit the ocean floor. The strain of my board lease almost pulled my ankle out of place, and everything went dark. I cursed myself. I knew it wasn't right to catch it—I knew it. My heart raced as I pulled myself up the surfboard leash. I swallowed some water before gasping for air at the surface. I got on my surfboard and I rolled on a wave to shore. Foamy seawater swirled around me. I ended up near a tributary that flowed into the sea. Tired, I sat on the beach. The nearest person was up a ways north of me. I figured it was about a twenty-minute walk back to the hotel. I sat there thinking of which tools to buy to replace the engine belt in her car.

Jamie found me. "You all right? I saw you got drilled," he said.

"Yeah. I got held under for too long; I don't know what's wrong with me."

"Is that it for you?" Jamie said.

"Yeah, I'm headin' back." I pushed back my wet hair. "The last couple of days have been hectic."

"No problem. What're you doing?"

"I'm gonna see Eva."

"I'll tell Scott."

"Thanks, man."

I walked back slowly. Jamie stood there and watched me.

"Dude, don't worry about Scott," he said as I walked away. "I'll talk to him."

"Thanks, man."

"Hey!" he said. "Put in a good word for me for Rosa."

"I will."

I got to the hotel room and showered. I put on a light blue shirt and black shorts. Slacks would have matched better with the shirt, but I didn't buy any and it was too hot. As I left the hotel room, Scott and Jamie approached.

"Hey," I said.

"Dude, look at you," Jamie said.

"What are you guys up to?" I said.

"We're gonna eat," Scott said.

"Yeah, I'm starving," Jamie said.

"Hey guys, let me see if we can all get together and hang out. I'll ask Eva to bring Rosa too—what do you say?"

They glanced at each other to confirm their approval.

"Yeah, all right," Scott said. Jamie nodded in agreement.

"I'm gonna see Eva now. I'll talk to her and work something out. Sound good?"

"Thanks," Jamie said.

No one looked back as we parted ways. I heard Scott and Jamie whisper as they entered the hotel room. If either one of them said anything stupid in front of those girls, that'd be the last time I hang out with those boners.

Before noon, Eva drove up to the entrance of the hotel. I got in and told her to take me to the auto parts store. She drove me to the only one in town. I told her to wait in the car. The place was a labyrinth filled with piles of auto parts of all types. There were even car parts hanging from the ceiling. It was organized chaos on steroids. Lucky for me, the guy behind the counter knew where everything was. By some miracle it only took him a few minutes to find me the engine belt I needed, an adjustable wrench, and a fourteen-piece metric wrench set.

We drove back to the hotel. It was so hot outside, Eva got out of the car and waited in the hotel lobby. The car was an older model with a simple belt system. After I replaced the belt, I took it for a test-drive. My hands were filthy, so I washed up at a gas station nearby and filled the gas tank. When I got back, I handed her the keys.

"All fixed," I said. She hugged me and kissed me on the cheek.

"Oh, you are fast. Gracias," she said.

"See? Not a problem."

"I didn't want to bother you."

"There's a restaurant upstairs. We can have lunch here if you like?" I said.

"Si, yes," she said.

We walked across the hotel lobby and up the stairs to the restaurant. I took a plate and got in line for the buffet. Eva stood behind me.

"Aren't you hungry?" I said.

"No, but I want coffee," she said.

"Did you eat this morning?"

"Yes, I had a banana and yogurt," she said.

"What do you want in your coffee?"

"Milk only, please."

I told her to find a table and sit. I came back with her coffee and milk. I got myself tacos and beer.

"Thank you," she said.

"You're welcome. It rained a little last night. I see little puddles here and there," I said.

"Oh yes, it rains a lot in August."

"When does the rainy season end?"

"November, December, and January are beautiful here. It's warm and dry." Eva put her coffee down on the table. "May I go to your room?" she asked.

I handed her the key. "Do you want another cup of coffee?"

"No." She placed her hand on my arm and smiled. Her hand moved with a tender touch across my forearm as she stood up. She looked back at me and stole a glance before going down the stairs.

The tacos were delicious. I finished my beer and waited a few minutes before realizing she wasn't coming back. My mind raced. I went back to my room. The door was slightly ajar. I opened it to find her clothes hung in the closet, and the drapes closed. Her long hair hung over her breasts as she lay in bed. As I undressed, she raised the bedsheet to show me her naked body. I lay beside her and she pressed up on me.

"I don't have a condom," I said.

"It's fine," she replied.

We kissed while our hands explored, then we made love. After a short respite she whispered something in my ear and we made love again. The room was quiet. Eva's head rested on my shoulder as she watched my chest move with each breath. I focused on the pencil-thin streak of light on her leg, resting on mine. She smelled like coconuts.

"What is it?" she said. "What are you thinking?"

"I'm not thinking of anything. I'm happy."

"I can't help but think," she said.

"Good things, I hope."

"Yes, good things."

We rested a bit longer before Eva got up, grabbed her bag, and walked into the bathroom. She was more beautiful naked. I wanted her to come back with me to New Jersey. I couldn't get enough of her.

The bathroom door opened. "Luke, do you want to go to the beach? I have time."

"Yes, let's go."

After a few minutes, she stepped out of the bathroom wearing a skimpy bikini. I rose quickly. "Give me a minute to get ready. You can take a spare bath towel," I said.

"I have one," she said.

I hugged her. "We better go or I'll throw you on this bed," I said.

"That's not a bad idea," she replied.

Later, a boy ran past us as we walked around the pool and toward the beach. We held hands. Passing the palm trees, the sand was soft and warm under my feet. People tanned in small clusters and children played on the sand. The ocean waves were calm under the afternoon sun. A breeze from the mountains flattened the waves and cooled the skin. I laid the beach towels and Eva put down her bag. We approached the water where three women stood talking as waves rolled and struck them below the waist. Eva and I stood nearby holding hands. The patchy clouds found their way to cover the sun for a short time. A fishing boat offshore sailed across the blue water heading south.

"You make me calm when you speak to me," she said. The salty air carried her scent of coconuts and her long hair touched my arm with light flaps. The light waves rolled against our legs.

"Would you like to learn how to surf?" I said.

"Oh, no. I'm not a good swimmer," she said.

"Surfing is so much fun."

"I like to tan on the beach. That is much better for me. I'm afraid of the water."

"My friends want to go out with you and Rosa. I was hoping for dinner. When is your next night off?"

"I work a lot, and most of the time it is at night. I am off tomorrow. I will ask Rosa."

"That would be great. My friends will love it and I will too."

Eva looked out and pointed at the water a few feet ahead of us. "What's that in the water?"

"What? I don't see anything," I said.

She took a few steps ahead of me. She turned to me and reached down where she placed her hands in the seawater as if to grab something.

"What is it?" I said.

Quick and suddenly, like a pretty devil, she swung her hands up and splashed salt water on my face. The wetness tingled across my skin. She did it again, before I realized it was another prank. I raised my hands to shield myself while she giggled.

"Oh, okay, it's like that," I said as I cupped my hands in seawater and splashed her back. By now, I was losing, becoming drenched. I ran up to her and grabbed her waist. She let out a shrill laugh, and I held her close. She wrapped her arms around my neck with a tender embrace.

"Now, I'm going to throw you in the ocean," I said.

"No, no," she said anxiously while giggling.

I loosened my grip and raised my hands around her back to hug her.

"Did you think I was gonna throw you in?" I said.

"No," she said, giggling. "Or else I will kill you."

Our foreheads touched and I kissed her. She relaxed in my arms, and we kissed again. I didn't know when we stopped. The sound of the ocean faded under the rapid undulations of her breath.

Chapter 8

The three of us got out of bed with equal excitement. Packed and with surfboards in hand, we headed to the front desk for directions to Playa Curvo. A woman greeted us, and Scott blurted out that we were looking for the blind man of Playa Curvo. Jamie and I chuckled. Remaining professional and gracious, the woman said she did not know the blind man of Playa Curvo but would tell us how to get there. She took out a sheet from under the counter and wrote down the directions. Of course, my best friends in the entire world made me drive, but you know, what are friends for. Feeling ambitious, we left and drove south, passing trees, mountains, and open, lush pastures. We knew we were close when we smelled seawater. Jamie was first to spot the ocean from between the trees. I was expecting to drive through the main street of a small town. Instead, we spotted a single sandy road that cut through the forest to the beach. On a whim I made the turn. We drove up to a flimsy metal gate made of one-inch pipe. Beyond it, the shore. No one was around. The place seemed remote and eerie to me. We never passed a home or a farm after we left Playa Sueños. I was about to turn the car and leave when Scott said he wanted to get out and open the gate. I said it was a bad idea, but he insisted. "There're no trespassing signs anywhere," he said. "The gate has no lock, so why not," he added. Scott was about to open the car door when Jamie pointed at two figures moving in the forest. As if out of thin air, two figures that fit the outline of an old man and a boy approached us. The old man carried a blind walking stick. His eyes closed and his mouth open showing only a few teeth, crooked and stained. The boy acted as his guide, holding his hand. He couldn't have been more than ten years old. A handsome boy who loved his abuelo and was careful. "Is that them?" Jamie said. The boy led the old man to us. The boy said something in Spanish and the old man held out his hand as a toll keeper would. With excitement, we collected some coins and I placed them in the old man's hand. As an added treat, Jamie handed the little boy a pack of Chiclets chewing gum he'd bought that morning. The boy opened the gate and waved us through.

The land beyond the beach was a lush pasture with grazing cattle. We had the endless coastline to ourselves—not a soul around. We got out of the car and punched each other with excitement. Scott got me good in the arm. I found a surf spot where the waves were smaller. I caught a few waves and sat on the beach. I thought of Eva. I wanted to buy her something. A necklace or a ring to remember me by. My heart filled with joy when I imagined a future with her. Jamie walked up to me, placed his surfboard on the sand, and sat beside me. Off in the distance, we watched Scott surf.

"The waves are larger here than at Sueños," Jamie said, shifting his wet hair away from his eyes. With his finger pointing, he warned me of a large sinkhole in the sand and to avoid that area.

"I'll go around it; thanks, bro. It's amazing here. I'm glad we came," I said.

"It feels like we're in Jurassic Park. I'm waiting for a velociraptor to come racing out of the woods."

I laughed. "Yeah, great movie . . . Don't forget to bring your camera tonight. I want pictures with everybody," I said.

"I'm definitely bringing the camera. Hey, did anything swim up to you out there?" Jamie said.

"What do you mean—like a fish?"

"No, it was small. As I paddled around, I felt a small pinch on my side. I was like whatever, but it happened again. Then I saw it. It was small, like the size of my thumb. It swam up and bit me then disappeared into the deep."

"Sounds like something didn't like the way you tasted," I said with a chuckle.

"Funny, bro, real funny. Are you going back out?"

"Yeah, I need a few minutes. If you're worried about that thing out there, you can wear my rash guard. It's in the bag."

"It's okay. I'm fine."

I took a few minutes to look around. I thought of the cliff again—never climbing one before. I'd go in the morning. I grabbed my surfboard and spent the rest of the afternoon surfing.

That evening, behind our hotel, we sat at the tiki bar drinking beer. The turnout was low. The bartender leaned over; his jaw was square, and his pale eyes gave him an earnest appearance. He served beer to a man who was alone. Next to me, an older couple ordered whiskey on ice. They tapped their whiskey glasses and smiled. Scott put down his empty bottle and giggled. Jamie looked around for the girls.

"What's so funny?" I said.

"I don't know," Scott said. "Something awesome is gonna happen tonight."

"I hope so. It's been a great trip so far," I said.

"It's true. The beach," Scott said with fingers up counting, "the surfing, the food, the women, and the beer. I got no complaints, dude." He paused and looked over at Jamie. "Dude, did you bring the camera?"

"I got it," Jamie said.

"Awesome," Scott said with a slight slur.

"Thanks for coming with us to Playa Curvo," Jamie said to me.

"Yeah, we weren't sure you were gonna make it, 'cause—you know—you're married," Scott said. They laughed by chuckling with their heads down and slapping the bar.

"Come on, guys." I finished my beer and placed the empty bottle on the bar. "I get it. I put you guys on the back burner and I apologize for that."

Scott didn't reply, but he showed a mild satisfaction on his face. Jamie leaned forward and tapped his finger on the bar. "At the end of the day, it's fine." He paused to look at Scott. "We would do the same, right?"

Scott nodded slightly, looking at his empty bottle. It was his fifth.

"Hey, Eva's here," Jamie said.

Eva's legs moved swiftly inside her pencil skirt. She nodded and waved when our eyes met. She was alone. Jamie nudged me slightly with his elbow. We stood up as she approached. We hugged. Scott and Jamie stood behind me, eagerly waiting.

"Eva, you remember my friends Scott and Jamie."

"Yes, hello." Eva smiled.

"Where's Rosa?" I said.

"No, I'm sorry. She has to work."

"That's too bad. I made reservations at the restaurant here," I said. "I hope you're hungry."

Scott, forgetting to let go of his beer, placed it on the bar. Jamie neared Eva and asked if she had been to that restaurant before. She nodded gently and said yes with a smile. His face brightened.

Island music played in the restaurant. Fire and smoke billowed from the grill behind the buffet table. The chef turned over a large rack of ribs; another chef prepared the rice, beans, and steamed potatoes. I sat next to Eva. Jamie and Scott sat across from us. The waiter arrived and gave us menus and he asked who would be eating from the buffet. We all did. The buffet displayed a mix of healthy and traditional foods. A rich assortment. The seafood looked fresh as well. The next important question was what to drink. No surprise, my boys kept ordering more beer. Eva got club soda, and I kept my buzz under control with a soda. I had an eye on Scott for any good reason to kick him under the table. My friends were last to get back from the buffet. Their plates stacked high with food. I understood their hunger after a long day of surfing, but being a glutton gives off a bad impression on people. As I expected, Eva made a wide-eyed glance at me.

"Un qué apetito," Eva whispered to me, hoping I understood.

"Si, hungry boys," I whispered back.

"I know it's a lot of food, but surfing makes me hungry," Jamie said sheepishly.

Their plates piled with ribs and chicken wings. A bowl of rice and beans made its way to the center of the table. Eva had the dorado, and me, the red snapper.

"The fish is very good," said Eva, after swallowing a morsel.

I shared my dinner with her. She gave me a piece of the dorado.

"The chicken is good too," Jamie said to respond to Eva's comment.

"We were at Playa Curvo today. Do you know about the blind man there?" Scott asked.

"No, I don't know Playa Curvo. I am always in Playa Sueños," Eva said.

"We heard a lot about a blind man that opens a gate to let your car onto the beach. It's amazing and weird to me, that's all," Scott said.

"Yeah, it does sound crazy," I said.

"Oh man, forget the blind man," Jamie said. "I got a confession to make." He paused. "I love Playa Sueños. I really want to live here."

Eva shrugged. "Yes, it's beautiful, but I want to live in America."

"Why?" Jamie said. "I mean, you have great beaches here, good food, and there's always something to do."

"There is no work here. If you find a job, the pay is very low. There's better work in America. Around here, if the tourists don't come, it's bad for everyone," Eva said politely.

"Jamie wouldn't know," Scott said. "He's never left New Jersey. I don't even think he's ever left our town until now."

"Shut up, Scott. I'm here, aren't I?" Jamie said sharply.

"Chill out, Scott," I said.

"Dude, all I'm saying is he doesn't get out much," Scott said, letting out a nervous laugh.

"Luke told me you're an artist," Eva said to Jamie.

"Yeah, I'm okay," Jamie said.

"He's pretty good, Eva. Don't let him tell you he's not," I said.

"It's only a hobby," Jaime said. "Luke makes me out to be somebody special, but I'm not. I can draw something for you and you can tell me what you think."

"Oh yes, I would like that," Eva said.

"I hope you come visit us in New Jersey. Don't believe what people say about New Jersey. It's really a nice place," Jamie said.

"I want to come to New Jersey," Eva said, smiling at me.

"I'm sure Luke will take real good care of you," Scott said with a wink and a nod. Scott spoke with an implied, derisive manner that made the blood rush to my face and the food lift in my stomach. Eva looked down and smiled slightly. I frowned and moved my lips to form words Scott understood. He shrugged and put food in his mouth.

"I don't think you need any more beer," I said to Scott. "It's water for the rest of the night."

Eva asked Scott what he did to pass the time back in New Jersey.

"I make bagels in the morning, and surf in the afternoon," Scott said.

"Tell her about what you're studying," I said to Scott.

"Yeah, I'm a student, too, but I haven't decided what to major in. I am thinking about communication. For now, I'm working at the bagel shop."

Soon after we told Eva our surfing stories, a server took our dinner plates away. Jamie got up, and took photographs of us. For dessert, everyone ordered coffee. Jamie asked for the three-milk cake, something he saw on the menu.

"What music do you listen to?" Jamie asked Eva.

"You mean American music?"

"Yeah, what American music do you listen to?"

"I like Michael Jackson, and Madonna."

"What else?" Jamie said.

Eva paused as she waved her hands. "My favorite music is Latin dance music. I love to dance."

"Well, I'm not a good dancer," Jamie said.

"You're not a dancer at all," Scott interrupted.

"He's right about that. I can't really dance," Jamie said.

"Do you have a girlfriend?" Eva said.

"No."

Scott let out a stupid cackle.

"You don't have a girlfriend either," Jamie said. "What are you laughin' about?"

"I have lots of girlfriends," Scott said.

"They're not your girlfriends," Jamie said.

"At least I got some, bro."

"Stop it," I said.

"It's true though. Jamie is pure as white snow."

"I'm done with you," Jamie said. When he stood up, he knocked over his chair and abruptly left the restaurant.

"See what you did?" I said to Scott. I looked at Eva in disgust. Scott picked up the fallen chair and placed it upright against the table. He walked away, slowly at first, but as if in fear, picked up his pace to pursue Jamie.

"I'm sorry about my friend. He drank a lot before and he's a bad drunk sometimes," I said. I wondered why I was friends with the guy. Eva looked at her watch, then reached to hold my hand.

"Drinking alcohol is very bad. I don't know why men drink so much," Eva said.

"They're very nervous. Drinking helps them relax."

"It's so bad. My father was like that too. Please don't drink like them," Eva said.

"I didn't know that about you. I'll cut back," I said.

Eva told the story of how her fatherless childhood began. How her mother did her best to ignore her father's alcoholism until it was too late. The last time she saw him was the night he struck her mother in the kitchen, and she fell. That night everything changed. The night Eva and her mother ran away from the only man in their lives. Talking about it made her eyes tear. It was the first time I saw her upset.

"I'm sorry about what happened to you and your mother. It must have been terrible. How are you now? Are things better than before?"

"Not so good, but yes, it's better. My mother is sick, and the money is not enough. I am doing the best I can."

I put my arm on Eva's shoulder and touched her hand. Eva thanked me and mentioned she was fine. She displayed a strong demeanor and expressed her desire to lift herself and her mother out of their current situation. Her expression then changed to a positive one, letting go of her past.

"Let's enjoy this dinner and forget your worries for a bit. How about we go dancing after dinner?" I said.

"I can't. I must work tonight. I want to see you tomorrow. Can you do something tomorrow morning or afternoon?"

"That's not a problem. Let's have breakfast tomorrow. The restaurant here at the hotel serves delicious breakfast. Is that okay?"

"That's good," she said. Eva kissed me. I smiled and kissed her back. "What time tomorrow?"

"How's eight thirty?"

"Okay, bueno."

I paid for dinner, and I walked her to her car. I apologized again, and I kissed Eva goodbye. I leaned toward the car window.

"Now, I've got to find out if Jamie killed Scott."

"I think Jamie will kill Scott," Eva said, smiling.

"Yeah, I think so too . . . Bye, beautiful."

I hurried back to the hotel. The room was dark and smelled of booze mixed with seawater and dirty clothing. The outside patio light brightened the hotel room enough for me to see Scott face down on the bed with his clothes on. He groaned on his pillow, giggling and mumbling to himself. I switched on the light to reveal the night table fallen over between the beds. Scott's surfboard dinged and leaning against the dresser. The recent struggle left the room with things strewn about and furniture shifted. Scott let out a steady, lazy *huh-huh* sound, then another giggle. I put the night table upright and pushed it back against the wall—luckily, it wasn't damaged. I sat down on the bed and looked at Scott with disappointment. Jamie wasn't there. Scott turned his head from the depth of the pillow. His eyes red and swollen, his body motionless.

"Huh-huh, Jamie hates me. Huh-huh," he said.

"Dude." I shook my head.

"He punched me. Huh-huh, he's done with me, bro," Scott mumbled.

"You can't blame him, dude. You destroyed him in front of Eva."

"Huh-huh," he mumbled.

I pushed the dresser against the wall and leaned his surfboard against the wall next to the other surfboards. "Man, you're a mess. Can you get up and take a shower or something? Clean yourself up, bro."

He didn't answer. His eyelids were closed, and his breathing was steady. "Dude, you need a shower," I demanded.

He rolled over. I took off his shoes and rolled him onto his back.

"I'll talk to Jamie, but don't do it again, especially in front of women—dumbass." He phased in and out of sleep. His jaw was swollen.

I passed the pool and walked down to the beach—no Jamie. I picked a direction and walked along the shore. Looking up, the night sky was a collective luminosity of stars. After walking for a while, I turned around and headed back. I found Jamie—even in the dark, I could tell it was him.

"Dude, you all right?" I asked.

"Where's the prick?" he said.

"The prick's in bed, licking his wounds."

"I couldn't help it. Nobody talks about me that way in public in front of me."

"I know, I know, he was definitely wrong, but give him some slack. He was drunk as hell," I said.

"I ain't hangin' out with that bitch," he said.

"We still have a couple days before leaving. Can you suck it up till then?"

"Nobody disrespects me like that . . . nobody."

"I know. I would have knocked his ass out, too, but this is Scott we're talkin' about. Our friend. He's the one who got us into surfing. He's the one who showed us the way. You can't ignore that." Jamie was still upset. He looked at the open ocean.

"You don't want to be friends with him anymore?" I said.

"No."

"Do me a favor. Give the guy one more chance. I know him; he won't do it again."

The seawater rolled up and sank into the sand; he crossed his arms. "He's already ruined my night. I'm not gonna let that bitch ruin the rest of my vacation. I'll deal with him till we get home, then I'll dump him."

"Damn, that's harsh. I hope it doesn't come to that. I'm sure you guys will patch things up tomorrow," I said with a hopeful tone.

"Hey, I want to thank you," Jamie said.

"For what?"

"The other night with the hooker. I'm glad you talked me into getting the hand job."

"Yeah, I thought so. I'm thinking the first time shouldn't be behind a bar somewhere with a stranger."

"Yeah, it was so mechanical. No feelings, ya know?"

"Yup, it's better doing it with someone you love."

"Ya know, I'm gonna stay here for a while," Jamie said.

"You want me to hang out with you?"

"No. I'll be back soon."

"All right. Don't hold a grudge. Nothing good comes from it. I know that from my own family. That pride crap makes you lonely."

"I'll sleep on the floor tonight. You can have the bed to yourself," Jamie said.

"No, we'll share the bed. You don't have to sleep on the floor."

"It's okay," he said. "I want to."

"Do what you want, Jamie. Take your time, buddy."

Chapter 9

I stepped over Jamie, who slept on the floor. I grabbed a shirt and trunks from my travel bag and entered the bathroom to change. I looked back before leaving; no one stirred. The sunlight was beginning to glow behind the eastern mountains. I took my sandals off before walking on the beach. The sand felt cool and soft between my toes as I ventured along the shore toward the cliff. In the dark ahead, tiny crabs moved along the sand, emerging from their burrows then back down again. Cool ocean water rolled up and touched my feet. I centered my sight over the vast sea, and its abiding presence brought me peace. I imagined where I was in the world as I drew fresh air into my lungs. I continued as far as the shoreline touched the stones of the cliff. I put my sandals on and climbed the rocks. I reached a clearing where I stood on a flat, sandy area. I looked out on the ocean below and the jungle above me. The rocks and boulders around me were scarred with pockmarks and crevices. A rugged place. A collection of twigs and sticks resembled an empty nest. A few feet away was a dead pelican stretched out and decayed—flies were circling its torso. I sat on a rock near the nest where I felt melancholy beside the final resting place.

The sun was above the mountains now, and the heat started. As I carefully stepped down the rock face, I looked down to see two pelicans fighting on the sand near the shoreline. Their wings locked in struggle as they struck one another with their beaks. I looked down at my descending steps to gain my footing. I glanced back at the duel where I was amazed to see one pelican inside the mouth of the other. The large gullet stretched and ballooned as its foe disappeared within its mouth. I looked down again to finish my final steps and landed firmly on the sand. I looked back to see only one pelican fly away. Unsure of what I saw, I took off my sandals and headed back.

I entered my hotel room. Eva sat on a chair facing the open glass door of the balcony. Jamie, Scott, and their surfboards were gone. I didn't envy the cleaning staff. The room was a mess.

She turned to me as I closed the door. "Where were you?" she said.

"I couldn't sleep so I went for a walk."

"Where did you go? I was waiting a long time."

"I took a long walk on the beach. It's beautiful here. I went all the way to the end of the beach to the cliff. You know—all the way down. How long were you waiting?"

"A long time—maybe half an hour," she said with slight irritation. "Your friends said I could stay and wait for you."

"I'm sorry—I lost track of time."

"I worry about you. There are bad people who can hurt you here. You never know what can happen."

"I can handle it, don't worry," I said.

"You say that, but you don't know. Tell me next time, Luca. You promise?"

"I will," I said softly as I got behind her, reached under her shirt, and pressed my warm hands against her belly. She let out a deep sigh. I moved her hair back and kissed her neck. She turned and we kissed and kissed again until she pushed me onto the bed.

Later, we faced each other in bed. My hand rested on her hip, caressing it back and forth. The breeze from the open balcony door rolled up our legs. Eva smiled.

"Leave with me," I said.

Eva smiled and put her hand on my face. "You are my man, but I can't," she replied with slight sorrow. "I want to go, but not yet. I will be ready soon."

"Part of me wants to rush things . . . Anyway, I'll come back after the fall semester, and I'll meet your mother."

"Yes, that's better. Can you stay for more than a week?"

"I have a few weeks off between semesters, so yeah. The spring semester doesn't start till late January. I'll call you a lot . . . What time are you going to work today?"

"Later this afternoon. I can stay and have lunch with you."

I kissed her many times. "You're so adorable. What do you want to do? Are you hungry?"

"Yes."

"I'm in the mood for something new. Any ideas?" I said.

"We can eat gallos or empanadas. I know a man who makes delicious empanadas, muy delicioso."

"Perfect; let's go."

Automobiles and motorcycles filled all the parking spaces along the street. The sidewalks were busy with people going places. A fruit vendor handed me a sample when he noticed my curiosity. He called the fruit Mamon Chino. I took off the skin and ate it whole. It tasted like a melon. Eva giggled at me. I followed her into the mercado. It looked like an indoor flea market back home. Vendors sold food, clothing, and other products and the air carried the smell of beef or pork frying on a skillet. Above the empanada place, plantains hung in bunches. Eva ordered two beef empanadas for me. She said it was the most popular item. She spoke to the man behind the counter as if they were friends. We sat at a small table next to the street near a vendor who sold beans and grains in bulk. Plastic bags filled with vegetables like garlic, onions, carrots, peppers, and more. I bit into my empanada.

"Mmm, delicioso," I said.

A light wind passed, moving her hair slightly. "I told you," she said.

"I have a serious question for you. Would you like to have a family one day?" I said.

Eva smiled. "Of course. I grew up with no brother or sister, so now I want to have a big family. I love babies."

"You would be a good mother, Eva. You're so caring."

"I want at least three children. I want my family to be so big and so wonderful . . . How many children do you want?"

"I don't know. I'll start with one and take it from there," I said.

We laughed.

"You only want one child? I think there should be at least two. I wish I had a brother or sister. That way they have each other. It's very important," she said.

"I guess you're right. I'm glad I have a sister."

As I bit into my empanada, a strange hand pressed down on the table. I looked up to see a man in his thirties, who began to hover over us with a crooked smile. After a quick look at me, he stared at Eva. He spoke to her in Spanish with a rapid, cordial tone, and with charm. After their short discourse, Eva looked at me stoically, almost nervous.

"Luca, this is Yeison," Eva said.

Yeison looked at me with his crooked smile, not showing his teeth. I reached out to shake his hand. His grip was strong and without courtesy. He looked back at Eva, boldly ignoring me. He continued his rambling. Eva nodded and gave him a forced smile. Yeison leaned off the table and asked me in broken English how good the empanadas were. I nodded in agreement.

"Do you like Playa Sueños?" Yeison said.

"Yeah, it's beautiful here. I'm enjoying it."

"Good, good. Eva will take care of you. She is good. She is very good," Yeison said.

I smiled and nodded with acceptance, feigning interest. They exchanged another line or two. Yeison asked me if I needed anything. I said no. He finished by saying Eva had his contact information if I needed anything and walked away. Eva studied my face. I finished chewing and held my drink.

"Who was that?" I asked.

"He works for my boss. Did he upset you?"

"Why would you say that?"

"You look angry," she said.

"No, it's just that he surprised me by showing up like that. To be honest, it felt awkward. What did you two talk about?" I said.

"He helps me and my mama. He brings things to us when we need it. He told me my mama is sick and I should go see her."

"So he helps you and your mother?" I said.

"Yes. He's a good friend." Eva gave me the rest of her empanada. I finished eating and we remained seated to finish our drinks.

"What does Yeison do for a living?" I asked.

"He's the manager at the restaurant where I work."

"But you said he works for your boss. I would think he *is* your boss since he's the manager," I said.

"No, my boss is the owner of the restaurant."

"Oh, so you report to the owner directly?"

"Yes, everybody reports to the owner, even him."

I wondered to myself, why wasn't her manager her boss? I let further questioning go to avoid conflict, but I thought of one more. "How come we never had lunch or dinner where you work?" I said.

"I don't like the food there," Eva said.

"What kind of food is it?"

"Asian food. I don't like it," Eva replied with a slight sneer.

"You mean like sushi—raw fish?"

"Yeah, I don't like it," she said.

"Do you want to leave and see your mom?"

"No, I can stay longer. I want to be with you as much as I can."

"Do you want to walk with me on the beach?" I asked.

"Yes, I like that."

We stepped out of the mercado and walked onto the beach, away from the noise of the street. The palm trees swayed gently. The sand was warm under the midday sun as our feet pressed and sank beneath it. I held our shoes in one hand and my arm over her shoulder. I took off my shirt and placed it where we sat. Eva leaned against me comfortably. We relaxed while hearing the sounds of the seashore.

"It'll be tough being away from you," I said.

"We must communicate. Call me or write me letters as much as you can. When you feel lonely, call me. When you feel happy, call me. When you feel anything, call me."

"I will, bella."

After a while, Eva had to go. We kissed and kissed again before she drove away. Going back to my room, my heart was full. To add to my euphoria, I prepared to go surfing. I put on board shorts and rubbed surf wax on my surfboard. A knock at the door surprised me. It was Yeison. He looked at me with bold eyes and a straight face.

"I must say something to you," he said.

"What's wrong?" I said, standing in the doorway.

He stood back from the door and put one hand behind his back. He said, "Eva is a puta."

I got annoyed. "What? What are you talking about? Why would you say that?"

"She . . . es una puta." He held out a piece of paper. "Go there and you see."

I began to close the door.

"No, no, no." Yeison stopped the door, reached out, and placed the paper in my hand. "Take it. Go here. You see."

I took the paper. Before I closed the door on him, he said if I needed anything, anything at all, he could get it for me—no problem. I nodded and closed the door.

"What a scumbag. You're probably stalking her," I said out loud as I sat on the bed and opened the paper; it was the address for the Jugosa Club. What a weirdo. Yeah, he was probably a stalker. I threw the paper on the dresser and grabbed my surfboard and left.

In the hotel lobby, I ran into Scott and Jamie on their way back to the room. I lost track of time. It was later than I thought. They were holding their surfboards and still wet.

"You're going surfing now?" Scott said.

"I wanted to hit the waves."

"All right, we'll catch you later," Scott said, sounding frustrated.

"Wait, wait. I gotta ask you guys something. Something came up. Let's go back to the room."

In the room, I sat outside and waited on the balcony. Scott and Jamie were cleaning up and getting changed. Sitting alone, I had a horrible image of Eva's body being pressed and ridden by Yeison. The thought made me stand up and kick the railing. I shook it off, walked back into the room, and sat on a bed. Scott was combing his hair and Jamie put on a shirt.

"A guy knocked on the door earlier. When I opened it, it was this older guy who told me Eva was a whore. I told him to go away but then he gave me the address and told me to see it for myself." I got up and grabbed the paper from the dresser and handed it to Scott. "He said she is working there tonight."

"Who's this guy?" Jamie said.

"Eva said he's her manager at work."

"Wait, Eva was with you when he knocked on the door?" Jamie said.

"No, actually, he interrupted us having lunch. He started talking to Eva while we were eating. After lunch, Eva and I hung out on the beach until she left. He must have followed me here."

"Dude, that's creepy. We should definitely check this out. I mean, don't you think?" Jamie said.

"Yeah, of course. It's bizarre, but you're right. Why would he follow me and even care about saying anything like that?" I said.

"Because it's probably true," Scott said. "Dude, Jamie and I see a lot of hookers here, and I know you like her, but I wouldn't be surprised if she was one of them."

"Dude, you're killing me," I said and put my head down between my hands. "God, why me, why? This is unbelievable."

"Whoa, whoa, whoa, we don't know anything yet. Calm down, Luke. Let's check it out first," Jamie said, looking angrily at Scott.

"Yeah, I didn't mean to say that, bro—sorry. He could be a stalker and said that to get rid of you. But I think we should go check it out," Scott said.

"Definitely, definitely," I said. "I gotta find out. Let's go," I insisted.

The address took us off Calle Principale down a well-lit street, past a dirty corner where graffitied walls lined the streets along with the bars and cheap hotels. We arrived at the Jugosa Club where the man at the door let us in and pointed to the open room down the hallway. The place was a strip club: loud and dark. Strobes and spotlights focused on the pole dancers prancing around on low stages surrounded by men eager to give away their money. The place was clean, almost honest if that's believable. A well-run business with girls hotter than the ones on the street. Scott and Jamie inspected the place with wide eyes. I told them to sit down while I bought them drinks. Even the bartender was beautiful, moving loosely in her Mariella halter top. I ordered two beers. When she finished removing the cap off the last beer bottle, I asked where I could find Eva Robles. She took my money and told me to wait. Her response troubled me. I brought the beer to Scott and Jamie who were already staring up the legs of a pole dancer. I told them to do whatever until I got back.

At the bar, the pair were waiting for me. A short man who stood beside the bartender. He made up for his height with muscular arms, slick black hair, and the guayabera shirt. We shook hands and he told the bartender to go away.

"You're looking for Eva? She has an appointment in a few minutes, you know."

"I only want to see her. That's all." My stomach ached, but superficially I was calm.

"How do you know her real name?"

"I'm her boyfriend. I just need to see her for a minute. That's all. It'll be quick."

He thought for a moment. "She's one of our best girls, you know—very pretty." He paused to look me. "Bien, since you know her, I will let you see her. It can only be for a minute."

"That's all I need. I'm sorry—what's your name?"

"Armando."

I followed Armando across the smoky room, past the pole dancers and away from the bar. My heart raced and I felt a slight pain in my chest. It's a different Eva repeated in my head over and over as I followed him. We entered a door, climbed a flight of stairs, and walked down a well-lit hallway past a few numbered rooms. We stopped at the door where a red heart-shaped origami hung above the number three. Armando knocked. My chest hurt more and more with each rap at the door. The door opened.

Chapter 10

She killed me when she opened the door. She killed my dreams, my future, my impression of her. I thought of walking away and forgetting her, but I couldn't do it. Know thyself, I once learned, but I did not. I realized years later that being attracted to someone is not a choice. Your heart wants what it wants—even to sacrifice who you are to get it. I first felt anger when I saw her, then betrayal. The truth will eventually reveal itself and you can no longer ignore your rational mind. I walked into her room; it was clean, like a hotel room. A bath towel shaped like a heart was on the queen-sized bed, and I smelled coconuts.

"Did you follow me?" Eva said irritably.

"No, but I should have," I said.

Armando saw I was upset and asked Eva if she wanted me removed. She said no. He stepped back but stood next to me, being protective of her.

"Your friend Yeison followed me to the hotel room and told me what you do for a living," I said with agitation. "When were you going to tell me about this?"

"I was never going to tell you about this," Eva said.

"So, you know how bad this looks."

Eva turned and sat on the bed. "After my mother and I ran away, we needed money. We had nothing."

"Yeah, but I can't believe you would do this. You're better than this, Eva."

"You don't understand," she said. Armando stared hard at me. I thought he would say something, but he let Eva talk.

"You're right, I don't. It doesn't matter anyway. I'm leaving and I won't see you anymore," I said.

"No, please, I love you," she said in a low voice. "Quiero ir contigo," she murmured.

"I'm sure you say that to all the men," I said and walked out. My mind raged, struggling to stay calm. I had ignored the signs around me with a woman I never knew or understood. My hopes and aspirations were ruined.

I gathered my friends and left that dreadful place. We stepped quickly down the dark, dirty sidewalk around the scammers and the desperate ones.

"Sorry, dude. I know you're upset, but don't let her ruin this trip for you," Jamie said.

"He's right. Let's hit a bar on the beach and talk about the next trip," Scott said.

I nodded reluctantly. I feigned interest as they spoke, keeping my head down. When the street sign read Calle Principale, we crossed and stepped down a narrow road to the beach. I thought she was genuine with me. I could see why some people became cynical, but my heart didn't want to be. Stop being so romantic, so innocent, so naïve. Could it be worse? I walked away from the most beautiful woman I ever met. How could I think that after only a week? It was too soon to forget her. Once I get back to school, I would forget her. I hoped I would. I followed the guys back to the tiki bar behind our hotel where we sat and ordered whiskey. After two shots, I began to relax. We ordered beer. From the moment we placed our beer glasses down, Scott proclaimed how he had never surfed so well in his life. The stories of our peaceful conquest of the ocean began. I only listened, taking gulps of beer during their intermittent laughter. Jamie brought up ideas for our next surfing trip. It would be somewhere on the Pacific side of the world, he suggested. A visit to the Fiji Islands or maybe Hawaii, the birthplace of the sport. One more round of beer on Jamie. Later, things moved without me moving as I peered at my giggling friends. Finally, they ceased, then a solemn quiet prevailed as if they ran out of gas. Suddenly, melancholy filled the air.

"I hate tomorrow," Scott said.

"Yeah, well, I hate today," I said. "Things were so much better yesterday."

"Well, I got you suckers both beat. I hate yesterday and all the days before it," Jamie said.

"It's about your dad, right?" I said with sympathy.

"Dude. That guy's a tyrannical prick. I can't wait to get out of there and get my own place."

"You got that apprentice gig with that plumber, so you should be out of there soon," I said.

"Yup. Once I get enough money saved, I'm out."

"Scott, looks like you're falling asleep, bro. We should head in. We have to get up early. Remember, the airport is a three-hour drive from here."

"Dude, whatever. I'm fine. I don't wanna leave," Scott said.

"Do what you want. I'm going for a walk on the beach to get a look at the ocean one last time," I said.

"Me too," Scott said. Scott stood up and stumbled. Jamie caught him and waved me away as he carried him back to the hotel room.

The ocean was flat like water in a bathtub, and the air was still. I walked on today's footprints in the sand until the seawater rolled up to my feet. I was so drunk that I had the urge to walk back to that whorehouse and take back what I said. Her stubborn ghost haunted me. I thought of her in that room. I kicked the sand with anger. My head spun unceasingly. I was done with Playa Sueños, and I was done with her. I heard something. I shook my head to clear it and it got louder. I stopped to listen—then silence. I listened harder. There it was again. It was the sound of weeping. A cry of sorrow. It came from either the ocean or my head. Yes, it was from the ocean, and it wept for Eva. My eyes teared, and I kicked the sand again with anger. I walked back, hoping never to return.

Chapter 11

"All right, we'll leave it here on the parallel axis theorem," the professor said. I finished my notes and closed my textbook. The lecture hall emptied. "See you next week," he said over the din of the moving chairs and the murmurs of the students leaving.

I walked out behind John Wagner, a study partner in my engineering program. "Are you going to Kent Hall tonight?" John asked.

"I don't know yet. I'm thinking about Butler," I said.

"I have a few questions I need your help on," John said.

"Sure, how about we meet at Butler around eight o'clock?"

"See you then."

I left through the main entrance of the Mudd building. A faint myriad of car horns blared from 120th Street. Under a gray overcast sky, the brick walkway was sopping from an earlier rain storm. The piercing wind gusts made late September feel like December. I took my time getting across campus, shifting my satchel, and thought about my next meal. A squirrel leaped across my path and disappeared into the hedges. Down the long stairs at the base of Low Library, I made a right toward Broadway. Along Broadway, a book cover showcased in a display window caught my eye. It was a picture of Martin Heidegger wearing a Nazi uniform. What the hell was he thinking? We all make mistakes, sometimes big ones. It's funny how much control our biases have over us. I should read more about him.

I descended into the subway on 103rd Street where it smelled like piss and diesel exhaust. I took the number one train down to 96th Street where I rented a spare bedroom from a writer who lived two blocks over on 94th Street. I never saw much of her, except at night when she left the dining room, where she worked, to pour herself more instant coffee. When she wasn't writing, she was out helping others in her workshops and lectures. She was a poet and published several books. She critiqued poetry as well. Luckily, I found her listing at the university admissions office. Since there were no more dorm rooms available at the time I was admitted, living with her was my best option. She preferred to be called DH.

When I entered, DH was chatting with a well-dressed black man. She introduced me as a young engineering student from Columbia. His name was Andre—an older Ghanaian who was learning poetry. I kept my greeting brief and broke away to my room where I dropped my backpack, grabbed money for dinner, and left. Broadway was take-out central. A person could order a wide variety of ethnic food any day of the week and have it delivered any time of the day—no problem. The night before, I had a gyro, but that night, I desired roasted chicken off the rotisserie. The local butcher was an older Hispanic man who reminded me a little of my father. He wore a meat-stained white apron. The heat from the oven made him sweat, making his glasses slide down the tip of his nose. He cut chicken with what looked like garden scissors. As I waited in line, I stared at his nose, waiting for him to push up his eyeglasses. He never did. It was annoying to watch.

A patron at the counter asked him about his daughter. When the butcher said she got accepted to graduate school, the patron congratulated him then joked how it would take another ten years to pay it off. All the old butcher did was smile and cut the chicken. After the patron left, I ordered half a chicken with a side of French fries.

When I returned, I found a note from DH on the kitchen table that read my mother had called. I called her back but no answer. I finished dinner and got ready to head back to the university to study. Before leaving, the phone rang. Her voice was low and anxious.

"Luca, I'm at the hospital."

"Why?" I asked eagerly.

"Tuo padre e malato. He could not breathe last night. Non so cosa fare. We've been at the hospital all day."

"Is he okay?"

"He's better now."

"What do you want me to do, Ma?"

"Your father wants you to stay in New York, but I want you to come home."

"It's that bad?" I said.

"Luca, I want you here. Talk to him and see what he wants to do. I'm worried."

"All right, no problem. Is Sofia with you?"

"Yes."

"Okay, I'll take the late bus home. I'll be in town by eleven tonight."

It was a Tuesday night at the Port Authority bus terminal. The early commuters were long gone and the line waiting for the bus was short. A young man in front of me held his suit jacket folded over his arm. His dress shirt crinkled and crumpled near his pants. He stood weary and pensive like the other late commuters. Behind me, a short Latina woman held bags of fruit and groceries. She looked at me for an instant and then looked away. The line for the bus was getting longer. I turned to face forward. I was sure Dad would be all right. He was a tough guy. I remember once he worked under a car with only a hydraulic jack holding up the vehicle. His body squirmed and wiggled as he crawled under it, reaching for the starter motor. "Give me the half-inch socket," he said. He turned the ratchet—*click, click, click*. The car rocked slowly at first, then swayed with each turn of the ratchet. I grew anxious. The car was up on two wheels with the old car jack straining to hold it. "Dad, the car is rocking; be careful," I told him. He ignored me. It was hard to watch. In the end, the job got done. Later, he scolded me and said, "You can't make money if you're scared of everything." He got paid forty dollars for that repair that could have killed him. I was fourteen years old at the time.

The bus arrived; I stepped on and handed my ticket to the driver. I took a window seat and placed my travel bag between my legs. Soon, the door closed, the lights switched off, and we left the city. I stared at the moving white subway tiles in the Lincoln Tunnel. My gaze drifted to the darkness outside and then down to the road moving under the wheels. I closed my eyes. Later, I opened my eyes to the low hum of the bus engine. I took a deep breath in the dark as I sat up and straightened myself on the seat. I looked across the aisle where a young black man was sleeping. Out the window, we passed the entrance of Fort Monmouth. My stop was next. I stepped off the bus behind a woman and her boy. I crossed the street and entered the parking lot. Sofia waved to me from the car. She was drained.

"Is Dad all right?" I said.

"It's been terrible," she said.

"How is he?"

"He's better now. They used a catheter to drain the fluid out of him. The doctor said he had pulmonary edema."

"What the hell is that?"

"It's when fluid builds up in the lungs."

"Why did that happen?" I said.

"I don't know. He's getting worse. I saw his feet the other day and they were swollen, like balloons."

"What the hell," I said. "How's Mom?"

"You don't wanna know. I don't get it. He's only sixty years old."

"I'm sure he'll be fine. He's tough," I said with confidence.

We entered the hospital room. My mother was adjusting my father's pillow, propping it lower to support his back. She put another pillow behind his head. I approached him without a word. His eyes were glassy and strained with an oxygen mask over his nose and mouth. His face sullen. Sofia sat down. My mother stood beside him, watching. Her eyes were red. I walked over and kissed her. I turned to my father and touched his hand.

"Sorry, Dad," I said gently. "How do you feel?"

He lifted the oxygen mask off his face with defiance—tired and short-winded. My mother told him to put it back on, but he didn't listen.

"I want you to stay in school. I don't want you coming here," he said.

"Voglio nostro figlio qui. He has to run the business mentre sei in ospedale," Mother said.

"I don't want him to work at the gas station. Appartiene all'Università," he said.

"No. He can go back to school later. Luca has to help in the business," my mother insisted.

"No!" he answered back with the last of his strength.

"Dad, Mom's right. The business can't run by itself. I can work there until you feel better; then I can go back to school."

"I'm okay. You can go back to school now," he said.

"Yeah, sure, you're okay," Mother said sardonically. "Look how you're breathing. The doctor said you have to rest."

"How long is he staying in the hospital?" I asked.

"Until he's better. A few days maybe," she said. "The doctor will tell us tomorrow."

"I can watch the gas station," Sofia insisted, but she was ignored without even a head turn.

"It's okay. It'll only be a few days. Can't leave the gas station alone; you know that," I said.

My father closed his eyes. He let go of the discussion and rested quietly.

"Michael, the doctor wants you to stay. Do what he says," Mother said, knowing he didn't care.

With his eyes closed, he nodded slowly. We waited for a response, but he fell asleep. I sat next to Sofia, hoping he would feel better so we could all go home, but nothing. I only felt myself become stronger. My mother asked me to follow her, leaving Sofia to watch him. We stood outside in the hallway near the nurse's desk.

"How did he get the pulmonary edema?" I said.

"Luke, your father is sick e lavora come un cane. He never watched himself and now he's worse. I didn't watch what he ate—now I have to. He has to stop working and you have to run the business."

"Okay, I'll take a semester off and run the gas station."

"Luca, money doesn't fall from the sky," she said. "You have to do this per la famiglia, or else we'll be on the street." Her eyes swelled with desperation. I put my hand on her arm and told her not to worry. My studies could wait until he was better.

"Yes, and you can go back after your father is better," she insisted.

"I will. Please don't worry. I'll call DH and let her know. I have to go back one last time to get my stuff and cancel my classes. It's not a problem."

I walked up to my father as he slept. His skin was dry, almost red, sun-beaten. I wanted to tell him everything would be fine, but I'd save that for my prayers.

There was little else to do and it was past midnight, so Sofia and I went home. Mother wanted to stay. She'd drive back later, she said.

The ride home was quiet. I thought of the time when I called my father at work to tell him I'd gotten accepted to Columbia.

He cheered. I'd never heard him so excited before; he was always so stoic. "A triumph," he proclaimed. Later, Lenny said how he walked around the shop and told everyone (customers too) about his son going to Columbia University. I was more interested in the university's robotics program. They had a great physics department as well.

The cold winds blew under an eerie autumn moon. Sofia and I walked to the back of the house, our path lit by moonlight. Inside, through the sliding glass door, Nicky-boy leaped with excitement. His wolfish pale silhouette pressed against the glass, eager to leave. I let him outside and Sofia went upstairs. I opened the freezer and grabbed a quart of ice cream. I took a spoon and went into my father's office. The checkbook was open on the desk. I thumbed through the bank statements. I saw a recent tuition payment for the fall, payments for a tanker truck of gasoline, and the utility bills. There was a lot of money transferred to another bank account. Hence, the main checking account showed a very low balance. As I sat down, my eyes gazed upon an overdraft notice; I lifted it and found another one—all from the same month. Checks paid to an architecture firm, land surveyor, and large money transfers to another bank made me feel he was planning construction on the land he'd purchased a few years ago. He never spoke much about what he did with money. He kept things to himself like the Sicilian he is. It made sense to buy a piece of land on a busy highway. His dream was to construct a building on it.

I put the ice cream back in the refrigerator and continued to review his finances. My mother came home and walked upstairs to bed.

Any profits made from the gas station were spent, not saved. It was unusual for him. He avoided risk like a young priest avoids a brothel; the urge was there but he abstained. He lost $4,000 once in the stock market back in the 1970s and he never partook in the secondary markets again. No, he was only interested in his business and real estate—that was it. He always wanted to escape the lease he had with the oil company, who owned the gas station. His wish was to be fully independent and not beholden to anyone. A commercial building on his land would represent the fulfillment of his toil and the ultimate achievement of his dreams.

It was very late. My eyes burned, so I went to bed.

Chapter 12

A maroon Oldsmobile rolled up to the last gas pump and stopped. I tightened the last bolt on a brake caliper on a Cadillac. "How long will Steve let that car wait?" I thought. I placed the ratchet in my father's toolbox and stepped outside under the gray October sky. Steve sat on a metal chair, staring down at his dirty, ragged sneakers. "Steve, can you get that?" I said eagerly, pointing to the Oldsmobile. He stood up with a mood of indifference and moseyed over to the pumps. I turned to the Cadillac to put the tire on. Al worked in the next service bay. The strong rattle of the air gun drowned out the rock music that played from the stereo on his work bench. I lowered the Cadillac and took it for a test-drive. Once back, I parked and finished the repair order. At pump three, a late-'60s white Volkswagen Beetle was left unattended. I walked out to help Steve. We arrived at the Beetle together.

"Steve, did you know these cars are air-cooled?" I said.

"What do you mean like—no radiator?"

"Yeah. When you ask the customer what they want, ask if we can check the oil."

I stood behind the vehicle and watched through the back window. The customer was a young woman with her blonde hair up in a ponytail. She had a stack of textbooks on the back seat. Steve told me it was okay to check the oil and to fill it up with regular unleaded. I lifted the rear hood door and we kneeled to see the motor. I pointed to the dipstick and the distributor cap and revealed to him no radiator. At first he said nothing as he looked harder to confirm it was true. He then let out a high, poultry-like cackle.

"Yeah, it's funny lookin', isn't it? That's definitely not a V-8," I said.

"Dude, it's ridiculous," Steve replied, putting his hand over his mouth.

"Hey, don't knock it, bro. If maintained properly, this engine can last for years. It's not fast, but it's tough."

With the dipstick out, I saw the engine oil was dirty. I told Steve to tell her she needed an oil change. Closing the hood, I heard her scold him about laughing at her car. He collected the money, and with his thumb pointed at me said it was me who laughed, not him. She scoffed at Steve and drove away.

"Thanks for throwing me under the bus, dude," I said.

"Whatever. She was ugly anyway. Who cares," Steve said.

"Who's the ugly one?" I thought.

"How's your dad doin'?" Steve asked. We walked back to the sales office.

"He's coming home from the hospital this afternoon."

"What? How long was he there?"

"About a week—he can't wait to get back to work."

"Good. I miss your old man. Did he tell you how he hired me on the spot?"

"No," I responded.

"I was walking downtown and heading to the amusement park when he drove up to me. He lowered the window and asked if I needed a job. I said hell yeah and jumped in. He never asked me any questions or references. He took me as I was. He gave me a chance, you know. I've been working for your old man ever since. It's been about six months now."

"What did you do before this?"

"I was over at the supermarket in town, but I left that job. My manager was horrible to work with."

"Are your parents nearby?"

"I live with my mom," Steve said.

"That's good," I said.

"Your father helped me out a lot. I really needed the money too."

"As long as you come to work and do your thing, he's fine with you," I replied.

"Yeah, but he didn't give up on me. He makes me feel good about myself."

"Yeah, he likes you. He's good at motivating people too," I said.

"I've been sober for a while now, ya know," Steve said.

"That's great. Congratulations—keep it up."

The pumps got busy with the afternoon rush. During a pause, I put my father's tools away and cleaned the service bays. Later, Al closed the garage doors, and I paid him. I put Steve's pay in an envelope. The temperature dropped further as the day progressed. I started the electric heater in the sales office. I felt the urge to call Jamie or Scott for something to do. After pumping gas awhile, I returned to the sales office and sat next to Steve.

"What are you doing after work?" I said.

"I'm going to the go-go bar down the road," he said, smiling. "I'm having a few drinks with Missy T tonight. She's a hot one."

"Really? Missy T?" I said. "What do you two talk about?"

"We talk about everything. I don't know. We talk about TV shows, even the bad ones. I leave it up to her sometimes. She's cool, man."

"Do you see her a lot?" I asked.

"About three times a week. I like her. I help her out with stuff, ya know?"

"Three times?" I said incredulously.

"Sometimes more. You have to see her. She's real hot."

"I need to make a phone call," I said. "Can you watch the pumps for a few?" Steve shrugged his shoulders and nodded in agreement.

I fished into my pocket for a few quarters. Steve leaned back on the folding chair, resting his feet on the windowsill. His foot knocked over the faded, dusty stack of franchise brochures. He tucked his hands deep into his jacket pockets. I put all my quarters into the pay phone and dialed. Scott's mom picked up.

"Hi, Ms. Lazio, it's Luke. Is Scott there?"

"Luke, how's your father?"

"He's better now, thank you. He's coming home today."

"Good. Good. Give him my best, okay? I'll get Scotty."

"I will; thank you."

Scott picked up the phone. "Dude, how's your old man?"

"He's coming home today. He's doin' better. Thanks, man."

"Okay, cool. Yo, the Ramones are playin' at the Trade Winds tomorrow night. You wanna go?"

"Yeah, most definitely," I said.

"Awesome, bro."

"Did you tell Jamie about it?" I said.

"Yeah, Jamie's going."

A few cars drove up to the gas pumps all at once. Steve leaned forward and the front legs of the folding chair hit the floor with a snap. He stood up slowly and stepped outside.

"Hey, I gotta go. The pumps are getting busy."

"Wait. Are you driving us or are we meeting there?"

"I'll drive," I said. "What time?"

"Come over at nine," Scott said.

"Al right, see you then."

I hung up and went outside. Steve and I walked past each other, brushing shoulders. He held a credit card. A customer asked for ten dollars of super unleaded. The car was a sun-faded Dodge from the last decade—even in the dark, you could see the rust spots on the hood. Why the hell would he put super in that thing? He'd burn out the rings and the valves. I squeezed the nozzle and locked the handle in place and moved over to the next car. The time passed quickly. Steve covered the inside pumps, and I covered the outside. I thought of the university and what I was missing. Being out a semester meant it could be an extra year to graduate due to core courses being taught once a year. I'd have to catch up during the summer.

Bobby arrived on time. His hair was still wet from the shower and he smelled like Irish Spring. He always carried his guitar, two packs of Marlboro Reds, and breath mints to start the night shift. Bobby was a confident, amiable guy who enjoyed playing the guitar when the station and the highway were dead in the early morning before dawn. He'd worked for my dad for many years until one day he left for Florida. Then, about a year ago, he came back and my dad gave him his old job back. His dreams of being a musician in Key West ended when he ran out of money. He never said that, but I knew this story from my father. At the end of our shift, I handed Steve his pay, and with swift determination, he walked out of the sales office and down the highway to see Missy T. I drove home, listening to Nirvana.

I walked into the house. My mother was in the kitchen. She said leftovers were in the refrigerator.

"Thanks, Ma. Where's Dad?"

"E' a letto."

"Is he awake? I want to talk to him."

She nodded. "Sofia is with him."

"Thanks."

"You don't want to eat?" she said with slight frustration.

"Later. I'll talk to Dad before he goes to sleep. It's about business."

"Can you do it after you eat?"

"I promise I'll eat later."

My sister sat at the foot of the bed, rubbing his feet. The bedsheets were drawn up to his neck. I sat beside the bed. His eyelids closed—he was enjoying the foot rub. I waited. He turned on his side and positioned himself like a reclining Buddha. His other arm was hidden under the sheets. He looked worn and frail. He opened his eyes, squinting from the lamp light. I got up and dimmed the brightness.

"You look better," I said. His hair was washed and combed back. His face was smooth, and he smelled like aftershave. "The business is fine. I deposited the money, and the workers got paid."

"Good," he said with a raspy voice. He cleared his throat with a long cough. "Did you get the check from Fazzi and Sons?"

"Yeah, they paid me."

"Did the check clear?" he said.

"I don't know yet. I deposited it today."

"Then don't say you got paid. Make sure the check clears."

"What did the doctor say? Any news?" I asked Sofia.

"Dad needs a lot of rest. The doctor gave us a diet to follow. He needs to watch what he eats."

"A few more days and I can go back to work, and you can go back to school," he said.

"Don't worry. Take your time getting better and everything will be fine," I said. He nodded softly and closed his eyes. Suddenly, he jerked his head back as if shocked with electricity.

"Aye! You're rubbing too hard."

"Sorry, Dad."

"That's enough. Thank you," he said. Sofia withdrew her hands and placed the bedsheets over his feet.

"Dad, the bank account is running low. I saw you transferred money to another bank. I'm a little worried about the low balance," I said.

He looked at me with one eye closed, an idiosyncrasy. "You remember the land I bought? I'm ready to build a garage, so I'm spending money on that. I have a separate bank account for the construction. The checkbook for that account is in the drawer behind the desk."

"Why didn't you tell me before? I would have helped you."

"No. You have to study. Don't worry about the land. I'll take care of it. I need a variance from the town and then Cangelosi can start building. The lawyer is helping me with the variance."

"What's the lawyer's name?" I asked.

"Fuchs. Expensive son of a bitch, but he's good," he said with disdain.

"Is Steve okay? He bothers me. Sometimes he sits and lets the cars wait. If I'm working on a car in the garage, he gets lazy. What do I do about this guy?"

"When he feels alone, he does that sometimes. You should go and help him. He's a good worker."

"Why is he a good worker? He looks lazy to me," I said.

"Because he goes to work every day and I want to give him a chance."

"All right. Whatever you say."

"Luke, there's a letter downstairs for you," Sofia said. I never got letters, so I felt curious and a little uneasy, thinking it may be from Eva.

My father closed his eyes. "Get some sleep. We'll talk tomorrow," I said. He nodded in agreement. Sofia and I walked around the bed. Sofia grabbed my arm to stop me. She lifted the bedsheet to uncover his feet. I followed her eyes to the right foot. She pointed briefly to a spot on his toe and covered it.

In the hallway, she turned to me and whispered, "I didn't see that spot there before—it's new, and I'm worried about it.

When I rubbed it, it hurt him. If he complains about it, we should take him back to the hospital."

"How's he walking?" I said.

"He's fine. He was a little slow going up the stairs, but okay."

"Does Mom know? Why didn't they see it at the hospital?"

"It's new and Mom knows about it. We noticed it earlier today when we washed him."

"Let him rest. He's happy being home. But he definitely needs to walk. He's been in bed too long, and he's weak," I said.

"I know. I'll walk with him tomorrow."

"The last thing he needs is another trip to the hospital. He hates it there."

"I know. He'll see the doctor soon anyway," she said.

I went downstairs and found the letter on the kitchen counter. My hunch was right. I often thought of Costa Miel. I had no regrets meeting her. She was beautiful and the experience was amazing. I'll never go back there. I lost respect for her; it was the lack of good judgment on her part. God, what about having some dignity for yourself? I'd rather sacrifice my time, money, and resources with a woman on a better life path. A woman worthy of sharing a legacy with me. I took her letter to the trash can. The faint smell of coconuts stopped me from dropping it in. I lifted the letter up to my nose. The smell flooded my mind with sweet notions and a yearning to read it. I put my rational thinking aside and brought the letter upstairs to my room.

Caro Luca—I miss you and the way you make me feel when you are with me. I know you are angry with me, but I was afraid to lose you. I want you in my life always. When I walk alone, past where we kissed, it reminds me of you. Please come back to me. Te amo siempre.

I have good news. I hope you are sitting down. I am very happy to say I am pregnant. I know you think this is not your baby, but it is. It is because I want a baby with you and no one else. Think deeply and you know it is true.

I want to tell you more. I live in a small apartment with my mother. I worked for Armando for many years, and he helped us so much. He is very important to us. I know you are angry with me, but I must make money this way for my mama and me to live. If I do not, Armando will be angry. Since I worked for Armando for so many years, he will let me leave soon and I want to be with you. Please change your mind and forget your bad feelings. My heart is yours, Luca. Te amo siempre.

Please come back. Call me so we can talk. I want to hear your voice so I can smile again. We are waiting for you, mi amor.

Eva.

I read the letter a few times. "Armando will be angry." What the hell did that mean? Why couldn't she just leave when he wasn't around? Wow, this was unbelievable. I should never have read the letter. And being pregnant with my baby? Yeah, sure. All the men she'd been with and it was my baby? Whatever. "I'm not your meal ticket," I said out loud. She was dangerous. Feeling annoyed, I put the letter in the desk drawer and went to sleep.

Chapter 13

As I left for work, I passed my father napping in the living room. The television was on. A scene repeated daily. He appeared older and worn out. Keeping him home to heal had drawn the life out of him. The man never sat idle and for him to do nothing made him simply wither away. I shook my head and walked up to him in his lounge chair. His mouth opened slightly as he slept.

"Dad, I'm going to work. You wanna come?" I said as I touched his shoulder.

My words turned him on like a light switch. He opened his eyes and said yes in his raspy voice. After making many promises to my mother, she reluctantly agreed to let me take him. She prepared food for us and got him ready. Although he moved with stiff joints and walked with a slight limp, he was eager to leave. I opened the doors for him and watched him carefully descend the porch steps, ready to catch him if he fell.

During the drive, he looked down often at his feet. I kept my eyes on the road and spoke about how the winter was coming fast. He agreed as he rubbed his knee.

The air was chilly when we arrived. October was being itself. The morning crew was happy to see him, especially Steve. My father limped over to a metal folding chair outside the sales office. His steps were labored, but his eyes were strong. The guys gathered around to greet him. He sat down, straightened his back, and placed his hands on his knees with authority.

"Hey, Mike, good to see ya. Are you back for good? We need you, chief," Lenny said.

"I'm here now," my father said with a confident retort. The guys laughed.

"Good man," Steve said. He stood beside Lenny, staring, hovering, while cars were lining up at the pumps. Their eyes fixed on my father's gaunt face.

"You look good," my father said to Steve.

"Thanks, Mike. You look good too."

My father nodded and winced as he rubbed his knee. Steve went to pump gas.

"Lenny, do you need anything from the back—cigarettes, small bills, or change?" I asked.

Lenny pulled out his shift money and handed me a twenty. "Yeah, we're low on Marlboro Reds. We can use twenty dollars in quarters too."

"I'll get you two cartons. Dad, do you wanna sit here or do you wanna come?"

"No. I'll stay here."

I got what Lenny needed and placed it on the counter in the sales office. Lenny gave me a thumbs-up and grabbed the cigarette cartons. He smelled like gasoline and cigarette smoke. We all smelled like gasoline mixed with something. I placed the roll of quarters in the cash register. Al entered the sales office from the service area. He welcomed my father back and told him business was slow, but steady. A lot of tire repairs lately, he mentioned. Yesterday, a lady who had her engine rebuilt came back angry about too much exhaust smoke. Al told her the motor needed time to break in, but she was adamant something else was wrong, and that we were to blame for incompetence. She made a scene and left, promising to come back. My father stood up and looked at Al (who was almost twice as tall as my father) with a stern glare. My father said, "When she comes back, tell her to talk to me." He pointed at his chest with repeated vigor. Al stepped back with a servile demeanor said, "I know you will, Mike, and I'm glad you're dealing with her, not me."

My father followed me to the private office in the back, which also served as a storage area. It was dark, windowless, and the air was stale. The smell of motor oil was pungent, and the floors were stained for decades. Boxes of cigarette cartons and candy were piled up on milk crates ready for vending, and the motor oil was stacked five boxes high. At the center of the office were worn, dirty office chairs surrounding a wooden desk from the postwar era. The air in the private office was always cool and maintained a chill even in the high heat of summer.

I pulled out a chair for my father and placed the shift money on the desk for him to count. A new hire was a no-show, and since our policy was to never let workers pump gas alone (except Bobby, the overnight guy), I had to find a replacement. I tried the new guy again but no answer. It's hard to find good help and there's always a no-show when I have a Ramones concert to go to with my friends. Nobody wanted to work a double so my next course of action was to grab the pile of old employee applications and start calling.

"Hey, Dad, the new hire is a no-show."

His thin body lifted with a slight wobble as he counted, but his eyes were sharp. "That lazy bum," he said with disgust.

"I know. I'm gonna make a few calls and see who I get."

"If you don't find somebody, call Bobby. He needs the money."

"Okay."

No one from the first few applications answered. I called Bobby who didn't pick up either. A bit frustrated, I called the next number and a woman with a heavy accent said hello. I asked for Youssef Hanna. After a moment of silence, a man with a soft, confident voice answered. I asked if he would be available to pump gas from 2:00 to 11:00 p.m. He accepted with sincere gratitude and added he would leave immediately. I put down the phone, and my father left the office. The money he counted was wrapped and ready for deposit. I put the money into the bank bag, locked it, and followed him outside where he sat in the same folding chair. Steve left and I pumped gas with Lenny until Youssef arrived.

Youssef rolled up on a bicycle—a thin man, wearing a blue baseball cap, dark slacks, and a heavy jacket. After putting down his kick stand, he approached my father and introduced himself with hat off and hand extended. I finished pumping gas and walked back to find my father and him having an amiable conversation. Youssef gracefully introduced himself to me.

"Hello. I am Youssef. Are you Luca?"

"Hi, nice to meet you."

"Yes, yes, I am here to work," Youssef said. Youssef's eyes were kind and he moved quickly with a savior's energy. He was about six feet tall and had a strong grip. I liked him right away and wondered for a moment why he wanted this job. He looked overqualified to me, with the characteristics of a military officer or a captain.

"My son goes to Columbia University. He is going to be an engineer," my father said with pride.

"Oh, Columbia. Very good; he is very smart," Youssef replied, looking at my father.

"Luca, give Youssef the shift money. Where are you from?" he asked Youssef.

"I am Egyptian."

"Oh, Egypt. Egypt is very close to Sicily," my father said with genuine approval.

"Yes, yes. You are Sicilian?" Youssef asked.

"Oh yes. I came to America a long time ago," my father said, waving his hand back to gesture the past.

Youssef laughed. He released a swirl of sound that carried everyone's spirit higher.

"Luca, show Youssef what to do so he can work," my father said.

"No problem."

Youssef was a quick study. I closed the service shop and grabbed the money bag. It was around six o'clock and the sky was dark with the faint glow of the twilight ending. I helped my father into the car when I remembered something.

"Wait, I forgot to fill the vending machines."

"Go do it," my father commanded.

"Aren't you hungry?"

"No. Go fill up the machines. You got the keys?" he said.

"Yeah, okay."

I opened the soda and the candy vending machines to inspect their contents. I went to the back office to retrieve what I needed and started filling. As I dropped each can into the chutes, a woman drove up and parked in front of the service bay doors. She stepped out and slammed her car door with anger. She chose me to go after since the repair shop was closed. Her eyes fixed on mine as I faced her holding a warm can of soda.

"Where's Mike?" she demanded.

"He's not here," I said. "Can I help you?"

"I want my money back for the crappy repair this place did to my car."

"The shop is closed. The mechanic is back in the morning. What's wrong?"

"What's wrong is my car smokes like hell and I can't drive it," she answered petulantly, pointing at her car. She moved close to me. I took a step back.

"Our mechanic will be back in the morning," I stated calmly. "He has to look at the car, so—"

"No, no, no!" she interrupted. "I will not take off from work so your horrible mechanic can fix my car again. I want my money back so I can take it somewhere else!"

"Hey!" my father yelled from across the lot. He approached slowly. His sick, pale complexion turned reddish with hostility as he moved like he was ten years younger. "I'm over here! You here to start trouble?"

Like a raging bull of Pamplona, she charged, pointing and shouting obscenities. "Goddamn it, Mike! You make me pay twelve hundred dollars for a broken engine. I want my money back!"

My father shuffled toward her, limping slightly as if without pain or disease. He pointed his pin-pricked finger back at her viciously. He yelled out over her outburst and repeated utter nonsense to drown out her voice: "Bla, bla, bla, bla, bla." Customers, workers, even babies in cars, watched in awe the verbal assault between my old man and this lady. I would have stepped in, but my father was venting his personal frustrations onto her. He didn't care about her or her car. He continued to yell at the sky, repeating the words *why why why* in a frightening manner. Soon, the woman backed off. The sight of my father's tirade disturbed her. She took a few steps back to regain some courage and with a final act of defiance said, "You're crazy, Mike! My boyfriend's coming to deal with you!" She entered her vehicle, lowered her window, and yelled out obscenities as she sped off.

I escorted my father back to my car. Everyone who watched went back to what they were doing as if nothing had happened. From my viewpoint, I saw nothing wrong with her car. The engine sounded normal, and hardly any smoke was leaving the exhaust pipe.

"I'm sorry about that, Dad," I said as I walked beside him, holding his arm.

"That bitch," he exclaimed. "Tell her to come back here. I'm not done with her," he said, panting.

I felt the heat on his arm, his adrenaline. He cleared his throat between heavy breaths. I sat him back in the car and finished loading the vending machines. On the drive home, I visited the bank and dropped the money into the night depository.

"I'll take care of the crazy lady tomorrow morning, Dad. I'll have Al check her engine," I said.

"There's nothing wrong with the car. The engine is new and has to break in; it's water vapor. That bitch," he said.

"It's okay, relax. We'll be home soon."

He gazed out the window into the darkness of the road. "Maybe we should have run the engine longer before giving it to her," he said in a calm voice. Soon, he was asleep. His head bobbed gently with the uneven road. His breath whistled through his nose. I wouldn't bring him back to work until he fully recovered.

"Dad, we're home," I said, touching his shoulder. He woke up with a sudden head lift, rubbing the bottom of his nose with his finger. I opened the car door and helped him out and into the house. My mother had dinner ready. A bowl of pasta was waiting for him. He wanted to go to bed. Before my mother could argue, he asked in a tired, raspy voice if I could bring him some cookies and milk. He ascended the stairs with slow, uneven steps, holding tight to the handrail.

"What's wrong with your father?" my mother asked me.

"Nothin'. He had a fight with a customer."

"Why did you do that? You can't have him work like that. He's sick."

"Ma, he's bored," I said as I poured a cup of milk. "He wants to go to work."

"Luca, your father is sick. He can't go anymore."

"Okay, okay, let me bring this to him." I grabbed a roll of Nilla Wafers.

"I'll be up after I clean the kitchen," she said.

I found him already in bed, lying on his back. He was only partially dressed for bed. His pants were still on. I grabbed him a clean undershirt. He sat up as I helped him dress for bed. I took his socks off. The black spot on his right foot had grown to about the size of a quarter. I'd tell Mom tomorrow. He leaned against the headboard. I pulled up a chair and sat beside the bed. I dropped one wafer in the milk to let it soak, and when the wafer was soft, I spoon-fed it to him. He wrapped his mouth over each spoonful. Milk leaked out from the side of his mouth, and I wiped his face with a paper towel. His eyes savored the milk and cookies with complete satisfaction. After a few more, he finished.

"Luca, I want you to make sure Cangelosi moves his ass with the building. I wanted to see the land today, but —"

"Don't worry. We can drive there tomorrow if you like. Where are the architect drawings anyway?"

"In the drawer behind my desk."

Mom entered. She said there was food ready if I wanted to eat. It was close to nine o'clock and I had to leave for the show.

"Do you need anything else?" I asked my father.

He shook his head as he slid down the headboard to sleep. My mother adjusted his pillow and asked him about his insulin. Knowing she had things under control, I got changed for the show and left to pick up the guys.

I drove up slowly outside Jamie's house. Under the dim porch light, the storm door swung open and crashed against the side of the house as it had many times before. Jamie stepped outside, raging. His long hair swayed as he took long strides toward me. I leaned over the passenger seat and opened the car door with a lift of the handle. Jamie wore an unbuttoned frayed flannel over his black shirt. He landed on the seat and slammed the car door, leaving the storm door swaying in the cool October night.

"Sorry I slammed your door. I hate that son of a bitch," he said.

"What happened?"

"I'm tired of being in that house with that bastard. If it wasn't for my mother, I'd be long gone by now."

"What's your mother got to do with it?" I said.

"I don't wanna leave her alone with him. He's crazy."

I drove away. I looked through the rear windshield to see Jamie's father step out of the house to close the storm door.

"Don't say sorry . . . You'll get through this."

"He hates everything I do, and he won't leave me alone. When he gets the chance, he puts me down and tells me what I should do. 'Why don't you do this' and 'why don't you do that.' It's like, why, why, why. I hate the prick."

"Yeah, your old man's a tough one."

Jamie sighed. "I can't wait to see the Ramones."

"Yeah, me too," I said. "So, you and Scott are good now, right? No bad blood?"

"Yeah, we're good. I got bigger problems than dealing with him," Jamie said.

Scott sat waiting on his front porch when we drove up. He ran over with light runner's feet. He wore baggy cargo shorts that were long and below his knees. His hoodie was unzipped and swayed in the chilly night air. Jamie opened the car door and leaned forward for Scott to jump in the back. I reached over and slapped his shoulder.

"Dude, isn't it too cold for shorts?" I said.

"It's gonna get hot in the pit, bro. You're gonna burn up," Scott said.

"He's right. Remember the mosh pit at Pantera?" Jamie said.

"Dude, of course—that was in the city. Phil was so awesome," Scott said, hitting his thighs repeatedly with the palms of his hands. He leaned his head forward between the front bucket seats, poised, eager, and with a smirk. "Awesome night, boys. Can't wait!"

Down Sycamore Avenue, the university campus was quiet. The streetlights glared like bright halos in the night. Closer to the beach, the wind picked up, and we turned left down Ocean Avenue toward the Trade Winds. We spoke of past shows and how we should cyclone the mosh pit. As we neared the venue, our excitement burgeoned into a blaze. We parked and hurried in line. We were shivered in the cold. The frigid air pierced our skin. We got closer to the entrance with great anticipation. Inside, we scurried for a spot near the stage, passing and leaning against the others. The venue was full. The deep blue lights dimmed. The amplifiers crackled and buzzed behind the black curtain and the crowd cheered. As if by a lightning strike, the curtain lifted and the stage erupted. The music sent the crowd into a frenzy. Joey's long bangs covered his face behind his sunglasses. He leaned forward to sing "Blitzkrieg Bop." I got pounded and stepped back as the mosh pit formed. Bodies hopped and crossed the floor with flailing fists and elbows. Some guy floated over the crowd until he was dropped like a sack of potatoes. He landed with a heavy thud. There were shouts, then quick, heavy tempos as the Ramones played the next song.

I pushed some punk into the pit, and he disappeared. Pinhead started. Someone pushed me into the pit. I ran full force into someone knocking him off balance. He disappeared. The force of the collision sent me flying into someone else, then someone else hit me. I swung my arms out to protect myself. The flashing strobe lights froze time into little slices. I crashed into the side of the pit before someone pushed me back in again. The air was heavy, and my mouth was dry. Everyone I touched was wet; the sound of music raged and passed on into memory. I bounced around like a lost atom in the sun. Where were they? I lost them. I pushed and pushed. Somehow, I appeared on the other side of the mosh pit again. Some dude gestured for me to hoist him up. I dropped my hands and interlocked my fingers. He placed his foot in my hands and I hoisted him over me where his body floated away over the crowd. I felt the floor shake. The crowd cleared enough for me to see the same guy on the floor in the fetal position. Somebody helped him up before I moved away. Jamie ran toward me, his face reddish in color, his eyes wide and wild. We were drenched with sweat, and the air was heavy with body odor.

"Where's Scott?!" he yelled.

"I don't know! This is awesome!" I said.

"Yeah! Hey, you wanna cyclone!" Jamie said.

"Na, I'm heading back in!" I said, waving my hand.

"Hell yeah!" he said.

I stood watching as Jamie ran into the pit and was gone. I hung back and watched the Ramones. I pushed into the crowd to cram it. The show ended as fast as it had started. The Ramones vanished from the stage with no encore, no nothing. The sharp white lights snapped on, and the crowd dispersed. Scott found me first, then we found Jamie.

"That was so awesome! I think I chipped the bone in my elbow!" Jamie said.

"Did you fall?" Scott asked him.

"A couple times," Jamie said.

We exited with the crowd like a herd of cattle. The cold air blew in from the exit, cooling us. Our hair and skin were wet, and our blood ran hot. The parking lot took a while to clear out. We were still pumped, talking over one another while we waited in traffic to leave. Scott said some dude had stepped on his foot and he thought he broke his toe. Jamie was an absolute chatterbox. He told of how he hit the floor and somehow a boot struck his head causing temporary hearing loss. I made it through the event with only a few bruises.

Scott interjected over Jamie's spiel: "Guys, I have to tell you something." Jamie continued with his story, missing Scott's words. Scott interrupted again, this time with a more insolent tone. Jamie went silent. We drove down Ocean Avenue along the shoreline. Scott reclined on the back seat.

"What is it—are you okay?" I asked, turning my head slightly.

"It's never a good time to say this so I better say it now. I'm moving to Florida to live with my dad," Scott said.

A lull ensued and the mood changed. We passed a traffic light and approached another.

"Wait, you're moving to Florida? Why?" I asked.

"I'm leaving tomorrow. He's got a good job waiting for me down there. I start working next week."

"Tomorrow? Wow, that's harsh," Jamie said.

"Yeah, I know. Sorry, I should've said something earlier about it. My dad's friend is growing his business, and he's willing to teach me carpentry, so I'm going."

"What about your mom? Is she cool with it?" I said.

"Yeah, she'll be fine. I'm going anyway."

"Since we're talking about life-changing events, I have one for you... Eva's pregnant," I said.

Jamie laughed. "Holy crap! This is too much. Wait! Are you moving to Costa Miel now?"

"Dude, are you sure it's yours?" Scott said.

"No, I don't think so," I said.

"I thought you stopped talking to her," Jamie said.

"I did, but she sent me a letter. I made the mistake of reading it."

"Dude, don't even think about it; just live your life. You should start dating again," Scott said.

"I will. I've been busy with the gas station and my dad."

"Hey, stop at the 7-Eleven for a sec. I'm thirsty," Jamie said.

I parked, and Jamie stepped out.

"Scott, we're gonna miss you, dude. It's gonna suck without you."

"I know, but I gotta go. Things aren't cutting it for me here."

"What about learning communication? What happened to that?"

"I should have said something sooner, but I didn't like it. I'm not the studying type."

"That's fine. If you're not happy here, that's fine, but I don't wanna to see you go, that's all."

"I'll come back and see you guys. You guys can come down to Florida anytime. The surfing's nice down there."

The car door opened with a rush of cold air. Jamie sat down and twisted the cap on his soda bottle, making low clicks. He took a long swig and swallowed.

"Sorry to see you go, Scott," Jamie said, not looking back, staring at the 7-Eleven.

"I know. Sorry, dude. I really wanna do this."

Driving back, I passed the signs for Long Branch. Scott rattled off some benefits for living in Florida—about the waves, the warm weather, and the work. "We'll go surfing at Cocoa Beach when you guys come down," he said.

Scott seemed jovial. It felt like he couldn't wait to leave. I also felt we wouldn't see him again. I thought of Eva and the way she looked at me the last time I saw her. The way I left her sitting there on the bed. It's crazy how things turn out sometimes. The girl is a tough one. I'll give her that.

I parked on Scott's driveway with the engine running.

"Hey, let's hang out. We'll play pool and drink," Scott said.

"I gotta go to work tomorrow," Jamie said. I agreed; I couldn't stay.

"All right, I'll call you guys after I get to Cocoa Beach. Step out with me real quick," Scott said.

We said our goodbyes. I gave Scott a hug. Scott turned to Jamie who extended his hand. Scott grabbed Jamie's hand and pulled him in to embrace. Scott turned and walked into his house, and he was gone.

The streets were bare as we drove under an occasional streetlight. The Ramones were forgotten, replaced by Scott's unexpected departure. I rolled down the window to let in some cold air.

"To be honest, I always had mixed feelings about the guy. I'm not really upset about him leaving," Jamie said.

"It's kinda messed up for him to say something on the night before he leaves," I said.

"C'mon, he's always been a selfish prick," Jamie said.

I stopped at a traffic light and let out a sigh.

"I don't wanna go home," Jamie said.

"Where do you wanna go?"

"Let's go to the Long Branch pier."

"The pier that burned down? There's nothing there except old burnt pilings and broken concrete."

"Yeah, I know. Let's go."

I turned the car eastward, toward Long Branch. I drove on, not knowing what to say—so I said nothing. I parked alongside the boardwalk. We went out and walked on the beach under the moonlight. It was cold. The moonlight dabbled and speckled upon the ocean, shimmering to the horizon. I thought of the first night I danced with Eva. The sea air rejuvenated me. We stepped onto the sand and climbed a jetty near where the old pier was. I took long strides over large boulders to the end of the jetty. Drops of seawater hit my pants, my shoes, anywhere it wanted to. We looked out onto the sea.

"What are you thinking?" I said.

"Nothing."

"I'm thinking we should drive down to Florida once Scott gets settled down there. What do you think?" I said.

"Yeah, I always wanted to see Terror on Church Street."

"I'll call him in a few weeks to see what's up," I said.

"You know what would be cool," Jamie said, looking down at the jetty. "I can make a human skull out of concrete and anchor it between the rocks here. How awesome would that be?"

"What do you mean, to anchor it to the jetty?"

"Pour hydraulic cement between the boulders and put the skull in the cement. It'll freak people out."

"Won't the cement cover the skull?"

"No, I'll have a piece of rebar sticking out of the bottom of the skull. The rebar will hold the skull to the concrete."

"Sure. If you make the skull, I'll help you do it."

"Cool. All I need is for you to hold the skull while I pour the cement. I'll also need you to look out for the cops." We chuckled.

Jamie turned and looked at the remains of the scorched pier. We jumped off the jetty. The cold sand was hard under my feet. The burnt wooden pilings stood like broken wooden soldiers marching into the sea. The salt water swirled around their bases and formed eddies. The top of each piling was black and charcoaled, wrinkled with creases. Farther out, near the last row of pilings, a twisted rusty iron bar protruded from the sea. A remnant of what once was a whimsical place. What else was under the sea—a *Claw* game, a concession stand, Skee-Balls? The fire destroyed everything a few years back. Now Jamie liked this place more than when it was thriving and alive.

I sat on a dirty, worn piece of wood on the beach and watched him walk around. I took a deep breath. He turned and paced slowly, the wet sand clumping on his shoes. Jamie stopped to look out past the pilings into the dark void of the sea. I sat down long enough to get bored. It was late.

"Hey, Jamie, let's go home. It's freezing out here."

"I want to stay a little longer. Sorry I dragged you out here."

"I'll be waiting in the car. Stay as long as you want," I said.

I made it halfway to my car. I pictured Jamie pacing back and forth along the edge of the dark, cold ocean, alone. I took two more steps and turned around and walked back to him. I lifted my collar to keep my neck warm.

Chapter 14

It was a dark, cold December morning. The frost glistened on blades of grass under the faint glow of the dawn. I let Nicky-boy outside. He ran off onto the yard and put his nose to the earth, moving around like a bloodhound. Someone will let him in later.

On my drive to work, I played *Bloodletting* until I felt melancholy enough to switch on the radio for the news. Youssef moved swiftly between the gas pumps when I arrived. His energy had been indomitable since he started a few weeks ago. Steve was doing his typical bare bones minimum (no surprise there). I drove a customer's Jeep into a service bay to change the oil. Al was working on a brake job one bay over. At the end of the morning shift, I counted the money. The morning shift was short ninety dollars; this happened often since Youssef had started. I became concerned. Ninety dollars is a large amount to be missing after an eight-hour shift. Neither Steve nor Youssef knew why. I had my suspicions but no proof.

Youssef entered the service bay. "Good morning, Mr. Luke," he said enthusiastically.

"Good morning, Youssef."

"I want to tell you something, sir."

"Sure, what is it?"

"Since I work here, I see a lot of customers with tire problems on Sundays. You know we sell more tires now."

Youssef mentioned he was an auto mechanic back in Egypt. He convinced me he could pump gas and repair tires on Sundays by himself when service was closed. We tried it and he did well. He sold a lot of tires too. The man was a natural salesman. All while pumping gas with Steve. For his hard work, I paid him a percentage from each sale and repair on top of his hourly rate. We moved our conversation outside in the cold due to Al hammering away on a rusted brake rotor. The early afternoon sun was bright but the cold, dry air chapped the skin. The highway traffic was busier because of the upcoming holidays.

Youssef continued: "We need more tires. We don't have enough. Last Sunday I had to turn people away. Also, customers don't know we sell tires when they drive by."

"They don't?" I questioned.

"No, I don't think so." He emphasized the lack of signage. I had a tune up sign and a brake special sign above the garage doors, but nothing else.

"Okay, I'll order more tires and call the sign guy to make us another sign," I said.

Youssef thanked me, shook my hand, and went home. Lenny arrived to work the afternoon shift. I told him the morning shift money was short again. We agreed someone was stealing money. In the past, I would keep an eye on the last hire, but with Youssef's strong work ethic, I had doubts.

Lenny and I pumped gas that afternoon. I got a phone call from my mother who told me my father was back in the hospital. This time for his foot. I wanted to leave, but she convinced me to stay. The nurse gave him pain medications, and he would be sleeping most of the day. The service garage closed at five. Al gave me his completed repair orders and left. I went to the private office in the back to prepare the bank deposit. While I counted the money, I decided to move Steve to the afternoon shift to work with Lenny, like it used to be. I'd work with Youssef in the mornings and see what happened.

I arrived at the hospital later that evening. The visiting physician told us gangrene had spread up his right leg and that he had to amputate. Surprisingly, my father was indifferent with the news. The rest of us were heartbroken. We all cried. The years of untreated diabetes had taken its toll. The antibiotics, good hygiene, and massages did nothing to stop it. It raced through him like a speeding freight train barreling off the tracks. The amputation happened immediately to prevent spreading. After a few days in the hospital, we took him home. From the car, I carried him into the house and placed him on the wheelchair. We rolled him to the kitchen table. My mother made espresso on the stove, and my sister sat beside him in case he needed anything. He appeared smaller, as if he'd shrunk in size. He kept his head down and his eyes closed, as if in concentration. I smiled and kept my demeanor upbeat. I kissed his forehead. The sight of the missing foot changed everything. How could this happen to a man who never sat still in his life? I refrained from talking. My mother poured espresso into a demitasse. No one said anything. Even Nicky-boy knew. The whole situation was disturbing, despondent, and hopeless. Nicky-boy got up and approached the wheelchair and put his chin on my father's leg. My father looked down at the dog and nodded.

"They did it," he said in a low, raspy voice. "They took it."

"I'm sorry, Dad, but the doctor said it was the only way to stop the spreading. Or else, why would he have done it?" Sofia said.

He lifted his hand and rubbed his nose. He winced, whined, and bent his head down so no one could see his face. I held my emotions back to be strong.

Sofia stepped behind him and rubbed his shoulders. Her eyes filled with tears, which flowed down her face. My mother placed the espresso on the dinner table and sat down. She held her hands together to pray, covering her face.

"I was strong before," he cried, letting out a moan with a session of deep breaths. "Now no more."

"It's okay to cry. Let it out," I said. With a deep release, he cried until he ran out of tears. It was the saddest day of my life. His breath subsided, and after he calmed down, he sipped a little espresso.

"I'm going to the courthouse soon to get that variance. Then we'll start building," I said. He nodded in agreement, looking down.

"When I was young, I was strong like you. I swam to the island of Lampedusa when I was your age," he said.

"I saw the photographs of you. You're very strong, Papa," Sofia said.

We drank coffee together. He appeared better. For a moment, I saw the strength come back to his eyes. "I want to talk to my brother," he said.

"It's the middle of the night in Milano. We'll call him tomorrow morning," Mother said. "You should go to bed."

He nodded in agreement. "A little more espresso," he said.

I carried my father to bed. The hospital gave us medical supplies to care for him. I went downstairs and noticed a second letter from Eva. The letter included two photographs. I wanted to keep it. I'd thought of her more over the last few weeks. One photo showed her posing next to a palm tree on the beach looking gorgeous. The other photo was Eva and her mother together. They looked alike. Her mother's name was Maria. They were both beautiful. I put the photographs on my desk and read the letter.

Dear Luca—How are you? I did not hear from you. Please don't forget me. You are my love and I want to talk to you. Call me or write to me. I am waiting for you.

I included pictures for you. My mother says hello and wants to meet you. My pregnancy is going well. Some days I feel sick, but the doctor says it's normal.

Armando understands my situation, but he makes me work until I cannot. As long as he makes money, he is happy. It's that simple with him. My health and the baby are most important to me, and he knows that.

Rosa wants to leave Armando, but he will not let her. Armando is stubborn and Rosa is a fighter, which makes a bad combination. I hope I am writing this well. I love to learn English and it takes a long time for me to write to you in English.

I hope you and your family are healthy.

I love you,
Eva.

Chapter 15

My father sat in his wheelchair watching television. The morning sun shining through the window showed the floating dust particles lingering in the air. His expression had a bored disposition and a yearning to do something else. I sat next to him and asked him if he wanted to go for a car ride. He agreed with a slow nod. In the kitchen, I told Mother I was taking Dad to the Twin Lighthouses and asked if anyone else wanted to go. Sofia, who sat at the kitchen table, said okay. Mom wanted to stay home. "The fresh air is good for him," she said. We prepared a few things and wheeled my father to the car all bundled up. I lifted him onto the passenger seat, and Sofia folded the wheelchair and placed it in the trunk.

We drove north past Long Branch to Sea Bright toward Sandy Hook. We turned into the Highlands and up the hill to the Navesink Twin Lighthouses. It was late December. The day was cold but the sky was clear enough to see Sandy Hook Bay and beyond. We made our way along the brick walkway to where the vista showed New York Harbor and the big city. The ocean was a deep blue and Long Island stretched out to the horizon. The skyscrapers of Manhattan were hard to see, but not the Verrazano Bridge. We sat near the old canon. The brown, heavy stone walls of the lighthouses were worn little over the past two centuries. The bold white numbers of 1862 displayed at the top-center of the façade. An occasional plane flew overhead, heading toward Kennedy airport. I sat next to Sofia on a bench and watched my father. His amputated leg was held up by the leg rest on the wheelchair. His sweatpants dangled over his knee, and the other leg weighed gently on his lonely foot. He sat with an offward glance, looking here and there. He looked down on his leg, examined it, and adjusted his sweatpants.

I whispered into my sister's ear. "I have good news. Last night the township approved the variances for the property. We can start building now. You wanna tell Dad? I know he'll be happy to hear it."

Sofia smiled. "Oh yeah," she said contently.

Sofia rose and kneeled beside the wheelchair. She placed her hands on his arm and looked into his eyes. She smiled. He replied to her with an inquisitive tone. Their talk was inaudible to me because of the wind in my ear. After a moment, Sofia got up and pushed him to me. He faced me with one hand tucked inside his jacket—he looked like an old Napoleon Bonaparte. He spoke in an interested yet weakened voice: "Sofia said we can build," he said.

"Yes, we can start building right away. I got the okay from the township last night," I said. There it was—that familiar look my father had when he thought too hard. It felt good to see him this way.

Under his crooked winter cap, and his nose dripping from the cold, he pointed his finger at me with energy. Unconcerned with his condition, he demanded I call Mr. Cangelosi immediately. He told me where to find the architect drawings (he'd told me where the drawings were once before). Sofia sat and listened intently. He explained the type of brick to use—it had to be specific bricks, he insisted. He carried on a few minutes longer until the wind picked up and hit us with frigid Winter air. Bothered by the cold, we went back to the car. I stopped for a moment at the sign for Marconi's wireless antenna. The sign read that the Navesink Twin Lights received their first wireless telegraph from a boat offshore back in 1899. A technology that changed humanity forever. The story inspired me to one day continue my engineering studies.

After lifting my father into the car, I asked Sofia to walk with me around the lighthouse. I told him we'd be right back.

"Sofia, I need your advice. It's important," I said.

"Sure, I have a few things to tell you, too, but go ahead."

"When I vacationed in Costa Miel, I met a girl. We hit it off and we had a great time . . . So, fast-forward to now. I got a letter from her saying she's pregnant." The last words I uttered stopped her cold.

"You didn't wear a condom?" she asked anxiously.

"She said I didn't need it."

"That was dumb! And you believed her? I thought you were smart."

"I know. I know. I should have, but we were in that moment and things happened. There's more . . . I found out she's a sex worker."

"What? Wait, she's a hooker?"

"I know. I know. She kept it secret from me, so I didn't know. I broke it off with her once I found out."

"So how do you know this baby is yours?" I didn't answer. "Okay, so first off, don't tell Mom and Dad. You have to make sure it's your baby first before you start telling anyone. They're going through a lot right now—we all are—and if they find out, it'll add more stress to our lives."

"I don't think it's mine, so forget I told you."

"Yeah, just leave it that way . . . Oh, I forgot to say, Uncle Silvio is coming to help us. He's flying in tomorrow," she said.

"Tomorrow?"

"Yeah, trust me, I didn't know until yesterday either. You know how they don't tell us anything."

"Yeah."

"By the way, Kelly still talks about you. She's still interested in you even after what you did."

"Isn't she going to college?"

"She's going to the community college nearby, so she'll be around. She loves you. She's felt that way ever since I've known her."

"I'll call her," I said.

"Really? Good, I'm glad. She's smart and pretty, and I think you're meant for each other."

The cold wind passed through our jackets and hit our bones. Sofia crossed her arms to stay warm. The temperature dropped further.

"C'mon, let's get back to the car. I'm freezing," she said.

***

Steve shouted obscenities at me before, during, and after he grabbed his last paycheck. He stormed out of the sales office with a wild swing of the door. I followed him outside, smelling the booze and the dank odor of his jacket. The sky was gray a week before Christmas. Youssef stood at a gas pump, filling a vehicle, bundled up and wearing a thick wool cap low to his brow.

Steve removed the check and threw the envelope to the ground in defiance. My heart raced as I followed him. He stepped onto the highway where he'd walked before so many times. I grabbed the discarded envelope and watched him head down the highway. He never looked back. Farther down the road, I looked at the go-go bar he frequented. The parking lot was empty and in large white letters over the go-go sign it read for lease.

I crumpled the envelope, letting my tension squeeze the paper into a small tight ball. Youssef approached me.

"That's it for him. I had enough of his crap. He's a drunk and a thief," I said.

"He has many troubles, Mr. Luke. May God help him," Youssef said in a gentle voice.

"I need someone to replace him. I can't have Lenny working alone. I'll go through the applications and make some phone calls. Do you know anyone who needs a job?"

"Yes, my brother," Youssef said.

"Well, if he works like you, then all my problems are solved," I said with a chuckle.

"My brother works in a restaurant at night. He has the time to work the afternoon shift. Is that okay?"

"Yes, definitely. He can work with Lenny."

"That's good. My brother will be very happy."

"Have him start right away."

I waited for Youssef to finish. He collected the payment and placed the cash neatly into his money roll. He stepped toward me with the energy and enthusiasm of a man with a purpose.

"Youssef, I'm curious to know more about you. You said you're from Alexandria."

He spoke as we walked back to the sales office. "Yes, it is a beautiful city, but you know I'm not Muslim." he said.

"Really? I thought you were."

"Oh, no, I am Christian, a Coptic. We are like Catholics but different."

"What's Coptic?"

He chuckled. "Coptic people follow their pope, not the one in Rome. Our pope is in Alexandria. Our love for God and Jesus is the same."

"I find myself talking to God more these days with my father being the way he is. His health is getting worse."

"I am praying for your father. He is a good man. Hardworking man. I respect your father."

"Thanks, Youssef. Why did you come to the U.S.?"

"I left Alexandria because it is better to make money in America. My uncle lived here in New Jersey for many years. He helped me and my brother come to America. Thanks be to God."

"I'm glad you're here."

The rest of the day I ran between the pumps and the service bays. The sun set, the streetlights illuminated, and the tension of Steve leaving faded. Youssef's brother, Sam, arrived and I put him to work with Lenny. Sam was quieter than Youssef, but he moved around the gas pumps with the energy of a badger. Feeling confident with the new hire, I deposited the money at the bank and went home.

I entered the house to see a face I had not seen in many years, my uncle Silvio. The man was a fantastic salesman. A dapper gentleman who exemplified what other salesmen strive to achieve. He made his success selling beauty products and supplies all across northern Italy. His sons had taken over the operation recently, leaving my uncle with plenty of time for his two passions: traveling and cooking. My uncle wore a gray V-neck cashmere sweater over a white dress shirt. His black slacks were pressed and debonair. He dressed this way every day. A practice every salesman should follow to succeed—dress for success, he would say. We shook hands. His mannerisms made me uneasy, as if he were inspecting me with inquisitive eyes. Mother and Sister prepared dinner. He let go of my hand and lifted a finger to his lips to silence me. He whispered that my father was sleeping in the next room. He returned to the kitchen to finish his espresso. He left the empty demitasse on the table and motioned me to follow him into my father's office. We made ourselves comfortable where I sat looking at him at the head of the desk.

"It's so good to see you. How was your flight?" I asked.

"Very good, very good," he said, being coy about his English. We spoke in Italian. He said, according to the doctor, my father would need to start dialysis treatment. I didn't know his kidneys were failing. He explained having diabetes for many years can cause that complication. I still felt hopeful. It may have been because of my uncle's presence. He was always so optimistic. He asked about how I was. I told him I had the business under control. I brought up the new construction and my scheduled meeting with Mr. Cangelosi. He knew nothing of my father's land or the construction of the repair shop. He shrugged his shoulders and said the new construction was my responsibility. I inquired about his family back home in Italy. He said his wife and two sons were fine—everyone was fine. He gave no details.

Sofia walked in and said dinner was ready. We got up and walked past the kitchen to the living room where my father was awake; I had set up a small bed for him there after the amputation. He wanted us to move his bed near the window, farther away from the television. We arranged the furniture as he liked and called in my mother for her approval. She thought for a moment and suggested the sofa be moved closer to the bed and the lounge chair closer to the television. The room was rearranged until everyone was satisfied. I put my father in the wheelchair and uncle Silvio pushed him into the dining room where he was placed at the head of the table. A bowl of lentil soup was waiting for him. Soon a basket of fresh Italian bread and a stack of chicken cutlets were placed at the center of the table. My father waited, and my uncle took the liberty of opening a bottle of wine. Nicky-boy entered the dining room and took turns sniffing us. "Are you ready for dinner?" my sister said to the dog. He whined impatiently and lingered under the table. Some of us lifted the tablecloth to watch him. His white, bushy coat shifted with his sudden movements.

"He's very smart," Sofia said. "He understands everything."

"He smells the chicken," I said, smiling as I peered under the table.

Nicky-boy whined again, lifting his face to my sister with the hopes of a morsel of chicken. My mother walked in and placed his food bowl on the floor. She mixed in pieces of chicken cutlets with the dog food. Nicky-boy stopped whining and left us alone. A large bowl of pasta bathed in pesto sauce placed at the center of the table meant dinner had begun. My uncle filled a plate with pasta and placed it before his brother. My father finished the soup and requested more pasta. My mother was last to sit. The steam lifted off the hot food. "Delicious," my uncle said. He poured more wine into his glass.

My uncle spoke to my father in Sicilian dialect. "Michael, why don't your kids speak Sicilian? Don't you speak Sicilian to them?"

My father shook his head in disagreement as he continued to eat his pasta.

"They don't speak, but they understand it," my mother said.

"Well, don't you think you should force them to answer you in our language? It's shameful to have them go through life losing where they came from."

"If they want, they can learn quickly," she said.

"But it's obvious they can't speak Sicilian. When will you teach them?" Uncle Silvio said.

"Hey, hey," my father interrupted. The room went silent. My father dropped his fork in his pasta making a loud clang. "We are not going back. We are not going back to Sicily, so English is all they need to know. If they want, they can learn it themselves. Can I eat in peace now?"

All eyes focused on Uncle Silvio. "Of course. I was making a point about keeping our culture."

"We are Americans now," my father answered as he picked up the fork. "That's it."

The silence continued until my uncle complimented my mother's cooking. "Allora, I want to practice English, then. I know my English is not good. So, it is okay?" my uncle said as he looked around for approval. "Good. Allora, Sofia, do you have a boyfriend?"

"No, but I'm going to college in September. I hope to find one there."

"Bravissima, Sofia. Remember, school first, boyfriend second." Uncle Silvio chuckled. "E you, giovanotto?"

"No, no girlfriend."

"No? That's okay. You study and make money. Then you get a girlfriend."

I chuckled. "Mom, let me know when you need me to pick up the fresh ricotta for the Christmas party," I said.

"Good. I am making fresh cannoli cream for the first time. I can't wait," Sofia said, smiling at Mother.

"I will make less food this year, only lasagna, lamb, and zeppole," Mother said.

"That's all?" I said as I winked at Sofia. Sofia giggled.

"Luca, I'm too tired," Mother said, annoyed.

"I'm just kidding, Ma. Besides, Sofia will help you."

"Yes, she will," Mother insisted.

"Everyone knows I like to cook, so. Mom will have a lot of help that day," Sofia said.

A heavy, short tapping on the front door interrupted dinner. Nicky-boy barked a few times. I recognized the tapping signature. I got up and hurried to the door before it started again. Jamie stepped back and away from the light behind me.

"What's up? Come in."

"No, I'll stay out here. I don't wanna bother your dad."

"No, come in. We don't mind."

"Can we talk out here?" Jamie said.

"Out in the cold?" I felt something was wrong. "Okay, let me get my jacket."

I stepped out onto the porch and switched on the front porch light. Jamie's shirt was bloodstained, smeared, and spotted lightly.

"What happened?" I said. "You okay?"

"I did it," he said with confidence.

"Did what? Where's your car? How'd you get here?"

"I beat up my old man. I had it out with him."

"What? You hit your father?"

"Yeah, I got him good. I had enough of him."

"Damn, okay. Start from the beginning. Tell me everything."

"It was one of those nights again. He was driving me crazy with his attitude. He complained about how I needed to change and about how I needed to be more like this and like that."

"Yeah, but he's said that to you before. What's different this time?"

"What's different is I had enough, and when my mother stepped in to stop it, I lost it."

"What do you mean—he hit her?"

"He pushed her and that's when I started swinging on him. I punched him in the face and he fell. After that, I hit him again, and again."

"That's crazy."

"It got worse. I straddled him and pinned his arms down and started whaling on his face."

"Wow."

"If it wasn't for my mom stopping me, I would've kept going. She stopped me though. 'It was shameful,' she said. She started to cry. After that, I ran away. I cut through the woods by the mall."

"Oh, man, I'm sorry. If you beat him that badly, you should go back."

"Na, I didn't beat him enough."

"But, Jamie, there's blood all over your shirt. It looks pretty bad. I'll drive you home."

"No. No, I'm not ready to go back. I can't." Jamie relaxed his limbs and sat on the porch steps. I sat next to him.

"Can you turn off the porch light? The lights bother me," Jamie said.

I stepped inside and turned off the porch light. The night air was still and cold, but not frigid.

"I was thinking about Costa Miel," he said, trying to calm down.

"Yeah, it was a great trip," I said.

"I miss it. The waves were amazing. The nightlife was fun, and the women were hot. Do you remember that first day there? The waves were enormous. They were overhead high."

"Dude, I know."

"Have you heard from Scott?" Jamie said.

"No, I've been busy. I have to give him a call. Scott had the right idea of going to Florida. At least the waves are better down there," I said. Jamie chuckled.

"Have you heard from Eva?"

"I did. That guy, Armando, is making Eva work while she's pregnant. I can't believe that wacko. The whole thing is unbelievable."

"I don't know what to say. I hate to bring it up, but what if the baby is yours? It's possible, right? Have you thought about that?"

"No, I seriously doubt it. I can't believe what she says anyway."

"Then why do you read her letters? Just throw them out and move on."

"I don't know. Part of me is still connected to her. Honestly, I miss her sometimes. I need more time to heal."

"Well, for the record, if you go back, I'm coming with you."

"I don't know. I need to move on is what I really need to do."

We sat idle for a time. In the comfort of the darkness. Jamie looked up with a pensive stare. I followed his eyes to the sky where the stars shared space with the moon. Venus sparkled and the faint glow beyond the trees reminded me of the lights of Calle Principale. Jamie had nowhere he wanted to go and we ran out of things to say. After a deep sigh, he asked me to drive him home.

Chapter 16

Down highway 36, the line of traffic cones steered me to the left. I drove slowly with the other cars like cattle herded through a chute into a single lane of traffic. I took the jug-handle and crossed over the highway to the construction site. The afternoon sun was low in the sky. I drove into the empty lot. Mr. Cangelosi was like I remembered him, only a bit grayer. He approached me from a distance kicking up dust where the old building once stood. I was a boy the last time I saw him. He was a plumber back then. Now, he ran his own construction company. Last I remembered, he installed a sump pump in our basement. He had this phlegmy, feeble voice that carried an inclination to clear one's throat. It was as if his voice box were partially paralyzed or damaged from an accident, or something. I parked alongside his truck. It was time to break ground and pour the foundation; hence our meeting.

"Luca, you remember me?"

"Of course." I leaned in closer to hear him above the noise of the highway.

"Last time I saw you, you were a boy. Now look at you—you're a man. How's your mother?"

"She's hangin' in there. It's my father—"

"I know, I know, I know—that goddamn diabetes. Oh my God. Your father's been sick for a long time with that."

"Yeah, he's getting worse."

"Oh my God. I remember years ago, when your father had the Pizzaiolo. I would go to eat lunch there, ya know. I have to tell you. When your father's sugar was low, he never stopped working. He was a lavoratore. Ya know what he did? When his sugar was low, he drank soda from the fountain until he felt strong again. He never sat down, that man. He kept working and working. He was a lavoratore."

"I almost don't wanna tell you, but the other day they amputated his leg."

"Oh my God. That goddamn diabetes. I can't believe it. I'm sorry for your father. I'm sorry."

"Yeah, it's terrible. We do the best we can to make him happy," I said.

"Ah, whatta ya gonna do. Mi dispiace. He's very lucky to have his family. You, your sister, and your mother are very good to him. He's lucky that way."

"Thank you, Mr. Cangelosi. I appreciate it."

"Okay, I got the drawings here. Everything looks good. The architect is a good one. The bricks will be here tomorrow, they say. By the way, the bricks your father ordered are the best—very expensive. Your building will last one hundred years."

"How much more are the bricks?"

"Eh, about twice the price."

"Really?"

"Yeah, that's what your father wants. I told him he could settle for the good bricks, not the best ones, but good ones. It would save you a lot of money, but he wanted the best."

"All right. He's been saving money and working for a long time. Whatever he wants."

"Yeah, sure," he said.

"My father told me to ask you a favor. He needs the building finished as soon as possible."

"I've known your father for many years. He helped me when I came to this country. I will go as fast as I can. Okay. I will finish in a few months."

"Thanks again, Mr. Cangelosi. Call me when you need the next payment."

We took inquisitive steps around the property, checking markers against the drawings. The building would be a six-bay garage with a small waiting area. We shook hands and I drove back to the gas station to finish my workday and deposit the cash at the bank. A routine I'd followed since leaving the university.

At home, the smell of gasoline wafted off my work clothes as I dropped them in the hamper. After a long shower, I put on house clothes, and read parts of Homer's *Odyssey*. In my bookcase were college notes, textbooks, and the few novels I thought worth keeping. Between the books, I pulled out a few of Kelly's letters she wrote me when we first dated. I unfolded them and placed them on my bed. Her words sparked fond memories of our relationship. I thought more of her recently. Over the last few weeks, I contended with myself that I may have misjudged my feelings for her. I thought often of our past and how I scrutinized my decision until I said to myself,

"What if? Yeah, what if? What if I stayed with Kelly Swanson?" I should have worked more on our relationship rather than given up. She did love me; there was proof of that in these letters. I remembered her kindness, her understanding. There are many failures on the road to success, I read somewhere. I know had the chance to make things right again. "Let me see where this goes," I thought. With an anxious, yet determined heart, I picked up the phone and called her.

"Hello," she said.

"Hi, Kelly, it's me."

"Hi," Kelly replied, waiting for my next word.

"I called because I wanted to know how you were. How are you?"

She paused. "I'm fine. To be honest, I didn't expect your call."

"I know. I don't blame you. I was very rude to you last summer." Her awkward pause pressured me to say the reason for my call. "I just want to say that I miss you. I miss your smile, I miss how fun you are, and I miss being with you." She remained silent, adding to the awkwardness. I thought she'd hung up, so I asked if she was still there.

"I'm here. What I want to know is why you gave up on us so easily?"

"I really didn't think it through back then. I didn't know what I wanted."

"Well, you didn't want me," she said petulantly.

"That was my mistake. I'm sorry to hurt you. I was confused. I was a confused dickhead."

"Oh, so you know."

"Yeah, but hear me out. Let me take you out to dinner so we can talk."

"Talk to me now," she said.

"I would rather talk to you in person. We can catch up. There's a lot to talk about."

"I'm busy for the holiday weekend, but I'm around next Tuesday."

"Sounds good. Is 7:00 p.m. okay?"

"Uh-huh."

"Okay, see you then. Tell your parents a Merry Christmas for me."

"Merry Christmas to your family. Bye."

I went downstairs. My father slept with his mouth open. His only foot was uncovered; it showed the gangrene had spread. My mother and uncle sat quietly at the kitchen table. They were jaded.

"I saw Dad's leg. It's bad now," I said.

"He's getting worse. He needs to see the doctor," my mother said. "I called the ambulance. They will be here soon."

"Okay, yeah, it's the best thing to do," I said. My uncle nodded in agreement.

We entered the living room. I switched on the light. My mother whispered to herself. I thought she said: "Mai possiamo ballare." I asked what she said. She let out a sigh and said in a low voice, "He was a good dancer once."

"Ma, he'll get better. We gotta hope for the best, right?"

My uncle took a hard look at the resting remains of a man who carried the shame of poverty with him to the new world. He told the story of the time he saved my uncle from drowning in the ocean when they were teenagers. My father held him above water long enough to escape the riptide. My uncle went on about how my father charmed my mother by playing the accordion and telling jokes. When they dated, my aunt, who was ten years old at the time, was their chaperone. My father would give her money to buy candy so he could have some time alone with my mother. I found my uncle's stories hard to believe. My old man never told jokes. He was serious all the time. I didn't get it. I never saw the sensitive, funny, or romantic side of my father. I feared him and respected him for the sacrifices he made for us.

The ambulance arrived. It beaconed red and white lights across the neighborhood, giving the neighbors a reason to huddle, gaze, and gossip. The paramedics carried him away on the stretcher. He was in a daze staring up at the sky. It was two days before Christmas. As a family, we did our best to keep our spirits high during the holiday season. Later, the medical professionals deemed it necessary to amputate his other foot. That plus the regular visits to a dialysis machine made it hard not to lose hope. He was only sixty-two years old. This was the man who had once saved his brother's life. The same man who became a successful entrepreneur and was now building a six-bay repair shop on his own land. Although the last achievement was not yet finished, I'd see to its completion and make sure he saw it standing.

Chapter 17

It was early evening as we neared the end of 1993. My father was home from the hospital. He sat up in bed near the living room window. My mother spoon-fed him his dinner of steamed oatmeal with a hint of olive oil. I sat on the sofa next to my uncle as we watched. Sofia walked in from the kitchen carrying a dishpan of warm water to clean him after feeding. Uncle Silvio got up and helped my sister place the dishpan near the bed. The silence bothered me; knowing our time together was special, I thought of something to say. All I could think of was if he wanted to go for a car ride, but he didn't want to go anywhere. Everyone focused on keeping him comfortable. My uncle faced his brother and pointed at me.

"Your son will see a girl tonight," he said as he smiled.

"Your English has improved," I said.

"I try," my uncle said. "Still not good, but I try."

My father moved his head away from the spoon and pronounced with vigor, "Is she blonde?"

"Dad, you know her. It's Kelly," I said.

"Good. I like her. She's blonde," my father said with more strength. "I like blondes."

"Daaaaad. You know you don't mean that. Stop," Sofia said. My mother shook her head to dismiss it.

"Your mother goes out and sees other men and leaves me here alone with my brother," my father said.

"Yeah, sure, I see other men," my mother said sardonically. "I buy food and your medicine. Where else do I go? I'm always here with you."

"You don't want me anymore," he said.

"C'mon, Dad. Stop it," I said. "Mom has always loved you. You know that."

He dropped his head on the pillow. Tears ran down his face; he sniffled. My mother stood up and walked into the kitchen. Sofia wanted to wash his face, but he told her to go away. He wanted to be alone. We walked into the kitchen where Mom began to clean dishes.

"Dad's depressed. He doesn't feel like a man anymore," I said to my mother.

"Your father is sick in the head now too," she said.

"He's definitely depressed," Sofia said.

"I'm tired," Mother said. "I'm so tired. Sono stanco di questo."

"Andare a letto. Dormirò nella stanza con lui," Uncle Silvio said.

"Yeah, Ma, go to bed. Zio will stay with Dad," I said.

"I'll stay too," Sofia said.

"Sofia, give your father his medicine at eleven o'clock. I'll get up early to clean him and get him ready for dialysis," Mother said.

"Okay," Sofia said. "Go to bed."

My mother's face manifested her suffering. The storm that was once far away was now here, and we were all in it, especially her. I never realized how bad it could get, taking care of him. There was a fear among us, a fear of the future, a fear he may give up. Another day of suffering was over, and all I wanted to do was leave and see Kelly.

Kelly Swanson was once the best attacker on the high school volleyball team. It was not her height that gave her the advantage over other players—she was only five foot four inches tall. It was her quickness and her agility to get past the blockers that made her special. Sofia was her teammate. Over the season, their bond on the court grew. My sister and Kelly developed into a powerful duo, passing and spiking enough victories for a winning season during my senior year. They were only sophomores at the time. Being friends, Sofia invited Kelly over for dinner on occasion, which was how I met her. Kelly laughed at my silly stories and displayed what I thought were positive cues toward me. Soon, I felt drawn to her as she was fun to be around. That year was an Indian summer and hot well into September. Kelly was over more and more and we spent a lot of time in the swimming pool. We played games and connected until that time when her eyes drew me to her lips and we kissed. Later, when I let my sister know, she giggled and told me it was obvious from the first. It was Kelly's intention to have me from the beginning.

Kelly's family lived in an affluent neighborhood near the Jersey shore. A traditional family where her mother stayed home and her father ran a successful architecture firm. She had a younger brother who rarely left his room but was cordial when you met him.

Her mother answered the door when I arrived. Mrs. Swanson was happy to see me. She let me in while we waited for Kelly. We exchanged pleasantries and Mr. Swanson walked in from the living room and shook my hand. They expressed their concern for my father's health and wished him a quick recovery. I didn't expect the gracious reception after I broke it off with their daughter the summer before. Kelly came down the stairs and rushed me out, leaving her parents waving goodbye at the front door.

On the boardwalk was a restaurant that sold hearty crab cakes. What better way to rekindle things than to bring her to the same place where we had our first date a few years ago. When I opened the door for her, I felt the comfort of the past, and my old mannerisms returned. She wore tight jeans, and under her light jacket a V-neck blouse that accentuated her breasts in a subtle way. We ordered crab cakes and drank beer. Kelly ate very little. She gave me some of her crab cake. Outside, the cold wind blew across the quiet boardwalk and against the window beside our table. I asked about her family. She said her mother was thinking about being a real estate agent and getting out of the house more. They planned a boat cruise to the Caribbean next summer, which Kelly seemed excited about. I asked about her brother. After getting his driver's license, he found a job working for a landscaper. We joked about how her parents were so pleased to see him finally leave his room and do something with himself. I gave her the latest on my father's condition and my life running the family business. She encouraged me to go back to the university after he got better. I agreed. Kelly shifted her sitting position and took a long drink of her beer.

"Do you have a girlfriend?" she asked.

"I don't."

"I'm going to say this because it's good to talk openly with someone you care about. What bothers you so much about me?" Kelly said.

Her question made me take a long drink. "I wish you were more agreeable with me. I hate how you told me to eat a certain way, and the way I dress. After a while, I just wanted peace in my life."

"But you were so grunge," she said jokingly.

"That's what I mean. You also hated my friends. It was all those things, but I care about you, and I did my best until I couldn't."

"You know I grew up to be independent. I grew up to be strong and make my own way in life, so I can't hold it in when someone bothers me. I want you to be a better man, Luke. Can't we respectfully disagree on stuff sometimes?"

"It's fine to disagree. That's what a relationship is about, right? Working on getting past disagreements. But I fell you were too disagreeable for me. What about the time you wanted to be vegetarian? I told you I didn't want to do it, but you made me feel like I betrayed you every time I ate a steak or a burger."

"Being a vegetarian is good for your health, so why not try it as a couple? Doing things together and growing together is important for a relationship."

"It's true you have good intentions, but if I didn't want to do it, why nag me about it? Also, why were you so rude to my friends?"

"I like Jamie; he's okay. It's Scott I don't like. He's a bad influence on you. I swear, unless he changes for the better, I'll always feel that way about him."

"He can be selfish sometimes, but I count on him, and that's worth a lot to me."

"You're childish when you're with them, and it bothered me. Besides, I let all that stuff go because I love you and I stayed. Isn't that enough?"

"If we start over, can you be more agreeable with me? Let me do what I want, barring anything stupid? I'm sure you'll let me know about it."

"So, you want to start over with me?" she said.

"Yes, I want you to be my girlfriend."

Kelly looked at me, smirked, and nodded in agreement.

I reached out to hold her hand. She looked into my eyes and smiled.

After dinner we made our way onto the boardwalk. We held hands as I led her to the car. It was cold. Our shadows passed quickly under the boardwalk lights. Her blonde curls flowed gently with the breeze. In the car, I turned on the heat and lowered the driver's-side window slightly to let in the ocean air. I touched her hand and we kissed. We kissed again. It felt like the first time.

***

It was a cold Sunday morning when I drove to the flea market. When Youssef found out how much I was paying for tires, he told me to visit the flea market and look for the tire man. There were hundreds of outdoor merchants selling things that day. I wandered down each aisle, passing old wooden tables selling trinkets and doodads. Near the back I found a carry-on trailer holding stacks of tires. Wooden boards surrounded the flat trailer and kept the tires secure. I hovered around the trailer inspecting each tire. The stack of thirteen-inch tires were near the back. As I peered along the trailer, the tire sizes increased.

The driver's-side door of an 1980s pickup truck opened and a man stepped out. He let out a high-pitched whistle as if calling a dog. I stepped away from the trailer to avoid conflict. He was obviously annoyed at me. His face had sharp Slavic features and black streaks swiped by dirty fingers. He had on worn-out jeans and a bulky, dirty winter jacket.

"Hi, I need tires. I run a gas station on Highway 36. Are you here every Sunday?" I said.

"Yes, yes . . . What do you want? You like my tires climbing on my stuff." His oil-stained fingernails passed over the tire grooves. "I sell very good tires. You can make good money from me."

"If I buy them in bulk, can I get a discount?"

"How many do you want?"

"I need about twelve. When I sell them, I'll buy more."

"Okay, that's good. You pick the tires. I'll help you."

When we finished, I shook his hand.

"My name is Luke."

"Demetri. Where's your business?"

"It's located in Keansburg on Highway 36."

"Oh, the one across from the supermarket."

"Yeah, that's me."

"Are you Michael's son?"

"Yeah."

"Yeah, yeah, you look like your father. Your father's a good man. He did me a big favor once. He's a good man."

"Thanks," I said. "Yeah. My old man's all right."

"No. I worked there. I pumped gas for your father. He helped me when I needed work. I have nobody here. My family's in Greece. I had some bad luck at the beginning, so when I didn't have money for rent, he let me sleep in the garage. I never forget this. The next day he gave me money for rent."

"Yeah, that's him. He was an immigrant, too, so it makes sense," I said.

"I paid him back so we're good now . . . After, I found a job at a restaurant. I was a cook in Greece, so I'm a cook now, you see. I sell tires for a second job."

"Well, as long as the price is right, I'll give you more business."

"You can take these tires—no charge, my friend. Pay me with the next batch."

"No, I can't do that. No way. You tell me what I owe you," I said.

"No. Don't worry about it."

"But you said you paid my father back." I studied his face. The motion of his arms and hands ceased. He moved his lower lip and gazed down in heavy thought. I made a low enough offer to wipe away what he paid for the tires but high enough to make him feel good. When he looked straight into my eyes, I knew we had a deal.

Later that day, after getting home from work, Mom said Jamie called. Our phone conversation was brief. He told me he would rather hang out than talk on the phone. I picked him up and we drove down to the shore. I brought Eva's last letter with me to give us more to talk about; it was still sealed. It was too cold for a walk so we ordered from the drive-thru and ate in the car. The ocean was calm under the dim stars and the bright moon.

"I'm sorry about your dad, dude," Jamie said.

"It's been tough, especially for my mom. She's been by his side the whole time taking care of him. She's a saint, really. I haven't seen you in a while. Everything all right at home?"

"Yeah, I wanted to catch up with you on that. Since that time I hit him, he's changed. He doesn't bother me anymore. He's been better with my mom too. It's crazy."

"Wow. That's crazy."

"Yeah, he's different now. Even his tone changed. He's calmed down."

"I guess hitting him back woke him up. You told him you're not a kid anymore," I said.

"Yeah, I don't know. It's that or he's given up on me, which is fine. I don't care. Either way, things are better now."

"That's insane. If I hit my dad when he was healthy, he would have killed me and thrown my dead body out in the yard," I said as I chuckled.

"Yeah, really. I thought the same thing, but it did the opposite. You know, I don't recommend guys beat up their dads, but in my case, I had no choice. The guy was driving me nuts. I felt I had no choice. Oh, and by the way, I started working for a new plumber. He's got me digging ditches all day."

"Yeah, you're looking buff, man. I thought you were hitting the gym," I said.

"No. I'm just paying my dues until my boss thinks I'm worthy enough to use a basin wrench."

We laughed.

"You wanna laugh more? I'm back with Kelly."

"What?! Why? That's not funny, bro. I thought you were done with her."

"No, I miss her. We're gonna give it another try."

"I remember you said she was too bossy."

"Yeah, well, I grew a set of balls and told her to change if she wanted things to work out between us."

"Well, good luck with that . . . But I do remember you two were good early on. I guess this means I won't see you as much."

"This time it'll be different. I'm setting a boundary for myself and more time with my friends."

"Okay, you said it. We'll see . . . Oh, you know she hates me, bro."

"Na, you're fine. She hates Scott, not you."

"It felt like she hated me. Anyway, good luck. I see no girl in my future right now. I'm so tired when I get home from work, I just chill in front of the TV until I fall asleep. I don't do much art anymore either."

"Don't stop drawing. You're so good at it. Promise me you won't stop."

"Yeah, I promise. My art teacher from high school calls me once in a while. He keeps bugging me about applying to the art college in New York."

"You should. The way you paint and the way you make the color pop off the canvas. It's awesome. Hey, I told you Eva's been sending me letters. I got her last one with me. I haven't opened it yet. You want me to read it to you?"

"Sure, if you want. I'm curious to know what's going on over there."

"Alright, here it goes."

Luca, I hope you had a beautiful Christmas with your family. Feliz Navidad.

I am very sad you did not write or call me. I want to talk and share my heart with you. The baby is getting bigger, and soon it will be in the world. I want you to be here when it is born. The doctor said the baby will come in May. Please come here to help me.

I am trying to be positive. That is how I am. I will not give up hope on you. I know you will be back to see me.

I love you,
Eva

Jamie rubbed his chin as I put the letter away. "Wow, she will not let go of you, man."

"I know. This is her third letter. She sent me a Christmas card too."

"She really talks like this kid is yours. Doesn't that worry you?"

"Yeah, a little, but how can I trust her? She sleeps with a lot of guys. She's trying to get out of there and she wants me to be her meal ticket. I'm not falling for it."

"I don't know about that. I think she really likes you. But yeah, her being a whore is tough to deal with. I understand if you want to move on."

"I did. I did move on. Kelly's better for me, in my opinion. She's purer. Remember, I only knew Eva for a week. That's not enough time to trust someone. You see what I'm sayin', Jamie?"

"Are you sure Kelly is pure?"

"Well, relative to Eva she is. I mean, yeah, she's been with other guys, but the count is low. She admitted to being with another guy that I know of."

"So now you're going out with Kelly, who's bossy—your words, not mine—and possessive. Okay, then, let me ask you a question: Would you rather be with a bossy babe or a girl who's relaxed and lets you do what you want? And more agreeable?" Jamie said.

"The second one, most likely. So, you don't think Kelly will change for me?"

"I don't. I mean, yeah, you guys were okay at the beginning, but I remember how miserable you were with her later on. Let me ask you one more question—which girl were you happier with?"

"Eva."

"Why do you think that?"

"Eva was more agreeable. I felt at peace with her, like a strong connection. I know our time was short, but if I could get past her promiscuity, she would be a keeper," I said.

"To be honest, and I say this as your friend, so don't get mad, but neither girl is right for you. You need to find a woman who's like Kelly but submissive like Eva. I'm just sayin'."

"I understand, but I hate to be alone. Even with all the crap going on, I need a girl in my life. I just can't work, go home, and sleep day after day."

"I'm not sayin' be alone forever. You should work on yourself. I was reading this self-help book and it said to set goals and pursue what you want in life. Not just money goals but relationship goals too. Write them down and look at them every day. You know, like how to make more money or the type of house you want or if you want to start a family, stuff like that," Jamie said.

"I gotta get my dad's stuff in order first. Then I'll focus on myself. In the meantime, I'm with Kelly. You know what I'm saying?"

"You know it, my friend. Seize the day, right? Isn't that the saying?"

"Carpe diem. The Romans knew what they were doing."

We laughed. I looked out into the night; the wind blew over the cold, dry sand. Staring out onto the water, I thought of the pelican at the cliff and the image of it flying away with another pelican in its pouch.

Chapter 18

Mortar oozed out from between the bricks under a heavy hand and the cold light of the sun. From my car, I watched the masons build a wall beside the discordant roar of the highway. The trowel smoothed the mortar before pressing down the next brick. The process repeated a thousand times before. A younger mason carried more bricks to the older masons and waited for the next instruction. I stepped out of my car with my camera to take pictures. Even if I got my father out of bed, he was too sick to care. His attention drawn inward on the knife-stabbing bed sores and the inability to move without pain.

Mr. Cangelosi stepped out from behind the trees, zipping up his pants. He waved to me without respect, almost waving me away, thinking I was and always will be a boy. He approached me with a confident swagger.

"Luca, how are you? You see what's going on. The walls are going up. You see."

"Yes, it looks good. Thank you."

"Yeah, we're moving fast, very fast. Depending on the weather. Eh, we could finish sooner."

"It's been a dry winter; now spring is here," I said.

"Yeah, yeah, of course, we get the money and keep moving."

"I'll take the next bill now if you got it?" I asked.

"Now? No, I have to make it first. Things change for me all the time, you know—the workers' time and the materials, you know. I will give you the bill soon. All right?"

"That's fine."

"Hey, Luca, you should be proud of your father. Yeah?"

"I am, Mr. Cangelosi. He worked very hard for this."

"Yes, yes, that's true. All right, let me get back to work. I will call you," he said. He walked back to his truck.

The elder masons stood on scaffolding, talking down to the young mason below who nodded in agreement. I positioned myself at an angle to the structure and snapped a few photographs. I walked around to inspect the walls and imagined how the place would look finished. I don't think I would have used such expensive material. We were running short on money and had to use the equity on the home to fill the gap. According to Mr. Cangelosi, the building would be complete in the next month or two.

I drove back to the service station. The outside pumps were busy as Youssef moved between the cars waiting for the next gas nozzle to click shut. As I entered the sales office, Lenny stepped out heading to the pumps. On the counter, next to the calculator, an envelope for Mr. Miller written in my father's hand. A loyal customer who brought his collection of Cadillacs for fill-ups and repairs. My father gave him a running tab, which he had to pay once a month. Turns out he was late by two months and owed around seven hundred dollars. Youssef entered the office and pointed at the envelope.

"Your father's friend needs to pay us a lot of money. I saw him two days ago and he looked at me like I was crazy when I asked him to pay the bill. Why do you give him credit?"

"I didn't. My dad did. He usually pays on time."

"A customer who doesn't pay his bill is not a good customer."

"Yeah, yeah, I know. I'll go to his house and ask for the money. He lives down the street. I'll go now," I said.

"You're the boss."

Al stepped into the sales office with a wrench in his hand. His hands were greasy with black under his fingernails. "Luke, make sure you get Mr. Miller to pay for his last repair." He pointed to a drawer in the counter. I took out an invoice for two hundred and fifty dollars. An alternator replacement for one of his Cadillacs.

"Okay, I'll get the money," I said.

"If you ask me, I would not give him any more credit," Youssef said.

"I'll take care of it," I said.

Around the corner, I walked down the sidewalk cracked by the thick tree roots of old sugar maples lining the street beside the picket fences and manicured lawns. I arrived at Mr. Miller's house. His lawn wasn't cut and clipped like his neighbors, but the size and location of the Victorian made up for the property's neglect. His familiar Cadillacs lined the driveway. Stepping onto the deep veranda, I opened the screen door and knocked hard. Mr. Miller opened the door. I'd never seen him smile, but this time he did. He immediately welcomed me inside. The home had a man's décor, as if a woman had never stepped foot inside, or if there was, her requests were ignored. There were no family pictures, only a large, framed photograph above the fireplace. In the photograph, Mr. Miller stood next to a racing horse poised in victory. Piles of paper and stuffed manila folders a foot high or more were strewn all around the house, even in the hallways. I followed him into his office where he asked me to sit down across from his desk. The choice of dark wood was ubiquitous, giving the home a dull, almost depressive ambience. Mr. Miller sat at his desk. Behind him, on an office table, more pictures of racing horses. On the wall, framed diplomas, the state bar license, and other academic accolades. He leaned forward on the desk with hands folded.

"How's your father?" he asked.

"Not good. Not good at all—he's on dialysis now," I said.

"Sorry to hear that. Luke. I've known your father for many years. He's a great guy. A hardworking family man. He would tell me often how proud he was of you."

"Thank you, Mr. Miller. I'm lucky to have him as my father. He's been struggling to keep his spirits high. I want to be optimistic but it's not looking good."

"Does he have a will?"

"Yes."

"That's good. So his estate is in order?"

"I think so. Everything is in his name. He mentioned he will pass on everything to my mother after his death."

"All his assets are in his name?"

"Yes, as far as I can tell. I do all the financing now and that's what I see."

"Your mother has nothing in her name?"

"No."

"That could be a problem. I recommend you tell your parents to consider signing a power of attorney document."

"What's that?"

"It's a document that gives your mother access to your father's assets in case he's incapacitated."

"Sounds like something we're interested in," I said.

"Look, have your mother call me so I can explain things to her. Give her my number. I would be happy to help."

"I'll do that. Also, the reason why I stopped by was to give you this envelope. It's the tab on gas and auto repairs for last month."

He removed the bill from the envelope and skimmed over it. "So, I'm short of funds right now. Let me get back to you. If your parents move forward with the power of attorney, can we discount my services for this bill?"

"I would rather you pay the bill in full," I said.

"I can do that. I should have the rest in the next week or two."

"I can't give you any more credit until it's paid in full."

"Don't worry about me. I've known your father for many years. We've always squared things, so it's fine."

"I can't extend your credit until you pay. Sorry, Mr. Miller."

"Do you know how much money I've spent at your father's service station? I go to him for all my fill-ups and repairs. Now, because I'm a little behind, you're cutting me off completely?"

"I'm not cutting you off. You are a loyal customer, and I thank you. But with my father gone, I'm making a few changes, and I'm not allowing credit to anyone who does not pay their last month in full."

"All right, fine. Let me cut you a check for half, and I'll pay you the rest later."

"That's fine. After you're paid in full, I will reestablish your credit."

He pulled out a checkbook from the desk drawer and wrote me a check for half the amount owed. I thanked him and left. A day or two later, Mr. Miller's check bounced. He no longer visited the shop. I suspect he went to my competition down the highway. I was mystified, with all his displayed wealth, he was unable to manage his finances. Lenny thought he bet too much on the horse races, but only Mr. Miller knew that. I was disappointed to lose him, but I'd get over it. I asked my family attorney about the power of attorney document, and Mr. Fuchs agreed. My father signed the power of attorney, which gave Mom control of his assets.

Coming home from work, I stepped into the house hearing the sound of moans. My father sat on the edge of the bed leaning his weight from one side to the other. We watched helplessly as he swayed and moaned.

"What's wrong?" I said.

No one spoke a word, as if frozen with grief. The constant pain of bed sores was too much. My family, including myself, knew it was over. His body had given up a long time ago. Now, his hope, and his tolerance, cried out for mercy.

"It's time to call hospice," Sofia said and left the room—too upset to stay.

Uncle Silvio looked at me and told me with his eyes it was time.

"Okay, what can I do to make his pain go away?" I said, knowing the answer to my question. My mother, exhausted, sat down on the chair near the bed. They tried to comfort him all afternoon, but the incessant pain overwhelmed him for most of the day. My uncle nodded in a gentle, slow acceptance.

"Call the doctor," my uncle said.

"Okay, Ma. Where's the phone number for the doctor?" She didn't answer me; instead, she pointed to the kitchen.

I remembered where the phone number was. The doctor answered my call, and filled a prescription of morphine; I drove as fast as I could to the local pharmacy to get it. When I got home, we gave him the recommended dosage and within minutes his moaning ceased. He was quiet again. The drug sent him under, and a necessitated quiet ruled the house. We replaced the bandages over his bed sores and covered him with fresh bedsheets. He slept as if nothing had ever happened. The pain was gone, and we were emotionally and physically exhausted. The ordeal left us weary, so we all went to bed. My uncle slept on the sofa next to his brother. The rest of us went upstairs.

The next morning, I opened my bedroom window for the first time since the fall. I got ready for work. Downstairs, the morning light from the window brightened the bedsheets where my father peacefully slept. I wondered why we waited so long to give him morphine. On the couch, my uncle turned over and woke up. His hair stood awkward and awry. He didn't sleep well. With a groan, he got up and made coffee. I leaned over to my father. His eyes opened. He smelled like morphine.

"Dad, I'm going to work now," I said.

He only looked into my eyes.

"I love you," I murmured.

His forehead was warm; I removed my hand and kissed him there. He closed his eyes. I went to have an espresso with my uncle.

"He's finally getting some sleep," I said. My uncle nodded as he sipped. "When can we send him back to the hospital?" I asked. He didn't understand my English, so I said it again in Italian. He stopped me while I spoke, cold, in mid-sentence, with his hand up. He told me in a quick, almost vicious, Italian, "He is never going back to the hospital. I thought you understood. Your father is on his own now. Nature will take over. I thought you understood that." His response startled me. The morphine made him seem normal, which gave me hope. I pushed his answer aside and sipped my espresso. I agreed and remained silent until I left for work.

Later, when I got home, everyone was committed to a chore around the house. My sister did the laundry. Mom cleaned the house. At the stove, my uncle brewed coffee. He did it about four times a day. The smell of espresso was festive. My father was in bed, without pain. After dinner, we gave him another dose of morphine and watched the nightly news with him. The news anchor spoke of President Clinton possibly sending troops to the Persian Gulf. My father slept. Sofia got up to kiss him and tucked him in. Mother did the same. Outside, the raindrops hit the window with light taps. The weight of each drop filled the pane until it flowed like tears.

Afterward, I called Kelly. It had been a few days since we spoke and the first time in a while the house was quiet enough to think straight. I took the next two days off for a day trip to

Pennsylvania with her. She was a decent cook and wanted to try a new restaurant there. The chef received good reviews in the newspaper. I hung up the phone, kissed my father, and went to my room. As I lay in bed, I began to compare the two. In the end, Kelly won, not because of beauty, or personality, but because I thought she would be a better mother. It was an unfair comparison since I'd only known Eva for a week, but if you looked at their families, Kelly won again. However, if life had placed Kelly under Eva's circumstances, I doubted Kelly would have sold her body to survive. I didn't know. I turned to my side and looked out the window. I missed the bats that flew around the streetlights in the summer. I closed my eyes and fell asleep.

***

The truss bridge over the Delaware River hummed as I drove over the metal deck. Kelly held my hand resting on the center console. We drove through the intersection and parked near the train station in the old town of New Hope. An old steam train departed for Lahaska. Kelly and I walked over a short bridge. We looked down upon ducks and waterfowl as they floated on the water. I bought a cigar for later and Kelly shopped at the boutiques along the river. She picked out something to show me, then put it back. She ended by buying a pink skirt. She looked pretty in pink. Walking along, I looked at her as we passed the Parry house and browsed the shops. My impression of her changed. She was genuinely concerned to know more about me and my family. She asked how I felt and praised me for my hard work. She was selfless and caring. I bought a bottle of wine for our meal. We were a little early for our reservation, but the host allowed us to sit where she wanted. Kelly asked a few questions about the menu and the server did her best to answer but had to ask the chef to confirm a few things. When Kelly was satisfied, we ordered. She ordered the pistachio crusted salmon, and I ordered a filet mignon, medium rare.

"The crushed pistachios on the salmon are delicious," she said. "We should try the linguine al pesto next time."

"The meat is so tender," I said. "Do you want a piece?"

"Sure, here, let me give you a piece of the salmon."

Kelly placed a little salmon on my plate. I cut the filet and fed it to her. As she chewed the meat, her eyes closed with joy. When she opened her eyes, I kissed her and held her hand tight and let go. She giggled.

"Oh yeah, that is delicious. It was cooked perfectly," she said.

"I didn't know you liked medium rare?"

"Oh yeah, the bloodier, the better."

"I guess you're not a vegetarian anymore."

"Nope, no more."

"You're awesome."

The dinner was enjoyed slowly. We ordered some garlic bread and a radicchio salad with goat cheese, which went well with the wine. Kelly was quiet as she finished her salmon. Another young couple entered and sat near us. The restaurant was small and had about a dozen tables. The town was known for its quaint and cozy setting, especially during the autumn and winter months. I dreamt one day of owning an old, drafty house for those reasons and those reasons alone—to live a quaint and cozy life.

"How long have we known each other?" Kelly asked, breaking my reverie.

"Uh, let's see. My sister introduced us over three years ago, right?"

"Yeah, like three and a half. Remember all the fun we had in the pool?"

"I'll never forget it. We used to sneak kisses without her knowing. Turns out she knew all along," I said, chuckling.

"Yeah, Sofia knew... I remember when I first saw you at your game against the shore team. The one where you scored the winning goal."

"Oh yeah, that one. That was one of my best games. That was the highlight of my short soccer career," I said with a chuckle. "I remember how nervous I was when I called your house for the first time and your mom answered. She asked me questions about who I was, and where I was from, and why I called. I was so nervous."

"My mom told me to watch out for you. Now she loves you." Kelly giggled.

"I'm glad she loves me. I would hate to be on her bad side," I said.

"I know it's early to ask this but when do you plan on moving out?" she said.

"I can't do much with my dad sick. I also have all the money going to the construction. There's a lot going on right now, but I know where you're going with this, and I do think we should live together."

"Me too. To be honest, I can't wait. There's this small house I drove by for rent. It's not far. I thought we should ask about it," Kelly said.

"Not yet. I feel guilty enough as it is."

"I know. I hate waiting though."

"Don't worry. We'll live together soon. We can do what we did last time. Would you like that?"

Kelly nodded and whispered yes.

"Okay, after dinner we'll go to that hotel in town. The one you like."

"Yes, now pour me the rest of that wine," she said enthusiastically.

"I should have gotten two bottles."

"We should get another one for the hotel room," she said. "I like this one—a cabernet."

"Definitely."

We shared a chocolate mousse cake. After I paid, we walked down a narrow street, over an old bridge, past the cast iron street lamps and the historic homes of old Bucks County. At the center of town, we entered a convenience store where I purchased another bottle of wine. Kelly pointed to a bag of potato chips. She said it was for the ride home. As I turned to pay, she stopped me.

"Are you forgetting something?" she said.

"No, I got the wine and the potato chips. What else do we need?"

She raised one eyebrow and puckered her lips, then it hit me. "Right, you're right. I forgot something."

"Okay, good. I'll wait outside."

I walked down the aisles until I found the condoms. I got a kick out of watching the cashier when I bought the twelve-pack of large condoms. She was an older woman who raised her eyebrows as she scanned the condom box. After I paid, she handed me the bag with a seductive smile.

Kelly and I held hands until we arrived at the hotel. It was an old stone manor built during colonial times. Our room had a fireplace, wide plank wood floors, and plaster walls. It's what you think when you visit old Bucks County. I lit the fireplace while Kelly opened the bottle and poured the wine. We stood face-to-face and raised our glasses and toasted to getting through the hard times. We turned to watch the fire.

"Thank you for your patience and not giving up on me," I said. "I love you."

"I love you too. I won't let you go, Luke."

I took the empty wineglasses and placed them on the table. I put my arms around her. She closed her eyes and leaned into me, pressing against my chest. Our lips kissed, and we pulled in tighter. We kissed again and again. I moved her hair away from her face. Her lips wet against mine. I took her hand and led her to the bed where we undressed each other slowly. When I kissed her breasts, her breath shortened. Our eyes met and we fell into bed. Our hands explored. We kissed gently and made love.

We lay together, and soon, we made love again. Afterward, Kelly fell asleep. I placed the bedsheet over her naked body, brushed her hair away from her face, and kissed her. The fire was out but the heat remained, giving a dry and comfortable feeling in the room. I sat on a chair and watched her sleep. I remembered how uninhibited Eva was in bed. She was a rock star. It's no way to base a relationship, but it helps. Kelly had improved, and I did love her, but how could I tell her to be better in bed without sounding disrespectful? She was so stiff.

Kelly began to stir. She opened her eyes slightly. When she saw me, she reached out her hand and told me to lie with her. I got up and slipped in bed beside her and held her close to me. I closed my eyes and enjoyed the smell of her hair until I fell asleep.

Chapter 19

The sound of footsteps and the bright light through the crack of my bedroom door woke me. My uncle moved with urgency. His hair in disarray. I got up quickly, as if I had been awake for hours, my heart beating at full gallop. I opened by bedroom door. His eyes were convincing, yet I did not understand. I thought he needed me to move my father or pick him up off the floor, or something else, but instead he embraced me. I remember I felt time slow as he looked at me with the eyes of a child, with no words, no mother, no brother. A fear struck me. He embraced me with terror and loss. My beautiful uncle let out a deep cry onto my shoulder. He trembled. A pain came from my chest. He let go of me and I followed him down the stairs as he sniffled. In the living room, my uncle walked past my father and sat on the sofa to weep. The same weeping a man may do two or three times in his life and the same weeping I did that morning.

My father lay in bed like an empty box—mouth opened, and stiff as though his essence escaped through his mouth. It had happened sometime during the night. His eyes looked upward at the ceiling. His soul was somewhere between the earth and the stars, but not in that room, not in that house. I looked out the window, but the world didn't stop like I wanted it to. I had trouble standing. I pulled over a folding chair and sat with my face leaning in close to him. My fear was replaced by doubt, then sorrow, then doubt again. Why, why did it have to happen? I felt sorry for him on top of everything else, destroyed by the disease and the other poisons now dead within him. A touch then nudged me aside to give room for my mother to lean over and kiss his forehead. I gazed through my tears when she said goodbye. Sofia sat next to me. Her face down on the bedsheets. Her cry pushed through the sheets and down to his skin. My wet eyes looked out the window to a lonely leaf on a branch shimmering in the early morning sunshine. I imagined a grassy field near a playground on a distant Sunday morning. My father and I took short steps and waited for Nicky-boy to catch up to us. The open field was wild and uncut. In the air, starlings dashed about and flocked together with more starlings. The trees along the stone path acted as spectators, watching us walk together. Nicky-boy sniffed about and wandered into the open field, untethered.

"How are you liking the university?" he said to me, looking down at the stone path.

"It's tough. I'm competing with the best students in the world. It's been stressful," I said.

"Remember, try to stay calm every day. Don't let your emotions control you so much. I know you're nervous—practice more self-discipline."

"That will be hard for me."

"I said try. When you're calm, you can think better. You're very smart."

"Thanks, Dad."

He looked down at the earth. "Don't worry, Luca. You'll be fine. No matter what happens in your life, you'll be fine."

The birds gathered on the treetops in a tight group. The starlings numbered in the thousands, coming from everywhere and out of the clear blue sky, packing themselves so dense I lost sight of the leaves between the wings and the beaks and the tails. My father continued walking toward the entrance of the woods, ignoring me. I stood hopeless — mesmerized as he stepped into the dark entrance of the forest. As I lost sight of him, the starlings, as if orchestrated by a divine conductor, flew up together to a colossal height and swirled about and ordered themselves into a twirling helix shape, flowing and changing with intelligence and determination downward and past me into the same entrance of the forest, as if following him. The flow of passing wings flapped vigorously and collided with other wings thick and dense, which clouded my vision until I found myself in a funeral home shaking hands with Al Smith who shook me out of the haze I'd been in for the last three days. It may have been his grip or his big American smile that shook me or the rhinestones on his shirt. He brought me back to the day of my father's funeral. The next hand I shook was of Jose Montano—my father's old coworker from the pizzeria days. Jose ran his own Pizzeria now. He told me my father was a great mentor to him. Next was Youssef and Sam Hanna. Then, to my surprise, Mr. Miller, then our neighbors, and on and on. The line was filled with people I knew from their faces alone. My mother, uncle, and sister were sitting with me across from the coffin where he rested beside the altar. Above us all was Jesus on the cross. Kelly and her family sat behind us. Uncle Silvio remarked with pride at the scores of people in attendance. Our priest, Father Joseph Mendoza from the Philippines, delivered the funeral Mass. He spoke in a low voice but with a heavy cadence. "Michael is with the glory of God now, in heaven. He has arrived in his eternal home. He is forever bound now to the glory of the Holy Spirit and the Lord Jesus Christ. He is here watching us. Not of flesh but by our side in spirit when we sleep, by our side in spirit when we eat, and by our side in spirit when we walk with joy in our hearts. Praise to the Lord Jesus Christ for He has victory over death. For everything there is a reason, and we are the Lord's. God has a plan for us all—have faith and peace in your hearts."

The Mass continued until Father Mendoza requested for all to pray. My mind sat blank. The Mass ended with a final blessing over the coffin beside the flowers and the statue of the Madonna. The lid closed. The pallbearers and I lifted the coffin and began the slow and solemn procession down the center aisle. We communicated through touch and the shifting weight of the coffin. The drag and weight on our shoulders made the coffin look heavier than it was, except for Al, who showed no strain. Youssef was in front, and on the other side was Uncle Silvio. Lenny and Sam held the rest of the burden. Our feet straightened and moved evenly. Church boys opened the main doors, letting in the afternoon light as we lumbered through and down the stone steps. The coffin was pushed in over the rollers and steadied to clear the door of the hearse. People exited under the soft blue sky and followed the hearse to the mausoleum for the final prayer. The tomb was sealed and the last tear was shed on that mournful day.

Back home, the house felt empty. We removed the bed from the living room and placed the medical supplies in storage. As I dismantled the wheelchair ramp, my sister told me Scott was on the phone. I put away the hammer and picked up the call.

"Sorry about your dad. My mom told me about it."

"Thanks, Scott. Yeah, the suffering is over. I wish he was around to see the repair shop finished. I don't know if I told you about the new garage he was building on the highway. He worked hard and saved for many years to build something he could call his own."

"Yeah, you told me once he was tired of the oil company telling him what to do at the service station."

"Yeah, the oil company owns the land and the station. My dad was the franchisee. He made good money, especially at the beginning, but the franchise fees kept going up and he made less and less money over time. I showed him pictures of the new construction before he passed. At least he saw the walls going up on the place."

"That's good, man. That's good. Your pop was a tough guy. I spoke to him a couple times over the years. I always respected him. Yo, I want to apologize for not calling you back. I had to get myself settled down here. A lot has changed for me over the past six months."

"Do tell, my friend. What's been going on with you? How are things down in the beautiful state of Florida?"

"I'm working as a carpenter with my dad's friend."

"That's great. That's funny—you know Jamie's a plumber's apprentice now. All you guys are getting into the trades. Are you busy?"

"Yeah, I'm working all the time. Sometimes seven days a week. That's another reason I didn't get back to you guys."

"Wow. What do you do on your time off? Are you still surfing?"

"Hell yeah. When I'm not working, I'm surfing, dude."

"Awesome. How's the girl situation down there?"

"I got my eye on one or two. I met one at a bar near me. She's a little older, but she's got it going on."

"Tell me more about her," I said.

"She's thirty-seven. I know. I know, but she's hot for her age. We're having fun."

"I'm not judging, man. As long as you're happy."

"Yeah, we're having fun. It's nothing serious. She's separated from her husband, so you know what I'm talking about. I'm just getting mine."

"I hear you, bro. That's great. Since we're on the subject of women, I'm seeing Kelly again."

"Dude, what're you doing? You know she wants to ball and chain your ass ASAP."

"Yeah, but I want to start a family soon, and I think she's the one."

"You think or you feel? There's a difference, bro. Anyway, if you want kids, then Kelly will definitely do that for you. I thought you wanted a few more years of freedom before all that."

"Na, I'm ready to start the next stage of my life. I've grown up quickly in the last year."

"Cool, that's cool. Hey, when I get my own place, you guys can come down and we'll go surfing in Cocoa Beach. There's an awesome spot I know."

"That's great. It'll be like old times."

"Old times? You make us sound old," Scott said. We laughed.

"Take care, Scott. I'll call you in a week or two."

"All right, brother. Peace."

A few days after my father's passing, I met the new franchisee. It was my last day running the service station. To make this brief, the Oil Company transferred the lease to a waiting franchisee, Mr. Patel, who by completing the transfer handed me a check for thirty thousand dollars. I thanked Mr. Patel and wished him luck. He was proud to say he would keep all the employees in place to signify nothing would change. I thanked him and gave him the keys to the property, then he shook my hand and thanked me back. I went to the private office for the last time to collect my father's things.

On the way out, I approached Al. "Well, this is it for me. The new boss seems to be a nice guy," I said.

"It's only the first day. We'll see. I heard he's getting rid of the service bays and building a convenience store. How much longer until your garage is finished?" Al said.

"Not much longer. The interior is almost done. Then the driveway and the landscaping. If I had to guess, about another month."

"Well, call me when it's finished. If you need a mechanic, I'm here for you."

"Thanks, Al. I'd love to work with you again. Take care."

I stepped out to the gas pumps where I shook Youssef's hand. "Goodbye, Youssef. You're a great man."

"Thank you, my friend. I am sorry it ended this way. I wish your father was still here. He gave me a chance when nobody gave me a job. I will never forget him."

The next day I sat in my room waiting for Uncle Silvio to leave. I opened Eva's last letter. My neglect had no effect on her. Regardless of being in love with Kelly, I felt a connection to Eva. When thinking about the last time I saw her, my stomach ached. A deep pain in the pit of my stomach. Her letters kept me drawn to her and maintained my curiosity.

The letter began with much consternation. Rosa was missing and she said Armando most likely sold her. Other girls at the club agreed. Armando had done this before, especially with girls who broke his rules. She went on to say, although Armando took her and her mother off the streets, he forced her into sex work to pay him. A situation she spent years doing to his satisfaction. "I worked for him like a loyal dog. And now, I have certain freedoms," she said. The only good news was her health. She was due with the baby soon and would send pictures to me. I put down the letter and my heart raced. The baby could be mine. She could also be writing letters to other men saying the same thing. But if she did that, she would've been taken by now. The letters would have stopped long ago.

I heard a tapping on my bedroom door. It was Uncle Silvio. He was ready and wanted to talk to me before his taxi arrived. We walked by his luggage on the way out and stepped outside into the warm afternoon air.

"Look after your mother. Okay? She is very tired," he said.

"I will. By the way, your English has improved."

"Thank you." He smiled. "You are the man now. When is the building finished?"

"One month," I said.

"Good. You will make a lot of money there."

"I'll do my best," I said to appease him. When the taxi arrived, my uncle stopped walking and turned and looked at me intensely.

"Stay hungry, capisci. Never rest. Life is best when you win, and you must always do your best. Your father did that."

"I will, thank you," I said as we walked back into the house. I carried his luggage to the taxi while my mother and sister said goodbye. I waited for him near the taxi. We said our final farewells before I walked back to the front porch and stood next to my mother. We waved as the taxi drove away. As we stepped into the home, I noticed the yard was unkempt. Without a word, I raked the leaves and trimmed the hedges. It was too early in the season to cut the grass. I finished, and when dinner was ready, I sat down in my father's chair in the dining room. My mother brought me a hot plate of pasta with pesto sauce, my favorite. Sofia came down the stairs. Before sitting, she grabbed the remote control and switched on my father's favorite news channel. I politely asked her to turn it off. Without objection, she switched off the television, put down the remote, and we all ate dinner together quietly.

Chapter 20

My open bedroom window brought in the early summer heat. I got dressed to meet Tom, a real estate attorney, about the lease agreement and the new tenant. We were fortunate to find a tenant for the new auto repair shop so soon. We were out of money after paying the final construction bill and the property taxes. It was a bittersweet day when Mr. Cangelosi gave me the keys to the completed building. I brought my mother that day to see it. Her eyes filled with tears as she stepped into my father's six bay service garage on the highway. "I wish he was here to see it," she said.

Downstairs, I waited for my mother. Sofia was working that day. She'd found a summer job in retail before heading to nursing school in the fall. I had to work as well, so I became a math tutor. In September, I'd be back at Columbia University to complete my engineering degree. I'd have to start my junior year over again since I left so early in the semester.

On the drive to the lawyer's office, I noticed my mother's hands were fidgety, picking her nails and tapping her leg.

"What's the matter? Are you nervous about something?"

She sighed. "Yes, your father never told me anything. He came home from work and I made him food and took care of things and cleaned the house. That's all I did since you were born. Now, I see all the bills and I don't know how to pay them. I don't know anything about that. Now, you and your sister go back to school and I'm alone. Sono preoccupata."

"First thing to do is to stay calm. I don't want you to worry. I'll teach you how to deposit the check you get from the tenant and how to write checks so you can pay the bills. After you do it a few times, you'll be fine. I promise."

"Your father took care of things before. Now, I am all alone—sono stressata."

"I know. I know, Ma. Me too."

"The closet has all his clothes, and I can't throw them away. I can't," she said, shaking her head.

"It takes time to grieve, Ma. For some people it takes a long time. It's okay if you're not ready. I'm still dealing with it too. Maybe you should do something outside the house. Not now, but when you're ready. Ya know, like find a job or take a dancing class. I know how much you love dancing." She did not reply. Her hands rested on her lap.

"Remember, I 'm here to help you. After you sign this lease with the tenant, we can finally pay the bills and save for the future," I said.

She remained silent for the rest of the drive; her hands stopped fidgeting. We arrived and met the new tenant. The contract signing went smoothly and would start at the beginning of the month. I gave the tenant Al's contact information in case he needed another mechanic.

Mother asked me to take her to the repair shop. I didn't see the point, but I did it. The smell of fresh paint was strong, and the clean floors had yet to show a drop of motor oil or a smear of dirt. The high ceilings gave the perception of spaciousness and professionalism. My mother surveyed the building as one would a final walk-through. I became curious when she told me to wait in the car. Without a word, I gave her the key. As I stepped outside, I passed a service bay window to see her pacing, her head down. She was ruminating as if in deep thought. I walked to the car, thankful of the man who was now at peace. I sat in the driver's seat and said to myself, "Don't worry, Ma. You're under his wing."

In the following weeks, Kelly and I were together often. I bought season badges to the beach where I got into the habit of applying lotion to her back and legs. Her blonde hair contrasted well against her tan skin. We had lunch most days at The Promenade, holding hands and staring at each other, ignoring the crowds around us. Kelly was quite an explorer. I enjoyed traveling as well. We took trips up to the Finger Lakes, Lake George, and once up to Stowe, Vermont, to hike up Mount Mansfield. One night, I woke and realized I had not received a letter from Eva in a while. She appeared in my thoughts at times, but less than before. Kelly constantly craved my attention, and I was back to making her front and center in my life. I saw less of Jamie and stopped surfing completely that summer. The waves don't get good until September, I would tell myself. Soon, I'd be back at school and Kelly would start at the community college and the summer of '94 would be over.

One quiet morning, I got out of bed early and took a drive to help clear my mind. I found myself near Sandy Hook. I drove up the short and winding road to the Twin Lighthouses where

I'd taken my father many times. Now only a memory. I sat on the bench near the canon to reflect and enjoy the fresh air. The peninsula of Sandy Hook was clear to see and stretched out into the New York Bay. The houses along the intercoastal waterway of the Navesink faded until all I saw were the memories of my father. What I thought of were not the times working or talking to him—no—I thought of those last few months of hell where he slowly decayed. The visits to the hospital and the dialysis treatment that kept him alive. The days and days of watching him in bed. Suddenly, I started to cry. I looked over my shoulder to make sure no one was there. Why did I always see him at his worst? I felt abandoned with only the thoughts of his final months to remember. Out over the ocean, where the sky meets the earth, I felt the suffering. I imagined if I could only reach my hand out to the horizon and pull him back. It was a silly thought. The horizon could never be reached. Every step closer to the horizon, it moves one step away. The tears flowed until my mind cleared. I wiped my face and stared at the moving boats on the water. The breeze and the sun were low over the sea. A new day was beginning, so I went home.

On a hot Saturday in early August, Kelly and I drove back from the mall after shopping for the upcoming semester. Kelly took a piece of paper out of her purse; on it was a written address and she asked me to drive there. The afternoon was young, and it was too hot to be outside, so I agreed.

"Is it far?" I said.

"No, I'll tell you how to get there. It's a house for rent I want to see."

"Why? We're back in school in a few weeks."

"C'mon, it'll be fun. I wanna see it. There's nothing else to do. Think of it as a learning experience."

"All right, let's check it out," I said, holding her hand.

Kelly expressed how handsome I looked wearing the shirt she'd picked out for me. We discussed the list of places we'd see in New York City when she visited me during the fall semester.

"Here, make a left here," she said.

The townhouse community was nestled between a shopping mall and a state highway. Kelly held up the address and read out the house number. I scanned the door numbers looking for 521.

"There it is; park here," she said, pointing to an empty visitor parking spot.

We got out and were greeted by the real estate agent at the door. He welcomed us in and showed us around the two-story townhouse. It was a two-bedroom with two and a half baths and a fireplace. The place was lived in with dirty floors and smudges on the walls. It looked as if the last resident had left in a hurry, leaving behind hangers in the closet and a body weight scale in the master bathroom. Kelly asked if the floors would be cleaned and the walls painted before the move-in date. The agent said no to the paint, but yes to the floor cleaning. The lease would need to be signed first, of course.

"What about the toilet seats? Can they be changed?" Kelly insisted.

"I can ask the landlord. I'll get back to you on that," the agent said. "Are you considering the unit?"

"To be honest, the price is high. If you can had the landlord drop the rent by like ten percent, we may consider it," she said.

"I don't know. The rent is priced at market and we do have parties interested."

"Then we'll get back to you," Kelly said peevishly. She walked out without a thank you or even a goodbye to the man. I thanked the agent and shook his hand. I followed Kelly, who was already waiting in the car. On the drive home she berated the agent for not being honest with the listing. She brought up the condition of the unit and that the rent was way too high. She spoke into an escalating agitation as if the agent had committed a crime and gotten away with it.

"Kelly, calm down. Don't go crazy over this."

The tension in her voice faded as she relaxed in the seat. "I can't believe they would show it like that. The pictures of the place looked totally different."

"We shouldn't even think of getting a rental until I get out of college—and even then, we should live where my job is."

"Well, I want to live near my parents. How far do you plan on moving?" she said.

"Like I said, wherever my job is. I'll try to find something close, but it could be out of state."

Kelly got quiet, thinking for a while. After a long pause, she said, "Okay, we'll talk about it after you graduate. I'm sure things will work out."

Kelly and Sofia helped my mother in the kitchen. I took Nicky-boy for a walk. On the desk in the home office was a letter from Eva. I put it in my pocket before leaving with the dog. After dinner, I took Kelly home. She wanted me to stay over and watch a movie, but I was tired and wanted to turn in early. I walked her to the front door and kissed her good night.

During the car ride back, I took the letter out of my pocket. There were pictures inside the envelope. My heart raced. I opened the letter and between the folds of paper were two photographs of a baby. It was too dark to see, so I drove into a parking lot and parked under a streetlight. One picture showed a naked baby posed on its side. Over the baby's head was Eva's New York Yankees baseball cap, which partially covered his face. It was a boy. He had plump arms and legs and was laughing with an open mouth. The other picture was a portrait of his beautiful smile, round shoulders, and brown hair. I squinted as I looked closer at the second photograph. My breath quickened as the image was clear and my heart knew he was mine.

Chapter 21

A man with a deep voice answered my phone call.

"Hello, is Eva there?" I asked, holding the phone tight to my ear. I waited for over ten minutes before Eva picked up and said, "Hola."

"It's me, Luca."

"Oh, Luca. Finalmente me llamaste," Eva said, sounding content and excited.

"I saw the pictures of the baby," I said in an earnest tone.

"Isn't he beautiful? I knew you would call when you saw his face. He looks like you so much."

"Eva, let me say something to you. It's important that you hear this. I didn't want to have a baby at this point in my life. I don't know if I should be angry with you or happy. Actually, I feel both."

"Are you mad at me? We have a baby now," Eva said with trepidation, then a pause. "Do you want him?"

I let out a heavy sign. "Yes, of course I do. I would never walk away from him. I just want you to know you deceived me and I wish you told me what your intentions were."

"Luca, we have a beautiful baby now and I love you. I want you here with us. When will you see your son?"

I put the phone down and took a few deep breaths. "Thy will be done," was all I could say to myself. The faint sound of her voice came through the phone. I put the phone back to my ear. "I'll fly down in the next day or two. I need to make arrangements. I'll let you know my flight information tomorrow."

"I'm so happy you are coming. So, you will come tomorrow?"

"No, maybe the day after. I have to get back before school starts. I'll call you tomorrow."

"Ti amo, Luca. Come to me soon."

I hung up and looked for my mother. She wasn't downstairs. I made my way upstairs to her bedroom. I stepped in to find her still in bed. It was 11:00 a.m.

"What's the matter, Ma? Are you sick?"

She turned herself over in bed. Her eyes were red. I knew what was wrong. I sat down next to the bed.

"I'm sad Dad's gone too. Even Nicky-boy's sad. He sleeps all the time now," I said. She took a tissue from the nightstand and wiped her nose.

"It's hard for me. We were married for twenty-five years. He died so young. I am alone now."

I didn't know what to say. I held her hand and waited. I gave her another tissue.

"I see you're doing a great job balancing the checkbook. We have a little extra money in the account now. Why don't you go and see your sister in Pittsburgh? Sofia and I are doing fine. Being away will help clear your mind."

She agreed with a slow nod. She had not left New Jersey in years and the invitation was already given at the funeral. A final tear rolled down her face before she sat up in bed. I told her I was leaving for Florida to see Scott for a week. She nodded and asked for her robe. I threw away the used tissue and asked if she needed anything else. She shook her head and went to the bathroom.

I knocked on Sofia's bedroom door down the hall. "Come in," Sofia said. She was reading in bed. I sat on her desk chair.

"I've got big news. It's a good thing you're in bed."

"Why, what's wrong?"

"Promise not to tell Mom. It's the last thing she needs to hear right now. Okay?"

"What is it?" Sofia said, annoyed.

"Promise first. It's a big deal."

"Okay, I promise. What is it?"

"Remember I told you about Eva and how she's pregnant? Well, the baby's mine."

"No. How do you know that? How do you know it's yours? How do you know for sure?"

I took the picture out of my pocket and handed it to her. Sofia inspected the baby's face for over a minute.

"You see the eyes, the skin, the hair," I said.

"Yeah, still, it can be somebody else's kid."

"C'mon, Sofia, you really think so?"

"Luke, you gonna let this lady ruin your life? You can start a family with Kelly and do it right. You're going to let this bitch take that from you? 'Cause you may not know this, but Kelly will leave you for this."

"I'm gonna see the baby."

She turned and sat on her bed. "You can't. It's a mistake. Let it go and move on."

"I can't do that."

"Think about it, Luke. This will ruin your future... Ya know what? Whatever. It's your life. I am telling Kelly though."

"I'll tell her," I said.

"Good, because it's not fair to her. I can't believe you're going with this slut instead of Kelly."

"There's a baby involved now. I can't let my boy not know me."

"You probably like her too," she said. I didn't say anything. Sofia looked down and let out a sigh. "You're my brother and I love you. And you're going to leave no matter what I say, so whatever. I can't stop you from wrecking your life. When're you leaving?"

"That hurts, Sis. But you're right. I am going to leave as soon as possible."

"Are you bringing her and the baby back?"

"No, I want to check on her and the baby. I'll help them financially, but I plan on coming back alone."

She let out a sigh. "I'll help if you need anything." She picked up the book she was reading and said, "Poor Kelly."

That evening, I took Kelly out. We drove into Red Bank to have a few drinks and something to eat, though I wasn't hungry. The night air was still. We held hands as we walked. Kelly nudged me to look across the street at girls parading in a small group dressed for a nightclub. She whispered to me, "I was never into the club scene." Ahead of us was a couple where the guy was dressed down and untidy beside a woman wearing something more formal. I whispered, "Even I know to wear better clothes than that guy." Kelly turned to me and said, "Are you sure about that?" I chuckled and looked down at my dress shirt. "C'mon, you gotta admit I'm dressed well tonight." Kelly replied, "Yeah, you're okay." We sat down at a small table next to the bar. She enjoyed ordering appetizers like a sampler or chips with her drink. It was seldom that I ordered whiskey with her. I like whiskey, but I would rather drink it with my friends. She would give me this look as if I had a problem whenever I ordered a Jack neat, or even worse, whiskey shots. She asked for chicken fingers and a light beer. I ordered a local brew from the tap. It was a normal crowd for a weeknight and the light above our table made Kelly's tan look darker.

"So, how was your day?" I said.

"It was good. I went for a jog this morning and got things ready for school. I helped quiz my mom for her real estate exam."

"Good. She's been excited about that. I'm happy for her."

"How about you? How was your day?" Kelly said.

"Well, my mom is still getting over things. We all are."

"Yeah, I'm sorry. I miss your dad too."

"My mom is going to visit her sister in Pittsburgh for about a week to clear her mind. She needs to get out of the house, you know."

"Oh yeah, I think it's a great idea. She needs to get away, and personally, I think she needs to go out and meet people."

"Yeah, so I'm actually going away for about a week as well."

"Really? When?" Kelly asked with concern.

"Like tomorrow."

"Why? I thought we were going to spend the weekend up in New York State."

"I can't. Something came up." I began to feel anxious. "Kelly, we promised each other to open up about communicating and say whatever's on our minds. Right?"

"Of course. We spoke about how important that is. What's going on?"

I let out a heavy sigh. "So I met a girl when I went to Costa Miel last year and we got serious."

Her eyes squinted. "I don't get it. Yeah, so? That was last year. What does that have to do with us?"

"I found out she gave birth to a child recently and she said it was mine." Kelly remained listening, waiting for me to add more. "Normally, I would discard it, because, you know, it can be anyone's baby, right?"

"Yeah," Kelly said as she shifted in her seat. "Go on."

"So, she sent me photographs. Look." I took the photographs out of my pocket and placed them on the table.

Kelly inspected them deeply. After a minute or two, she put the photographs down and put her hand on her forehead. "You know what? I don't feel well." She sniffled and put a napkin to her nose. Her eyes welled with tears.

"You okay? You want some water?"

"No, it's my stomach. I can't. I can't. Just take me home." Kelly got up from her seat and stood waiting for me. Her hand on her stomach. I got up and she followed me to the car. I wanted her to say something, but her eyes were empty and detached. On the drive back, I told her I'd be back in a week. She didn't answer. Nothing, nothing I said made her respond to me. She kept looking out the passenger window. I knew she was angry. When I reached for her hand, she pulled away. I shut down and drove a long and quiet ride to her house. No words or glances were exchanged. I parked in front of her home. Before she opened the car door, she hissed, "I don't know who you are anymore." She scurried across her front lawn; I stayed in the car. Something in me let her go as she walked into the house and closed the front door. That night I turned from side to side with my eyes closed hoping for sleep. Instead, I saw Kelly walking away down a long hallway with numbered doors. She passed door number three and disappeared into the darkness. Then I dreamt I was standing alone in a convenience store. Ahead of me, Kelly was talking to the cashier. Her back to me. She turned to face me. Her blonde hair was long and curly and beautiful. I stood motionless by the exit. She looked through me without emotion as she walked out the exit where she disappeared into the crowd. I walked out to follow her but she was gone. The people formed a line and marched around the parking lot as if on parade, holding red flags and some playing horned instruments. I looked for her again, but the parade was in the way. I felt lost and I realized my car was parked in the next town. I began the long walk to my car, away from the parade, down an empty street that stretched all the way to the horizon.

Chapter 22

I looked out the airplane window. The late afternoon sun revealed a vivid landscape of clustered tiny houses surrounded by the brown of scattered trees and open plots of grass. The same mountain range I remembered from a year ago with patchy clouds over them. We were close to landing. I thought of Eva and the baby; she never told me his name. I closed my eyes and thought of meeting my son for the first time. I was both excited and nervous. To relax, I pictured the day I surfed with Jamie and Scott at Playa Curvo. I remembered the blind man and the little boy and wondered if they were still there.

The airport was busier than I remembered, making me believe more people were discovering the beauty of this country. This time a pickup truck was available to rent. Wow, Jamie and Scott would have loved that.

I stepped outside into the sunshine holding my bag—the air was humid and the sunshine felt warm on my shoulders. It was around eighty degrees. I got in the truck and headed west. The roads near the city were freshly paved, which was a pleasant surprise compared to last time. Farther along, the roads reverted back to their dilapidated condition. Luckily, the pickup truck handled the heavy bumps and potholes well. I passed wet mountains and lush forests. I had to pull over for a minute when I saw alligators sunning themselves near a riverbank. I'd read on the airplane that the fresh and fertile landscape was the result of the many volcanic eruptions in the past. It reminded me of Sicily. Sicily, however, is not in a tropical zone, which made me think you can grow more in Costa Miel. I would rather live in Sicily though—it can get too hot for me here.

I learned the road signs: *Ceda* means "yield," *Estacionar* means "park," and *cinturon seguridad* means "seat belt." It took two hours to arrive at Playa Sueños. The sky darkened with the advancing twilight. Eva's directions led to a narrow road not far from Calle Principale. I drove past a hostel, a liquor store, and some houses between empty lots to find where she lived. The address led me to a two-story apartment complex with six units above and below one another with an office to the side. All the apartment doors and windows faced the parking lot. The office there had its shades closed. Eva lived on the second floor. The property was surrounded by a metal fence and a security gate, which was the only way in or out. The apartment building was old and worn as if suffering from steady neglect over the years. In contrast, the security gate and the fence looked new or well maintained. As I entered the gate, a pickup truck was leaving. I looked at the driver, who appeared familiar. He looked like the man who followed me last year and handed me the address to where Eva worked. Her so-called friend of the family.

A young woman looked down at me from the second-floor railing. I parked my truck and looked up to see she was gone. I grabbed my bag and Eva walked out of her apartment. She wore a light, colorful, striped sundress. She moved quickly, but carefully descended the stairs. She had loosely curled her long black hair, looking angelic. She extended her arms and we embraced. My eyes closed and the smell of coconuts made me feel at home in her arms. I stepped back to look at her; her smooth skin shined and her eyes were like black pearls above her beautiful smile.

"Wow, let me look at you," I said, letting a good ten seconds pass. "Wow." She looked thinner than I remembered. She leaned back a little as I held her hand, then pulled her in for a long hug.

"I hope you're hungry," she said. "We made some food for you." I thanked her with a smile and a kiss on her cheek.

We climbed the stairs holding hands. As we ascended, I felt I was being watched. Curtains in apartment windows moved slightly and shadows disappeared. Eva led me to her apartment. There it was again—a curtain moved behind another window. Down the way, a door opened. A young woman peered out at me and then retreated and closed the door. The scene was almost eerie.

The door to Eva's apartment opened and her mother, Maria, stood before me. Her hands at her side. She wore an apron. She was shorter than Eva but similar in appearance. She put her hands together and prayed out loud. Her voice cracked. I looked over at Eva who consoled her mother and said something in Spanish. Maria cleared her throat and said "salvador" over and over again until Eva told her to stop.

"What's wrong?" I said.

"No, nothing. She is happy to see you," Eva said while helping her mother to the small table near the kitchen. Maria sat down.

"Really? I didn't know my presence made happy people cry."

Maria got up and hugged me as if I were her son missed after a long absence. Eva told me to sit while they brought me dinner. I smelled cooked vegetables and fried oil. I asked if I could help but she refused and told me to be quiet because the baby was sleeping. The apartment had only one bedroom and the furniture was old. The only thing that hung on the wall was a wooden crucifix. The sofa faced a small television lying on a rickety stand. Above the window and behind the sofa were Christmas lights strung up; they were off. I thought working for Armando would have more to show for it. I looked around and realized there was a lot I didn't know about her.

Eva placed a bowl of ceviche on the table. The raw fish soaked in lime juice smelled delicious. Her mother brought a small bowl of bean soup and stuffed bell peppers. Eva went back to the kitchen and brought fritters and a carafe of water. She motioned for me to help myself as I slowly filled my bowl with ceviche. Maria sat next to me and watched until I was ready to eat before taking a stuffed bell pepper. We started eating.

"How was your flight?" Eva said.

"It was fine. I was lucky to arrive on such a beautiful day."

"We have many beautiful days here. Soon, the baby will be awake, and you will see him."

Her mother smiled at me, looked at Eva, and said something to her in a slow, gentle tone as she maintained her smile. Eva thanked her and put her hand on my shoulder all while speaking with graceful approval.

"My mother says you have gentle eyes," Eva said. I thanked her mother for the pleasant words.

A knock at the door broke up the peaceful dinner. Maria's expression changed to one of frustration. Eva got up and I followed her. Maria went to the window to see who it was. Maria said something to Eva in Spanish. We opened the door to a man who wore a scowl under his dark mustache. He was lean and wore a gray short-sleeved shirt and slacks. He looked quickly at me, then to Eva. They exchanged words in Spanish. Eva answered the man with yes and no responses, then he walked away. I closed the door and locked it.

"What did he want?" I said.

"He said Armando wants to meet you tomorrow morning for breakfast."

"What time?"

"Nine," Eva said.

"No problem. Are you coming?" I asked.

"No, he only wants to see you." Eva turned to face the bedroom. "It's time to see the baby."

We entered the bedroom and the baby was resting between two pillows in the center of the bed. The baby looked at me when I entered. His eyes like mine. Eva picked him up, and gave me the baby to hold. I smiled at his heavy stare. I asked if Eva fed him. She said yes. I asked his age and she said he was three months old. His birthday was on May 19. He looked into my eyes, smiled, put his hand in his mouth and drooled over his sleeve. We giggled. Maria entered the bedroom. I asked for his name. Eva said she wanted for me to name him. We all left the bedroom and sat at the table. I put him on my knee and we admired him. His plump legs had beautiful rolls and he had a thick head of brown hair, like mine.

"You want me to name him?" I said.

"Of course. He's yours."

"He's yours, too, Eva. Are you sure?"

"Yes."

"Okay, we'll call him Michael."

"Michael," Eva said and looked at her mother and in translation said the baby's name was Miguel. Maria giggled and repeated the name Miguel and looked at me with joy.

"Wait. Yes, let's call him Miguel instead of Michael. Miguel is better."

I looked at a crack in the wall near the window and said, "You should tell the landlord to fix that."

"It's up to Armando," Eva said.

"Armando owns the building?" I said incredulously.

"Yes, he owns many things. He has a lot of money."

"What about you? What's your situation here?" I said.

Eva said Armando was generous when he wanted to be. As long as you did what you were told. The men who worked for Armando dropped off food and supplies to the girls in the apartment complex. According to Eva, the baby lacked nothing. Armando kept the women there like prisoners and gave them little money. That made them hide their tips, which added up over time with hopes they could use it one day. Armando knew this, which was why he kept most of the money to himself. When the girls complained, he cut back their supplies to maintain his control. New girls who resisted took longer to understand this. If the lack of supplies didn't send the message, then physical harm put them in line. There was no way out.

I began to understand the inhumane conditions the women were in. Rosa resisted and tried to escape. When she was caught, Armando sold her away. Eva told the story as if siding with Armando, saying Rosa had it coming, being so disagreeable. Maria listened with her head down, demoralized. The baby was quiet as he stared with eyes wide open, playing with a spoon.

"Why aren't you more upset about this? This place is insane. Why don't people ask for help?" I said with frustration.

"There is nothing we can do. His men are watching us, and a lot of girls have nowhere to go."

"The police would be a good start," I demanded.

"Armando pays the police. They're our customers too. It is hard to trust them," Eva said. "When someone goes to the police, Armando knows, then he will sell us away to another place like this."

"That's unbelievable. Wait, what about the car? Can't you just drive away?"

"That's Armando's car, not mine. He likes me so I'm allowed to drive when he allows me."

"So you're allowed to drive his car?"

"I worked for Armando for many years. He saved my mother and me after we left my father. We respect him. Yes, it is hard for me at first, but we survived. I survived."

"But you're his prisoner? Wow, this is too much." I paused. "Okay, I understand you're afraid. I'll help you get out of here. What do you think Armando wants to talk to me about?"

"He wants you to take me, my mother, and the baby. I worked enough for him. He says it's time for me to go. Some say I'm getting older. The men want younger ones."

"Okay, so then let's go. Get your stuff and let's leave," I said.

"We can't leave. He wants to speak to you first," Eva said stoically.

"I can't believe you're not upset about this. What if I don't want to talk? I'm telling you to pack your things and we go."

"No, Luca. We can't. A man is outside watching us. He has a gun. If we leave, he will kill us," Eva said, remaining calm.

"Okay, I'll meet him tomorrow and find out what he wants."

I gave the baby to his grandmother and helped Eva clean up. I washed the dishes. The rest of the evening I learned how to prepare baby formula and change diapers. We fed Miguel every four hours. Late that night, as I fed the baby, Eva woke and sat up in bed to watch me. Maria insisted on sleeping on the sofa in the living room; she wanted to give us privacy. Eva mentioned her mother's depression was less severe once she knew I would come. Maria was much like my mother, submissive, and more traditional. The differences between them were the men in their lives. Maria married a cruel man who coped with his unresolved issues through intoxication. His physical and mental abuse drove her and Eva away to save themselves.

After the baby finished the formula, I burped him, then put him in bed with us. I lifted the bedsheets and adjusted my pillow. Eva smelled like soap, her hair grouped over her shoulder. She lay on her side, facing me. I held her hand. Her smile pulled me in. My other hand touched her face and we kissed. We kissed again. I stopped when I realized there were three of us in bed. Earlier, when we cleaned the kitchen, I asked her how she was able to be with so many men and remain sane and controlled. She said she was like a robot with her customers—disconnected emotionally. Armando was always there to protect her, but most customers were good men, not crazy. She admitted she had this ability to separate the sex work from life at home—she was born with it, she said. I admired her mental strength. Her past bothered me, but she appeared so detached from it that I could let it go over time. She was the mother of my child and I couldn't give up on her because of her past mistakes. As she closed her eyes, my heart filled with joy with the two I loved beside me. I could never leave them now. They were part of me.

Chapter 23

It rained overnight. The morning sun dried up the small puddles, giving the air a heavy moisture. I took a deep breath as I waited outside the apartment complex for my ride. Behind me, I felt the staring eyes of helpless onlookers. I turned back and a random curtain closed with the scare of being revealed. I felt anxious. A small car drove up and the window opened. The driver handed me a piece of paper. I unfolded it to see an address and the name: Café Neto. I looked at the driver for guidance but all he did was point down the street. I told him I understood. He rolled up the window and drove away. I walked down the street for about ten minutes to Calle Principale; across the street was Café Neto.

The large open-air dining area in the café offered a beautiful view of the Pacific Ocean. The tables and chairs were new and the ambiance was relaxing and inviting. Armando sat alone at a table near the corner; he waved me over when he saw me standing near the entrance.

Yeison stood by him like a henchman waiting for orders. The long scar down his face was new to me. I didn't remember it from last year.

Armando stood up and shook my hand. "Please, sit," he said. "Do you want something to eat or drink?"

"Coffee, please," I said.

"We have the best coffee in the world here in Costa Miel. The beans come right from the mountain, you know." Armando put up two fingers for the server to bring two coffees. "So, tell me about yourself. Where are you from in the United States?"

"I'm from New Jersey, but my family is from Sicily."

"What brought your parents to leave their country?" he asked me in a curious tone. He stirred a little sugar in his coffee.

I said that there was little opportunity for work in Sicily. I brought up the Belice earthquake of 1968 for my parents' final reason for leaving. The earthquake's aftermath left them homeless, and as a result, they immigrated to America to start anew. Armando shared his own story of an earthquake he experienced a few years back. The earthquake's epicenter was offshore so most of the damage was caused by the tsunami it formed. Playa Sueños sustained minor damage, but tourism ceased for a time, which was bad for business. It seemed business was all he cared about—nothing else. As I sipped my coffee, my stomach turned, thinking of how he trafficked and exploited women for *his* business. He showed no empathy. I looked out at the ocean and thought of how unfair the world could be for some. I nodded as he spoke. He paused to finish his coffee.

"You are a lucky man," Armando said.

"I am? Why do you say that?"

"I say it because Eva has picked you. You are the one, and I know why she picked you. I can see it. You are good looking, intelligent, and young with a good heart. I can see this in you, you know." Yeison frowned and turned away to hide his frustration. Armando continued. "Eva is one of my best girls. She worked for many years, and she has never complained, and I made a lot of money with her, and now, it's time for her to go. She worked her way out, as I promised, and I am a man who keeps his word, you know."

"Thank you," I said. Yeison stared at me; his facial scar was more pronounced, as if swollen with his temper.

"You want another coffee?" Armando said.

"Yes," I said. Armando looked over at the waitress and put up two fingers. He continued. "Luca, I'm a businessman. And I am very good at what I do. So, you know I can't let her go without something. For me to give her away is not good business. She can still make me a lot of money. It's true she's older now, but still beautiful, and her customers will pay a lot of money to be with her. You understand?"

"Yes," I said, remaining calm.

"Okay, so then you understand I'm losing money when I give her to you." Armando paused to watch me nod in agreement. "Okay, so, it's important for me to get something from you, you know?"

"I understand, Armando. What do you want from me?"

"Only money. For you to take Eva, I want five thousand dollars."

"Okay, I'll do it, but I need a few days to get the money." My hand trembled slightly as I held my coffee. Yeison stared at me with malice, standing closer to Armando. I was afraid to think what he would do to me if Armando wasn't there.

"Bravo, Luca. Yes," Armando said, telling Yeison to bring the guaro and a few glasses. Armando got up and left while Yeison pulled up a chair and placed the bottle and some glasses down. The bottle label read aguardiente. I pushed my coffee aside and avoided looking at Yeison. He opened the bottle and sat down.

"What is it? Que es esto?" I asked Yeison.

"Guaro," he answered insolently.

Armando came back holding a few cigars and a book of matches. He sat down and proceeded to cut the cigars and hand them out. He struck the first match and held the flame up for me. I inhaled until I felt the smoke in my mouth and watched the tip of the cigar burn. The cigar smoke was smooth in my throat.

"What is guaro?" I asked.

"It's made from sugar—like rum. It's good," Armando said.

"Sounds good. Do you drink it straight?" I asked.

"Yes, we like it like this. Do you want ice or water?" Armando asked as he poured.

"No, I'll take it straight."

"Good," he said.

We puffed from the cigars. Armando raised his glass. "To the new father," he said. Armando glanced at Yeison who was sulking and said, "Ah, leave it alone." Yeison looked at Armando with frustration and said he was fine. Armando snapped, "Then congratulate him. He's going to be a father."

"Salud," Yeison said in a weak voice, followed by Armando who said it louder. We drank guaro.

"What do you think?" Armando asked after placing his glass down.

"It's very good. The cigar is mild too. It goes well with the guaro," I said.

Armando leaned back into his chair and puffed his cigar and looked at me inquisitively. "So, Mr. Luca, what are your plans?"

"Give me a few days to get the money. I'll have cash for you then. I hope that's fine."

"Yes, yes, I know. You can stay with Eva, that's fine too. I will have one of my men drop off more food and supplies for you, you know."

"Thank you."

Armando tapped his cigar on the ashtray. "You see, I want you there so my girls can see you. When you take Eva back to America, the other girls will understand and do the same thing, you know—be like Eva."

"I understand," I said.

I wanted to leave, but Armando spoke about the great surf spots in and around Playa Sueños (Eva had told him I was a surfer). He asked me to surf with him and I agreed to appease him. The guy gave me the creeps. When there was a lull in the conversation and the cigars burnt low, I said I had to leave and take care of my son. Armando chuckled a little. He took the cigar out of his mouth and pointed at me. "Luca, let me give you some advice. I am a father, too, so listen to me. Never be your child's friend; be his father. Provide a structure for your son to follow, and guide him the best you can. And remember, he did not ask to come to this world—you brought him here. He's your biggest responsibility and your greatest joy. The rest you will have to learn on your own, you know." He turned to

Yeison and laughed. He demanded more guaro. Yeison poured and we drank.

A wind swayed the nearby palm trees and a gust of ocean air passed over our table, spilling ash from the ashtray. The wind intensified, causing the patrons and the staff to move away from the open vista of the beach. We became curious with the sudden event but remained seated. Another gust of wind was followed by an enormous pelican flying toward the café from the beach. It landed and perched itself on the railing beside the tables, startling the patrons as it folded back its wings. I recognized the pelican from the cliff. The one that swallowed the other pelican on the beach. The wind died down and the waitress opened her arms to scare it. It did not move—unafraid and confident. I stood up and said I would contact him in a day or two. Armando nodded as he kept looking at the pelican, ignoring me. He asked the waitress to shoo it away. Armando and Yeison got up and left the café through the kitchen entrance. As I stepped across the dining area, I felt the pelican staring at me. The waitress grew courageous with one more swing of her arms the pelican turned around and flew back toward the sea.

Walking back to the apartment complex, I thought about how to get five thousand dollars. As I climbed the stairs to the apartment, I felt eyes staring again. Maria opened the door; behind her, Eva stood holding the baby. They followed me to the table where we sat. The women were eager to hear me speak. I said with confidence that Armando and I had settled on a deal, and in a few days, we would leave for America. I reached out to Miguel and touched his tiny hand and smiled. Eva and Maria sat waiting for me to say more about the meeting. After an uncomfortable pause, Eva asked why it would take a few days. I said I had to make a phone call to get the money. After the money was here, I'd give it to him and we could leave. Their mood changed from uncertainty to acceptance. Eva gave Maria the baby and embraced me. She thanked me with a kiss. I looked down at Maria who remained reserved and cautious. With nothing else for me to say, everyone went back to their duties. After the baby was fed, Eva wanted me to burp him. She placed a cloth on my shoulder and told me what to do. After I put Miguel to bed, I told Eva I had to leave and take care of things.

I left the apartment and approached the stairs. The door to one of the apartments opened slightly as I passed. In a low tone, almost a whisper, a woman's voice called out from behind the crack of the door. It was from the face of a pretty woman, looking tired and distraught. I stared back at a single pair of eyes under her long blonde hair. Her mascara followed her tears and in a quiet desperation I heard her say *ayuda*. The encounter shocked me and left me upset, thinking what Armando and his men were doing to these women. At that point, I understood their fear and hopelessness and why Eva behaved the way she did to survive. I did nothing but nod at her and continued toward the stairs. I looked up at a security camera mounted above. Being more aware, I noticed other security cameras mounted in inconspicuous places. I walked down the stairs and into the parking lot where a man sat in a parked car. He looked at me with inquisitive eyes. He didn't stop me. I must be the only man besides him in the apartment complex. Maybe there was another man in the office, but I couldn't tell. The shades were always closed. I left the complex and walked down the street. It took some time to find the Onyx Club. It was the only place I could think of to ask for a phone. As I hoped, Ryan was still working there. I squeezed in at the bar between a guy in a Metallica T-shirt and an older man sitting on a barstool. I put a ten-dollar bill on the counter and Ryan walked right up to me. Island music played from the speakers overhead. I ordered a local brew from the tap.

"Hi, Ryan. That is your name, right?" I asked.

"Yeah, that's me."

"You probably don't remember me. I came here with my friends about a year ago. We're from New Jersey. You said you were from South Jersey—Cherry Hill area."

"Yeah, I remember you. Where're your friends? They out surfin'?"

"No, I'm here alone this time. Do you know where I can make a phone call?"

"There's a pay phone down that hallway near the restroom, but if you're calling the States, you'll need a phone card. We sell them here if you need one."

"I'll buy one. Hey, Ryan, do you see a lot of sex workers in Playa Sueños, or is it just me?"

"Yeah, there're a lot of them here. Costa Miel is a poor country so we get a lot of girls who come here to make money. This town brings in a lot of tourists, so there's heavy demand for it.
"

"Do you know if some of them are held against their will?"

"You mean like a sex slave? I guess there would be, but I don't know about that," Ryan said, wiping the bar counter with a wet towel.

"What if I told you I knew where women were held against their will and forced to do sex work?"

"You mean like a pimp? Sure, in Playa Sueños, no doubt about it," Ryan said.

"Yeah, but these women can't leave even if they want to."

Ryan ceased wiping the bar and stood pensive as he rolled his lips inward. "Hey, there's this lady who comes in here like twice a week. She goes around town and talks to girls about getting off the street. Maybe you can talk to her. She'll be here tonight around five o'clock."

"Why? Is she a cop?"

"No, she goes around and looks for girls who need help and who want to get out of the sex business. She can probably help you."

"What's her name?"

"Esperanza. She usually sits at a table and approaches girls at the bar she thinks needs help."

"All right, I'll talk to her." I tipped him and went to the pay phone.

Before calling, I thought of what to say to my uncle Silvio. The only person I knew with that much money to spare. It was a lot of money, but with the recent happenings back home it was an opportune time to ask for it. He answered with an apologetic tone once he heard my voice. He asked how we were. With regret, I told him how much debt we incurred from the funeral and the construction. He expressed his sorrow and understanding. I went on to say how we received a few unexpected medical bills and how my father had no life insurance before ending with, "We need five thousand dollars to be fine—can you help?" He kept quiet for a few seconds. He stated his concern for our family, and after a brief pause, said he would wire me the money. I thanked him profusely, letting him know I would pay him back. He told me how much he loved his brother and regretted the terrible situation we were in. He ended by saying not to worry about paying him back but that the five thousand dollars was all he could give. I appreciated his generosity, and after saying I loved him, I expressed my desire to visit him one day.

Leaving the club, the afternoon was filled with people coming in and out of shops and restaurants. The walk to the apartment complex was a blur. I kept looking down as I concentrated on the future and the possible outcomes.

Maria let me in. The baby sat on the floor in the living room. She passed me and hovered over him, holding his hand to prevent him from tipping over. I closed the door and waved to Eva who was in the kitchen scooping rice and beans on a dish. I sat down next to my son who looked at me deeply with fresh large eyes and plump cheeks. I picked him up and took him to the table where he sat on my knee. Maria sat down next to me, and Eva brought plates filled with food to the table. I poured the water in my glass and waited for Eva to sit down before eating.

"I have good news. I should have the money by tomorrow."

Eva smiled and translated to her mother. Maria smiled and whispered, "Mi salvador."

"By the way, how do I contact Armando?"

"You can go down to the parking lot and tell the man in the car. There is also a man in the office," Eva said.

"Okay. So, there's always a man here?"

"Yes. There is always a man here. They change during the day and night, but Armando always keeps a man here."

"This place is terrible," I said.

"Sí, yes," Eva said.

"How many girls live here?"

As she chewed, she looked at me with inquisitive eyes and shrugged her shoulders. "Sometimes the place is full and other times no."

"When I left this morning, a woman asked for help."

"What did you do?" Eva said.

"Nothing. There's nothing I can do." I paused. "What'll happen to these girls after we leave?"

Eva put down her fork and wiped her mouth with a napkin. She remained calm and looked at the baby before answering me. "Armando is giving them a place to stay, and food, and they make good tip money. They work for as long as Armando needs them and then they can go."

"I don't think so. Look at what happened to Rosa. Armando sold her, didn't he? He is selling you to me. He sells them when he's done with them."

Eva answered back with an agitated tone. "I don't know what he does. Armando can do whatever he wants. I don't know. All I know is I worked very hard for him and he kept his promise to me. Some girls don't understand how to be with him. I love Rosa and I told her to listen to Armando but she didn't listen and now she's gone."

"I'm sorry to say this but it sounds like you are defending Armando. Aren't you upset?" I asked gently.

Her voice was beginning to crack. "I'm afraid. I'm afraid of him. Armando has power here in Playa Sueños. If I do what Armando says, we can survive. I can't worry about everybody. I can't. I only care about Miguel, my mama, and you. That's it."

"I understand. I'm sorry to upset you, but I feel sorry for the women here. I wish I could stop this madness."

"Luca, you're a good man, but you can't save everybody. There were other girls before me who worked with Armando and he let them go. I saw it. But the girls who fought him lost everything. I saw that too. Please give him the money and we can go."

"I can't believe you did this for so many years. I would've gone crazy. I know you haven't worked recently. I assume it's because I'm here."

She nodded.

"I'm going out this afternoon. I'll be back after dinner," I said.

"Why, where are you going?"

"I'm going to the Onyx Club."

"No, stay here with me and the baby."

"I want to go out for a drink and talk to Ryan. You know, Ryan, the bartender. I just want to talk to him."

"Don't tell him about this place. He'll tell the police and it will make Armando go crazy. Promise me."

"I want to ask Ryan a few questions, that's all."

Eva got up and threw her dish in the sink. She snatched the baby from me and went to the bedroom and shut the door. Maria kept her eyes down on her plate, eating. I motioned to Maria in the direction of the bedroom. She understood. Maria waved me away and smiled. I got up and knocked lightly on the bedroom door. When I heard nothing, I walked in. Eva sat on the bed holding the baby. She rocked him gently.

"You know, I haven't seen Miguel cry once since I've been here," I said.

"Why would he? He's my little man," Eva answered with confidence.

"And Miguel has a wonderful mother," I said to the baby, sitting beside her. I leaned in close to Miguel. "Miguel, your mother knows how to take care of you. Eva is a blessing to us all." Eva smiled and kissed Miguel on the forehead. She continued to rock the baby gently.

"Miguel, your father is wonderful too. He wants to save everybody who asks for help. He is a superman," Eva said with light sarcasm.

"I know you're worried, but to let this insanity go on would be criminal. It would leave me hollow inside to walk away without saying something to someone, anyone."

"It is something you can't stop, Luca. I know this. Armando pays important people to look away. Some important people use his Jugosa Club. There's nothing you can do, mi amor. Please believe me."

I kissed her on the cheek. She didn't smell like coconuts anymore; she smelled like the baby. We spent the afternoon playing with Miguel, fed him, and put him to sleep. I reminded myself to buy a toy truck or a toy train for him next time, though he was more concerned with sleeping and eating.

At five o'clock, I left quietly. In the parking lot, a few girls jumped into a sedan and were driven away—going to the Jugosa

Club, I supposed. I ignored the watchman sitting languidly in his car. The sun was low in the sky, marking the start of another wild evening in Playa Sueños—the largest coastal party town in all of Costa Miel.

After what I'd seen over the last two days, a paranoia had grown within me, especially being in that part of town. I thought I was being followed. A man behind me looked similar to the watchman from the apartment complex. It continued for another block or two before I changed direction and took a different way to Calle Principale. As soon as I could, I turned down another street, glancing over my shoulder every minute or two. He was no longer behind me. I walked faster and glanced back to make sure he was gone.

I arrived at the Onyx Club. I made my way around the crowded dining area to the bar. I had to wait to talk to Ryan who was busy making drinks. When I had the chance, I asked him if he saw Esperanza. He nodded and pointed to a woman sitting alone at the end of the bar. Her face was older, but her hair was young and long and wavy. She appeared hyperaware of her surroundings and watched you with inquisitive eyes.

"Hi, my name is Luca. Do you speak English?"

"A little," she answered with slight apprehension.

"Ryan, the bartender, told me to see you. I hope you can help me. It's about the Jugosa Club."

"What do you mean?"

"It's about the girls working there." My nerves jumped when a person knocked into me. "Can we talk in private? I think I'm being followed."

Esperanza nodded, looked over at Ryan, and pointed to the kitchen. Ryan gave her a thumbs-up. Esperanza told me to follow her. We walked behind the bar and into the kitchen where servers and cooks worked steadily, exchanging words and plates. Esperanza stepped into a low traffic area near the large refrigerator and told me where to stand so I wouldn't be in the way. She looked at me intensely.

"What are you saying about the Jugosa Club?" Esperanza asked.

"It's not the club. It's about the girls who work there. I'm staying at a place where girls from that club are being held against their will, like prisoners."

Esperanza sighed. "Yes, I know this. Armando Castro is a pimp. Do you know anything about Armando?"

"Not really. I met him twice. I probably know as much as you do about him."

"Then we can't do anything," Esperanza said with frustration. "The federales want him but they can't catch him."

"What do you mean? I know where he keeps the girls. Can't we get the federales to raid the place and get the girls out?"

"No, it's not like that. The federales need to catch him trafficking the girls. The girls are afraid to say anything and the local police are in his pocket. So, only the federales can stop him, but they cannot without a reason."

"You're telling me, after all these years, the police—sorry, I mean the federal authorities—can't catch him in the act?"

"They can't. Well, not yet. Armando is very good at what he does. He knows who to pay and he knows what to do."

"What do you do?" I asked.

"I help girls get off the street and start a new life without sex work. I have a place where they can go and live a quiet life."

"Do you find a lot of girls who want out?"

"Very few."

"Why?"

"The girls who come here are poor and they need the money to help their families back home. They make a lot of money here. Men come from all over the world to Playa Sueños to pay good money for sex, so there will always be sex workers here. The problem is trafficking."

"So the demand will always be here?"

"Si, si, it will always be this way."

I shook my head in disappointment. "Ya know, I'm buying my girlfriend away from Armando."

"Que? You're buying a girl?" Esperanza said with amazement.

"Yeah, I'm paying Armando five thousand dollars for Eva Robles."

"Oh, wait, wait, wait. If the federales see you make the deal with Armando, then we can arrest him."

"That's what I want. I want him arrested. How can I help?"

"So you want to help arrest Armando Castro—are you sure?" Esperanza put her hand on my shoulder. "It can be dangerous for you."

"I'm sure."

"Okay, I know someone you should talk to. His name is Diego. He works for the federales. I will call him. When will you meet Armando?"

"I'll get the money tomorrow, then I'll contact Armando to set the meeting."

"I will call Diego and tell him to be here at the club tomorrow and wait for you."

"Okay, I should be here late morning or before noon."

"We will be here all day waiting for you."

We parted in opposite directions. Stepping out onto the street, the deep night sky wrapped itself around the bright lights of Calle Principale. I felt like being alone, so I turned down a narrow road that touched the sands of a windy beach. I took my shoes off and wandered toward the water's edge where I sat and thought about what I'd gotten myself into. My feet pushed deep into the cool sand as I thought of what Eva had said earlier about Armando. Esperanza had a good reason to say he was dangerous. Half the town was either corrupt by his money or scared by his muscle. Could I really stop him? Was I naïve to trust Esperanza? What if I paid Armando and he killed me and kept Eva anyway? That could easily happen. The more I thought of the possible endings, the more I wanted to renege with Esperanza. I tried to forget and looked at the waves crashing and remembered surfing with my friends a year ago. We were careless and free back then, just a bunch of drunken dudes having fun. I looked up at the stars, hoping for a sign. This time, neither the stars nor the ocean said anything to me. I was alone and afraid.

Chapter 24

The next morning I woke to the sound of voices and the smell of brewed coffee. The baby and the jet lag left me yearning for more sleep, but my desire to finish the deal with Armando got me out of bed. Eva and her mother prepared scrambled eggs, bacon, and toast for me. I ate with relish. Eva moved about the kitchen holding Miguel, using one hand for cleaning. I asked Eva if she was hungry. She said she'd eaten earlier. Maria sat beside me and kept to herself, drinking her coffee. Her eyes tired and disengaged.

"Why is your mother sad?"

"She is like this sometimes. It's her depression."

I looked at Maria curiously and smiled. She glanced at me, then looked down at her coffee. "Eva, tell your mother we'll be out of here soon. That should make her feel better."

"I did, but it doesn't matter with depression. She has to relax. I told her to sleep with the baby after I feed him. The baby makes her feel better."

"Any idea where Armando wants to meet me? I should have the money by lunchtime."

"I don't know. He is very careful."

"That's what bothers me," I said, eating my toast with marmalade.

After breakfast, I had time to play with Miguel. I covered my eyes as we played peekaboo on the floor in the living room. His heavy giggles and bouncing cheeks lowered my tension and lifted my fear of the future until I had to leave.

Once again the complex was quiet and eerie—no curtains moved or shadows faded as I passed. After a long night of working, it made sense. I approached my rental car and the watchman glared at me; his eyes piercing me with suspicion. He sat there looking at who came and went. Sometimes I'd see one walking along the fence, like a guard at a prison. The girls were chauffeured to the club. Taken back and forth throughout the night, like a shuttle service. Once, a Cadillac drove in and two men got out and entered an apartment. I turned away from the window so as not to dwell on what I thought was happening.

I arrived at the Western Union in the late morning. From what I could see, I wasn't followed. The money came through; I put it in a small paper bag and stuffed it in my pocket. I headed for the Onyx Club to meet with Diego and Esperanza.

Esperanza sat at the small table near the bar. Next to her was an older man dressed in plain clothing. He was not what I imagined to be a federal officer. They directed me to the kitchen area to the same private spot as the day before. Esperanza introduced me to Diego. We shook hands. Diego was relaxed and lacked the intensity I was expecting from a man trying to arrest Armando. His calm demeanor worried me. I felt a little better when he showed me his badge.

"Esperanza told me you met with Armando about buying a girl. How long ago was this?" Diego said.

"Just yesterday. I had breakfast with him at Café Neto."

"When will you meet him again?"

"I don't know. I got the money this morning. He told me to contact the guard at his apartment complex when I was ready."

"Okay, good. So, Luca, in order for us to arrest Armando, we will need to record him doing the transaction with you. Do you understand?" Diego asked with a careful undertone.

At that moment, my chest pounded. He spoke to me like I was one of them. "How do we do that?" I said. My hands trembled slightly.

"That depends. I don't think Armando will meet you at Café Neto. If so, you must wear a wire, a small microphone under your shirt. Did he search you last time?"

"No, but I think his men are following me," I said.

"Maybe, but since you're not from here, he is very cautious."

"He knows I'm from the United States. I don't believe he thinks I'm a threat. I just want to bring Eva, my baby, and her mother back to the United States with me."

"We will follow you to make sure you're safe. If we see anything happen, we will protect you. I have two men on this. I will also have a man sitting in the café when you have the meeting."

"How long has Armando been doing this?" I asked.

"Too long," Diego said, looking at Esperanza. "Esperanza, tell him about Armando."

Esperanza shook her head slightly. "Armando is a monster, Luca. He has been buying and selling women for years. He is smart and he pays for people to be quiet, and if not, he will kil—" Diego broke in and touched her shoulder. She ceased, knowing she'd said too much.

Diego continued talking for Esperanza. "Armando is a criminal and needs to be put in prison for a long time. What you're doing is brave and we are grateful. When we arrest him, many broken families will be reunited and Playa Sueños—no, the world—will be a better place." He went on to say he'd be at the Onyx Club for the next few days and to tell him immediately when and where I would meet Armando.

I felt a deep ache in my stomach, similar to when my father died. As Diego and Esperanza walked away, I felt little comfort with Diego's men following me. My father would want me to save my family. I felt indecisive, not to mention afraid. I may give Armando the money and seal the deal. I never agreed to wearing a wire. What if they search me? They didn't last time. Oh my God. Oh my God. Help me. God, help me. The pit of my stomach ached.

Diego's men followed me to the apartment complex. They drove off as I entered the gate. I got out and walked over to the watchman in the car and told him I wanted to meet with Armando. He nodded and pointed to my apartment and gestured for me to wait inside. As I turned to go up the stairs, a man opened the door to the office. It was Yeison. He froze in the doorway and started at me intensely as I walked by. A storm raged in his eyes, and the scar on his face was larger than before. I got used to the staring and the curtains moving as I passed. Before I could knock, Maria opened the door. Eva was in the bedroom with Miguel. Maria asked me if I was hungry. Before I could answer, she waved me over to the kitchen, where she took chicken and rice out of the refrigerator. I had no appetite, but I smiled and thanked her. She warmed up the food for me on the skillet. I sat down and watched Maria. She reminded me of my mother, empathetic and nurturing. She placed the heated meal on a plate and brought it to me. I poured myself water and took some bites. I gestured if she was hungry by pointing at my stomach. She said no, then poured herself some coffee and sat next to me. "Es un hermoso dia," I said slowly. She nodded in agreement and smiled. "Puedes hablar espanol," she said. I replied, "Estoy aprendiendo." When I finished, she got up and opened the refrigerator and asked if I wanted something sweet. I put my hand on my stomach and gracefully declined. I thanked Maria and went to the bedroom where Eva fed the baby. Miguel's eyes were drowsy as he drank from the bottle. He sucked on the milk bottle with a healthy voracity. Soon, Eva handed me the empty bottle and burped him.

"I got the money, and I'm waiting for a meeting time."

"Did you talk to the police?" Eva asked as she gently patted the baby's back, rocking him slightly.

"Yes."

"So you will help them?"

"Yes."

Eva let out a heavy sigh. "I was thinking about Rosa. She was like a sister to me." Eva let out another sigh and sniffled. "Armando sold her because of me." Her eyes began to well up and her voice cracked. She continued to lightly pat the baby's back. She cleared her throat. "One night, Yeison wanted me. Sometimes Armando lets his men take us. Yeison always wanted me, so one night he did. Yeison and another man were driving us back from the club. I was lucky to have Rosa in the car with me. They stopped the car and he put himself on me and he told Rosa to watch, but she was not afraid of him. She scratched his face and he screamed. There was blood everywhere. After that, they took her away and she was gone. She did that for me, Luca. She did that for me." Tears ran down her face. I took the baby from her and laid him on the bed. I put my arm over her shoulder as she wept. I sat closer to her. Her tears flowed. It was the first time I ever saw her cry. I held her closer. Catching herself, she turned to look at the baby. She sniffed a few times and wiped her face with the baby's blanket.

"I worry about the baby now. If you can't arrest Armando, he will take the baby away from me. If Armando kills you, it will be the end for all of us." Eva lost herself and began to weep again.

I stood up and became angry with myself. I wrestled with the thought of either helping or not helping Diego. I paced back and forth, taking in deep breaths. Maria walked into the bedroom. She looked at me, then to Eva. Maria approached her daughter to console her. I put my hand up to my face and paced, ignoring Eva's crying. I tried to collect my thoughts before the sound of three heavy knocks came from our apartment door. The banging shook our hearts and everyone froze as though our time of reckoning had come.

Chapter 25

Again, heavy knocking reverberated throughout the apartment. "It's time," I said. Eva wiped her face, stood up, and walked to the door. I followed. Maria stayed with the baby. It was a henchman with a message. He spoke rapidly in Spanish to Eva, who nodded in agreement, and ordered her to repeat his words back to him. I recognized him as one of the watchmen. He nodded and walked away. I closed the door and stood there as if waiting for results of a grim medical diagnosis.

"Armando will meet you at Bernardo's Surf Shop in half an hour. He said to bring the money and wear surf shorts," Eva said.

"Half an hour?" I said.

"You should leave now. That place is outside of town at the end of Calle Principale. It's easy to find."

"All right, I'll change and go."

Eva embraced me and we kissed. Our foreheads touched. "Padre nuestro," she whispered. "Oh Dios. Dios nos salve." We kissed again. I got changed, and hugged Maria, who cried in my arms. I told her everything will be fine. It will be over soon. Maria sat near the window and watched me leave, like many of the girls trapped there, hoping for salvation.

I passed the door of the woman who'd asked me for help. Our eyes met through the dusty windowpane; her mascara running. The watchman stared at me. I took deep breaths. I put the money on the passenger seat and drove away, not caring who followed me. No time to contact Diego—Armando definitely knew what he was doing. I wonder if he knew I'd spoke to Diego. At this point, it didn't matter. I'd give him the money and get the hell out of Playa Sueños with my family and never come back.

Calle Principale ended at a crossroads at the edge of town near a small parking lot beside the beach. The other road led up to a mountain and away from the coast. The place was quiet and bare with only a small café and a surf shop for beachgoers who want to get away from the commotion of Playa Sueños. I parked on the side of the road near the café. An occasional vehicle sped by, turned, and drove up the mountain. Armando stood under the sign for Bernardo's Surf Shop, holding his surfboard upright. His board was stained with wax, brownish and dirty with sand. He wore only surf trunks. A tattoo of a pimp skeleton stood out among his many tattoos on his sturdy physique. I approached him with consternation, but nonchalant and composed. We shook hands.

"The surf is good today," he said.

"Yeah, last summer my friends and I surfed farther south from here. Do you always surf here?"

"No, I surf in different places, you know. I wanna surf here porque I like the place across the street." He pointed to the café. "The man there makes the best empanadas in all of Playa Sueños. After we surf, we go there and eat."

"Sounds good," I said.

I followed him into the surf shop. Armando and the man behind the counter conversed like good friends. I rented a funboard rather than the shortboard I usually ride; it's less work for me to catch the waves. Before we stepped onto the beach, he asked me to remove my shirt and put it in the car, which I did. He spoke to me with such amiability I almost forgot who he was.

We paddled past the breakers, staying about ten feet apart. A well-formed swell made us jockey for it. I looked at Armando, who gestured for me to take it. The waves were about head high. The sparse white clouds under the deep blue sky made for a beautiful afternoon. I surfed waves back to shore. Armando was an impressive surfer. He rode a competitive shortboard, telling me he had a lot of experience. I paddled out and sat on my board to rest; the closest surfer I could see was far away. We took turns riding the waves without much interaction. I witnessed his competitive nature and tenacity to one-up me on the waves. My mind was on our meeting and my hope that he would keep his word. Over time, as the afternoon sun went down, there were fewer waves to surf. I became impatient. I wanted to pay him and leave. Armando paddled to me and sat on his board. We floated on our surfboards as the swells passed, waiting.

"What do you think? You like the surf here?" Armando said.

"It is a good spot. But to be honest, I haven't found a bad spot yet."

"Oh, we have bad spots. When you're here so long, you know them."

"I have the money in the car. Are you getting hungry?" I asked.

"One or two more, then we eat," Armando said, moving his board closer to me. "I want to tell you something, Luca." He paddled closer to me.

"What?" I said. We were an arm's length from each other.

"You know, after we make the deal. I want you to wait for me at the apartment. I want the girls to see you taking Eva away with you."

My eyes flashed between him and his tattoo, a skeleton wearing a pimp suit. "Okay," I said.

"And something else. I say this because I know women and I know Eva. I want you to remember this."

"What's that?"

"When you're back in America and everything is good and everything is fine, don't be surprised if she wanders from you. Don't be surprised if she hurts you, because she will hurt you." Armando pointed to his chest, his finger dripping seawater. "You know, don't blame Eva for that, because a puta is always a puta. Blame yourself for buying a puta," he said with an arrogant tone.

My eyes shifted from his cold stare to a bird flying over the ocean. It flew effortlessly above the waves as it came toward us. As it neared, the wing span widened as the creature revealed its enormous size. It was the pelican again. The same one at the cliff I climbed last year and the same one at Café Neto. Armando followed my gaze with an unexpected curiosity. The monster of a bird flew over us, casting a shadow across our eyes. With its passing, the sea around us lifted, then crested. A gust of wind offshore hit the top of the crest, forming a mist, causing the air to rainbow. Armando drifted into me. When our surfboards touched, I lunged at him, compelled by my hatred and my stark desperation to extinguish his light from the world. My arms locked around his neck as I committed to squeeze his throat. We fell off our boards and into the sea where the rush of water filled my ears and I heard Armando cry out as his mouth filled with seawater. I clutched him with mighty volition. His hands reached back. I held on. I held on, unyielding. Armando grabbed my hair and kicked, but I tightened further, battling my desire to breathe. The water got cold as we sank deeper into the darkness. My eyes closed and my mouth clenched. He let go of my hair and swung wildly to reach the surface, but he couldn't, and the darkness turned pitch black. My heart beat uncontrollably, and I yearned to breathe but was too frightened to let go. I felt the pull of my ankle leash from the surfboard. I became lightheaded and swallowed water. Armando suddenly ceased to struggle, going limp and motionless. I let him go and swam up to the surface. I felt faint and at my limit before a heavy gasp filled my lungs with precious, cool air. The ocean swirled around me as I gasped again. Not knowing where I was, I got on my surfboard to rest. I took in breath after breath until my head cleared. Seeing I was alone, I paddled back to shore and sat on the beach to rest. My heart raced and my heavy breathing continued. The man from the surf shop ran past me to look for Armando. Then two men approached me from what seemed like nowhere. It was Diego and his deputy. Diego kneeled beside me and placed his hand on my shoulder.

His deputy remained standing, looking out to the ocean while he spoke into his two-way radio.

"You okay? Where's Armando?" Diego asked me.

"I don't know. We were surfing and suddenly a wave hit us. I was under for so long," I said.

Diego stood up and spoke to his deputy in Spanish. I stood up and unleashed my surfboard. The man from Bernardo's Surf Shop ran back to his store.

"There's a surfboard on the water. Is that Armando's surfboard?" Diego pointed beyond the breakers. I nodded in agreement. Diego spoke into his two-way radio.

"Diego, I'm worried about Eva and the baby," I said.

"Yes, we will go, but I have to find Armando first. We have more police coming."

"We have to leave right away. I'm afraid for them," I said.

"Not yet!" Diego snapped. "We must find Armando. Was Armando alone with you?"

"Yes."

Diego spoke into his two-way radio, giving orders. A few minutes after, a rescue helicopter flew in and hovered over Armando's surfboard. The sea rippled and sprayed from the forced air of the helicopter blades. Two men in rescue gear jumped out of the helicopter and splashed down near the surfboard. The noise and spectacle attracted locals to gather on the beach. More police officers arrived. They worked the scene and kept the bystanders at a safe distance. Diego placed his hand on my shoulder.

"Armando may have someone nearby. I will tell one of my men to go to the apartment and make sure Eva is okay."

"Your men may not be able to get through the security gate," I said.

"We know what to do," Diego said confidently.

From the tumultuous surf, the rescue team carried Armando's lifeless body to shore. Attempts were made to resuscitate him before the paramedics arrived. The lips on Armando's face were blue and his hair caked with sand. He was gone. Would they know I did it? But whatever happens to me, at least that monster is dead. A monster with no remorse or empathy toward the living.

Diego answered a call from the two-way radio; the voice cracked and strained and yelled as if in combat. Diego's eyes widened as he heard the message. Something was wrong. He answered back with an irate tone: "No hagas nada. Estoy en camino." I closed my eyes and put my hands to my mouth. Diego got off the call and told me to follow him. "Quickly," he snapped.

Chapter 26

I drove close behind Diego's car as we shot down Calle Principale. Over a small bridge, past shops, eateries, and hotels—past the side street that led to the Jugosa Club. My heart raced with the twilight as I swerved around and passed cars and scooters. We turned up the road that led to the apartment complex. A small crowd of locals parted to let Diego drive through the entrance. The gate was broken down but the police kept people out. I parked along the street and ran over. I moved through the crowd and yelled out to Diego. Diego told his men to let me in. He was briefed by his fellow officers. The office door and windows were broken with shards glass strewn everywhere. The watchman's car had bullet holes in the windshield. All the apartment doors were open except for Eva's. A few policemen stood outside the door to her apartment with guns drawn. There were women in the parking lot who were either crying, angry, or yelling. The scene was chaotic. Diego held his pistol at his side as he crossed the parking lot.

"Luca, stay calm. Upstairs a man is holding hostages."

I put my hand to my face. "Oh my God. They're hostages," I exclaimed.

"Stay calm." Diego put his hand on my shoulder. He looked directly into my eyes. "Look. Look at me. We arrested one man. There's one more upstairs. I'm going to talk to him. You must stay here. I'll go upstairs and talk to him. I'll let you know what's going on later. Do you understand?"

"Can I come with you?" I said.

"No, no way. It's too dangerous—forget it. Stay here with my men." Diego walked away. The back of his neck shined from sweat. Before Diego could climb the stairs, policemen on the second floor yelled out for everyone to back up. The door to Eva's apartment opened. The policemen closest to the door waved people away—some went down the stairs. Yeison stepped out of the apartment, holding Eva at gunpoint. The scar Rosa put on his face was red and pronounced. Miguel was in Eva's arms.

Diego stepped back away from the stairs and from the parking lot looked up to get a better look at Yeison. Diego raised his hands in surrender. "No tengas miedo! No tengas miedo!" Diego shouted to Yeison. "Nosotros no te haremos daño! Calma, calma!"

Eva winced as she held Miguel tight to her chest. I froze, hoping he would let her go. "Give him what he wants!" I yelled to Diego. The policemen aimed their weapons at Yeison, a man who lacked the charisma and the intelligence of Armando, but not the cruelty. People shouted and tensions were high. Diego and Yeison went back and forth about releasing Eva and the baby, but Yeison refused. Yeison demanded everyone to leave so he could drive away in his car. Eva kept her eyes on the baby and did her best to remain calm. During a precarious lull in the negotiation, Eva shifted her body in such a way as to give a nearby policeman the confidence to fire. The sound of the gunshot froze the crowd as the policeman's bullet hit Yeison in the neck. Yeison let Eva go as he stumbled. Eva fell to her knees, almost dropping Miguel. She got up quickly and ran to the stairs. Seeing the opportunity, the surrounding officers began to fire, hitting him multiple times but not before Yeison fired one shot into Eva's back, making her fall. She never made it to the stairs. The rapid release of gunfire caused bystanders to scream and others to run in fear. Everything happened so fast. I panicked and pushed my way past the police and up the stairs to Eva. I hyperventilated as I turned her over. Her back was wet with blood. Miguel cried. His face scratched from the fall. I pried the baby out of Eva's arms. A policeman took me away to allow the paramedics, who were already there, to help on her. Miguel cried in my arms. I looked over to the policeman who'd shot Yeison in the neck. He was consoled by fellow officers as they stood over Yeison's body. The scene was chaotic with people moving all around. I didn't see Maria. Diego gave orders to clear the apartment complex. We were corralled and moved off the property and onto the street where we joined the anxious crowd at the gate. No one was permitted near the apartment building and heavy police presence guarded the main entrance. The area was closed off and labeled a crime scene. Feeling lost and helpless, I stood outside, holding Miguel, hoping to see Eva or Maria. Soon, all the girls from the apartment complex were taken to the police station. Police cars and ambulances came in and out of the complex. I waited with Miguel in my arms for over an hour. The crowd thinned, and Miguel began to cry again. It was getting late. I was about to leave when I saw Diego step outside one of the apartments. I waved and called to him. A policeman told me to stand back. Diego walked down the stairs and approached his vehicle. I called out again to him and he saw me. His face grim.

"Diego! How is Eva and Maria?" I asked desperately.

Diego shook his head and said, "I'm sorry. No one lived."

I stepped back and pressed my face against Miguel's little shoulder and wept. "No, no, God, no, no, no. I failed. I failed. I failed you, my little boy. I failed."

Chapter 27

Over the next two days, I stayed at a hotel with my son. Esperanza was gracious enough to visit me. She kept me company, fed the baby, and assisted with the funeral arrangements.

I keep my emotions to myself, and I am proud to get through hardships on my own. But Esperanza constantly asked how I felt. She had a way of talking with genuine caring and openness. Being vulnerable, I found myself crying on her shoulder more than I expected. She had seen her share of suffering on the streets of Playa Sueños, yet she remained strong for herself and for others. I felt she knew what I did to Armando that day, but I never told *anyone*. A secret I will keep forever. She was content with the women freed and the Jugosa Club shut down. A small victory in a world that at times is corrupt and takes advantage of the meek. The event at the apartment complex changed Esperanza's direction with her activism. Although she would continue her work to help women out of the sex business, the demand for it would not go away. She would begin a vigorous campaign with the hopes of changing the local laws in favor of a safer and more empowering reality for sex workers in Playa Sueños, maybe in all of Costa Miel.

I struggled with whether I should call my mother and my sister. I'd be home soon and arriving with my son would completely shock them. Once I told them my story, they'd never be the same. A phone call about my situation would make them worry and panic, so I would rather not. When I arrived with Miguel, they'd accept it because they had to. A baby is a blessing, and things would carry on.

I couldn't find information on Eva's father. I wanted to give him the news for the sake of closure. Eva and Maria had moved on from that man many years ago, so that was that. As far as other relatives, I had nothing to go on. There was no paperwork retrieved from the apartment. I wasn't even allowed to go back and check because the complex was still a crime scene. I had to let it go.

I decided to call Jamie. I had to call someone back home, and since he was an understanding friend and knew what was going on, I felt it was the right thing to do. At first he was surprised about what happened to Armando, being an experienced surfer. The whole situation at the apartment complex left him stunned. He finally apologized about not being in Costa Miel to help me. He expressed his deep sympathy for Eva and her mother and reiterated his availability to help with anything I needed. He insisted on flying to Costa Miel immediately. I told him all I needed was a ride home from the airport, nothing else. After some back-and-forth, Jamie reluctantly backed away and said he would be happy to pick us up at the airport when we arrived. He was looking forward to seeing Miguel and learning something about babies.

The morning of the funeral, the sky was gray and it began to drizzle. Miguel and I met Esperanza at the funeral home. She picked a place near the center of town with close walking distance to the cemetery. I spent all the cash I had on the funeral. The burial plots were in a beautiful location at a high point overlooking the cemetery. I made one wide tombstone, which displayed pictures of Eva and Maria forever side by side. Below their names, the stone read in Spanish: "Not My will, but Thy will be done."

The priest arrived early. He spoke kind words to me and blessed Miguel. People walked in and crossed themselves over the coffins, then walked over to me and the baby to offer their sympathies. The saddest faces were the women who looked upon my motherless child. Little Miguel, with a fresh bandage on his face, looking on, not knowing the gravity of the moment. He would reach out his little hand and turn his head as he shifted in my arms. I would bring him back to visit when he was older. He'd learn and try to understand the suffering his mother and grandmother endured. Would I break down one day and tell him what I did? I doubt it, but I'd worry about that in the future.

Diego was there. He shook my hand and offered his condolences. He asked to speak to me in private. He handed me a bag. In it were some of Eva's personal belongings. Along with some pictures, there was a notebook. In it were Eva's drawings of clothing designs and full dresses in color. One drawing looked similar to the yellow dress she wore when we first met. I felt she would have been successful if she had the chance to pursue her dreams. Eva was strong and intelligent with the grit to persevere in this world, but that's not enough. You also need to be at the right place and at the right time, which can make all the difference.

"This is all I could get from the apartment. There wasn't much," he said.

"Thank you, and thank you for your help," I said with sorrow.

"Believe me, I wish it ended differently. He would not negotiate with me. He was like a trapped animal. The good news is Armando is gone," Diego said, pointing to the ground. "He will no longer traffic women, and Yeison is gone too." Diego let out a heavy sigh. "I found out Yeison was told you were helping me. We don't know who told him. Yeison knew a lot of people in town. His informant could be a local policeman. We're investigating that too, but for now we don't know." Diego paused and let out another sigh. "We do know that cold bastard shot Maria when she opened the door for him. After that, the place went crazy. My men were nearby and heard the gunshot and broke into the gate. Yeison had another man with him, but he gave up without a fight. Yeison was a killer who snapped and lost his mind." Diego paused. "It was a terrible day. I'm sorry for your loss. I did the best I could."

Tears ran down my face. I wiped my nose and put Miguel in the stroller. "I wish Eva was here," I said as I tried to calm down. I took a few deep breaths. "If Yeison knew I was talking to you, then why didn't Armando know?"

"I don't know that. Either Yeison didn't tell Armando or Armando knew and waited to do something about it later.

Anyway, it's a good thing those devils are dead. I'm afraid to think what would happen if they were still alive."

"I was lucky in that way and not lucky in another," I said, looking at Miguel.

"Yes, yes," Diego said, looking at Miguel. "The baby looks good. You will be a good father." He shook my hand and left.

A few young women from the apartment complex arrived. One looked familiar to me. After a closer look, it was the girl who'd asked for my help. She looked at me as I stood near the stroller. When our eyes met, she broke away from the others and approached me, keeping her gaze on me. She opened her arms to embrace me.

"Gracias," she said as she held me for a long time. One of my most vivid memories was when I saw her sad face peeking from behind her apartment door. I walked away at the time not knowing what to do or how to stop Armando's madness. She didn't speak English well, but well enough for me to know she was seventeen years old and from Eastern Europe. Her nightmare started over a year ago when a few men drove up and kidnapped her after she left a dance club. From there she was moved and used until Armando bought her. Her name was Elena and she was leaving to go back home to her parents, far away from Playa Sueños. She gave me her phone number and told me to call her anytime. She thanked me again and left with the other girls.

Around noon, the sky cleared. The priest led the procession, which attracted the curious and those generous enough to follow on foot behind the hearse. The procession grew enough for me to look back and forget Eva for a moment. The people of

Playa Sueños were warm and respectful. Though I suffered, I felt some relief knowing Armando and Yeison were gone.

Past the cemetery gates, everyone gathered around the empty graves. As the priest spoke, I remembered a time when Eva and I were on the beach. I held her in my arms under a bright sun as the ocean flowed gently over our feet. I missed her smile, her touch, and how she spoke to me. Her ghost will always be with me.

The priest ended his sermon, the caskets were placed in the ground, and everyone parted in peace. I put flowers on the tombstone and sat there with Miguel to be alone for a while and say goodbye.

On my last day, I took Miguel to the beach but not before strolling down Calle Principale for the last time. The street was busy with tourists like it always was. With the club closed, it didn't stop the pleasure seekers. The need to procure sex will always be there. Another club will take its place and it goes on and on.

The sun was strong and the sand hot. I placed Miguel on a large beach towel by the water. I adjusted his hat and made sure his skin was protected against the harsh rays of the late afternoon sun. He rolled onto his belly and jerked his plump legs with excitement. He stared back at me with a wide, innocent smile. I kissed his little feet. As the day ended, people collected their blankets and bags and left the beach after another beautiful day relaxing beside the undulating sea. I sat Miguel up to face the water. The wind folded up his wide-brimmed hat. I began brooding about Eva's absence as I stared at my boy. He looked at me and pointed to the sea. I looked out, and above the waves, under the low light of the setting sun, flew the same pelican I knew, the one in my thoughts. Miguel babbled at it as it flew in the direction of the cliff that descended into the sea. As we watched it fly away, I said to myself, in a faint voice, "Thy will be done."

About the author

Giovanni B. Sciurba was born in Sicily and raised in the vibrant cultural landscape of the United States, blending two worlds that have shaped his storytelling. With an engineering degree from Columbia University, Giovanni's analytical mind is tempered by his deep passion for literature, allowing him to craft a compelling narrative that weaves together rich characters, complex emotions, and a thrilling plot twist.

A lover of both adventure and human connection, Giovanni draws on his Sicilian roots and his experiences living in New Jersey to create stories that explore love, sacrifice, and the shadows of the human soul. Under a Pelican's Wing marks his debut as a novelist, showcasing his ability to blend suspense with romance, and to delve into some of life's most difficult and powerful themes.

When he's not writing, Giovanni can be found exploring places that inspire him or reflecting on stories of the people around him. He currently lives in New Jersey, where he continues to write and explore the world, one story at a time.

www.ingramcontent.com/pod-product-compliance
Lightning Source LLC
Chambersburg PA
CBHW071416300726
48976CB00006B/2114